ATHERTON

THE HOUSE OF POWER

PATRICK CARMAN

ATHERTON
THE HOUSE OF POWER

LITTLE, BROWN AND COMPANY
New York ~ Boston

Little, Brown and Company

Hachette Book Group USA
1271 Avenue of the Americas, New York, NY 10020
Visit our Web site at www.lb-kids.com

First Edition: April 2007

ISBN-13: 978-0-316-16670-6
ISBN-10: 0-316-16670-7

10 9 8 7 6 5 4 3 2 1

Q-MT

Printed in the United States of America

For the people of Aduana Dos

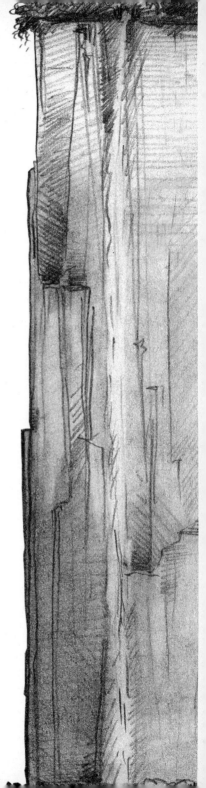

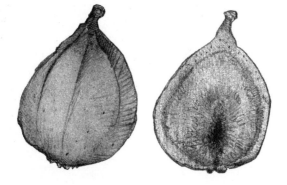

TABLE OF
CONTENTS

PART 1

PART 2

PART 3

After days and nights of incredible labor and fatigue,
I succeeded in discovering the cause of generation and life.
Nay, more. I became myself capable of bestowing animation
upon lifeless matter.

DR. FRANKENSTEIN
FRANKENSTEIN, 1818
MARY SHELLEY

PART
ONE

*"It won't be long now.
Things are already beginning to change."*

There was a long, static-filled pause,
followed by a distant response.

*"I know, I know. I hope we haven't moved
too quickly. I'm not sure they're ready yet."*

*"Why must you always talk such nonsense?
We've waited long enough."*

*"I agree. It's just . . .
We have no idea what's going to happen."*

*"That's always been your trouble, Luther. You're
indecisive, always wavering. It sometimes makes me
wonder why I've kept you around these long years."*

*"One thing is certain —
some people are going to be very unhappy."*

There was a strange sound from
the other end of the line, as if a secret moment
of quiet laughter had occurred.

*"Indeed — there will be some miserable people.
I do believe you are about to be one of them."*

"What do you mean?"

*"Luther, you can't have seriously imagined I would
allow you to use my creation for your own gain."*

The voice trailed off, replaced by the cracking and popping of electricity in the air. Then it returned.

"You know as well as anyone that this place is mine. I formed it. And I won't part with it. I won't have you meddling in my business any longer."

"Dr. Harding, what on Earth are you talking about?"

"It belongs to me. It's my creation and I'll do with it as I please. I believe I've had enough of being told what I can and can't do. Our time has come to an end, Luther."

"What do you mean to do, Maximus? You cannot disengage from the rest of the world."

There was a stillness, then labored breathing and the sound of heavy objects being moved.

"Goodbye, Luther."

"Maximus? Maximus!"

Static poured from the receiver.
Then the line went entirely dead.

What did it mean? Had he gone mad?

Dr. Luther Kincaid looked up and whispered into the night sky.

"May God forgive us our reckless making of a new world."

CHAPTER 1

A BOY WITH A SECRET

In Mr. Ratikan's grove there lived a boy. He was not well-to-do, but his needs were met and he was happy most of the time. His name was Edgar.

Some would say that Edgar was skinny like all the other boys who worked in the grove, but they would only be half right, for everyone knows there are two kinds of skinny children: Some are fragile as paper while others are nimble as wire. Edgar was the wiry kind, strong and quick as a jackrabbit.

Deep in the heart of the grove, a thick canopy of leaves hung low overhead, and in the heat of the day it was a cool, quiet place to lie in the grass and take a nap. But Edgar was not the kind who enjoyed sneaking off to nap under the trees like some of the others. He was far more likely to be found doing something mischievous, which is precisely where we find him as our story begins.

Somewhere in a silent part of the grove, Edgar had been swinging violently back and forth on one of the tree branches, trying to gain enough speed to fling himself across the grassy path to a branch five feet or more away on the other side. Twice Edgar had let go too late and flown through the air feetfirst, landing on his back in the middle of the path with a terrible *thud*.

Undeterred, Edgar made a third attempt, which sent him careening through the air so fast he smashed into the tree's trunk and was rewarded with a bloody nose.

The ruckus caught the attention of the owner of the grove, Mr. Ratikan, a tall, hunchbacked man who was always determined to put an end to Edgar's fun.

Edgar was in the middle of his biggest swing yet, brushing the leaves in the tree with his arms as he came forward. When he swung back, Mr. Ratikan struck Edgar on his bare feet with his walking stick.

"Come away from there this instant!" yelled the angry man. Mr. Ratikan had chalky white skin, and his mouth was perpetually turned in a scowl, making his thin lips and long mustache seem like nothing more than red and brown ribbons around an unhappy mouth.

The walking stick had failed to knock Edgar free. Swinging his feet high up in the air, Edgar let go, arms and legs flailing. This time he caught hold of the branch on the other side. But the moment he did, the branch snapped off and he crashed to the ground.

This was exceptionally bad luck for Edgar, since nothing made Mr. Ratikan quite as irritated as someone damaging one of the precious trees in his grove.

"Now you've done it!" Mr. Ratikan shouted, poking Edgar in the ribs with his walking stick.

"I was only having a moment's fun before coming to find you," said Edgar as he tried to dodge the stick, his voice cracking and dry. He scrambled to his feet and dashed behind the trunk for protection, wiping a bit of blood from his nose.

Mr. Ratikan's walking stick crashed against the trunk of the tree, barely missing Edgar's head. "Get to work on the saplings — and don't you stop until you've finished twenty!" He rapped the stick against the tree once more, and Edgar jumped back. "If I *ever* catch you playing in the trees again, there'll be no dinner for a week!"

Edgar sized up the space across which he'd flown. Though he would have to work an extra hour for his misbehavior, it had been worth it.

"GO!" cried Mr. Ratikan, slapping his walking stick over and over against the tree and hoping to catch one of the boy's fingers in the process.

Edgar sprinted down a winding pathway leading through the shade of the grove until he was well out of sight of Mr. Ratikan. *That was a reckless thing I did back there,* he admitted to himself, despite the fun he'd had. *It won't do to stir up watchful eyes. Someone might see what I've been doing.*

Edgar slowed to a walk as he reached the oldest stretch of trees, where the limbs grew wide and long. Little bits of light were shooting between the leaves, and he tried to catch them in his hand as he went. Edgar was easily amused, and he would have made a good friend for someone, but he stayed by himself a great deal. He was a boy with a secret, and he kept it well.

Edgar made his way along the twisting path until the canopy of leaves fell away. He had come out into the full light of day where there was a cliff wall reaching so high into the air he couldn't see where it ended. Down its side, roaring vigorously, a waterfall crashed to the ground, and Edgar observed a familiar sight nearby. Several men stood around the pool at the bottom of the waterfall, guarding it from anyone who might approach out of turn. While three of the men stood on alert, others rationed water in small wooden buckets to a line of people from the village. There were three such waterfalls coming from the top of the cliffs, but this was the only one near to the grove. The others were far off in places Edgar had never been.

The careful distribution of water was one of the troubles of living in Tabletop, but Edgar thought it must be better than life in the Flatlands beneath him, where the water supply was limited to what little spilled over the edge of Tabletop. It was hard to imagine anyone below surviving for very long. In the world of Atherton, those in the Highlands above controlled the flow of water, and they could do with it as they pleased.

Suddenly there came a sound of a twig snapping from somewhere nearby in the grove. Edgar froze, wondering what he might do if Mr. Ratikan came out from the shadows again, swinging his walking stick. *I should have known he would follow me,* Edgar thought with regret.

"You've got twigs and leaves caught in your hair," came a small voice from behind a tree.

Edgar felt some initial relief that it wasn't Mr. Ratikan, but he still wasn't altogether happy when he realized who was speaking to him.

"Come out from there, Isabel."

A head of tangled, dirty hair emerged from behind the trunk of the tree, then a brown forehead, and finally a dark eye with a thick black brow hanging over it peered out.

"Did Mr. Ratikan knock you down again? Did he hit you with that awful stick of his?"

As usual, Edgar ignored her questions. "Why must you always follow me, Isabel?" Edgar shook his head back and forth to free the rubbish from his hair, but the twigs and leaves only danced back and forth like little animals clinging to a nest.

"I can get those out for you," said Isabel as she leapt out from behind the tree. She was tiny compared to Edgar, younger and skinny in a way that made Edgar think he might be able to snap her in half if he wanted to.

Edgar brushed the leaves and twigs from his mop of brown hair, and then he turned to go.

"Oh, but you can't just *go*," said Isabel. "You need to tell me what happened. Did Mr. Ratikan throw you to the ground? Is that why you've got leaves in your hair?"

Edgar was about to scold the girl as an older brother might do when he felt a slight rumbling beneath his feet. Isabel felt it, too, and they both stood quietly, trying to understand what it was. It had happened before — this faint trembling of the ground in the grove — and so the two were not so surprised by it. Still, it was a little stronger this time, as though someone were banging a drum in the ground beneath them, trying to get their attention.

"My father says it's nothing," said Isabel, "but it does feel strange, doesn't it?"

The feeling stopped, and Edgar began to walk away without answering. It was getting late and he still had twenty trees to trim.

"We'll talk tonight at dinner," said Isabel. "Whatever Mr. Ratikan did to you, it'll be our little secret."

She ran back into the grove, content for the moment to let her imagination run wild about how Mr. Ratikan had beaten Edgar with his walking stick.

Edgar licked his dry lips as he walked the last little path toward the sapling field. He would have to wait until dinner to get a cup of water, but Edgar had grown used to this routine — everyone had — and soon his mind was on other things.

Edgar gazed out past the edge of the grove. He often daydreamed about what his world might look like from far away, and he had devised a rather accurate image in his mind. Atherton was situated on three circular levels, each one wider than the one above it. The broad Flatlands were at the distant bottom. Edgar thought that if a person fell off the edge of the Flatlands, they would fall forever. Tabletop, where Edgar lived, was a large plateau at the top of a steep rock face rising from the middle of the Flatlands. And then there were the Highlands, the most mysterious place of all. It sat at the top of the imposing cliffs in the center of Tabletop. People who lived in Tabletop often wondered what they might find in the Highlands. There were rumors of giant animals and abundant water, of powerful people and beautiful places.

Edgar, too, had always been curious about the Highlands, though he'd never been there. Travel between the three levels was strictly forbidden. No one from Tabletop knew what was at the top of the cliffs, because no one was ever invited.

ATHERTON

House of Power   THE HIGHLANDS

TABLETOP

FLATLANDS

DR. HARDING
2. 12 2092

CHAPTER

2

LOOK FOR ATHERTON

By the time Edgar finished trimming his twentieth sapling, late afternoon had come to the grove. Trimming was one of the more time-consuming tasks, though fortunately it wasn't very difficult, because Edgar would need his energy when evening came. The moment he was finished with the saplings he started off toward Mr. Ratikan's house for his evening ration of food and water.

When he arrived for dinner, all the other workers from the grove were already in line. Not everyone from the village worked in the grove, because there were a great many other tasks to be done. There were sheep and rabbits that needed tending and figs from the trees to be processed. Animal bones and parts that weren't eaten or used to create useful items had to be taken to the edge and thrown into the Flatlands along with other debris from Tabletop. But all the work stopped when dinner hour ar-rived in the grove, and everyone came to Mr. Ratikan's house.

Isabel spotted Edgar almost immediately. She waved at him to join her in the line, but Edgar tried to ignore her. Soon she had left her father's side and moved to the back of the line, where she proceeded to bother Edgar immensely with a lot of questions he didn't want to answer.

"That Mr. Ratikan is awful, don't you think? Did you get some water today? I got a little, but hardly any. I wonder what we'll work on tomorrow. Do you think we'll go to the third-year grove? I like the third-year grove best."

Isabel talked until the two of them reached the front of the line, and she proceeded to ask some of the same questions of Mr. Ratikan as he rolled his eyes, filled her bowl and cup, and tried to move her along. Mr. Ratikan wouldn't let anyone onto the steps that led to a tiny porch in front of his door, for enter-ing his house was forbidden. This made it difficult for him to get rid of Isabel without picking up his walking stick and wav-ing it at her.

"Why must you always try to hit people with that horrible stick of yours?" said Isabel, her dark eyebrows set in a scowl.

Mr. Ratikan responded by pinching his face in such a ghastly expression that Isabel snatched her cup and bowl and scurried away from the house.

When Edgar arrived at the front of the line, Mr. Ratikan's at-tention was turned away. There was a strange sound coming from the direction where Mr. Ratikan was looking, and Edgar turned to see what it was. A man who had become sick was standing against a tree. He was leaning over, as though he were trying to throw up, though nothing was coming out of his mouth.

"Pay attention, boy!" Edgar turned back to the porch and found his caretaker looking directly at him. Apparently Mr. Ratikan had seen all he cared to of the sick man in the grove. He squinted with one eye, trying to decide how little he could offer to the boy and still expect a good day's work from him.

"Did you finish the saplings?" he asked, scratching at the edge of his greasy moustache with one hand, and pointed his walking stick at the boy with the other.

"Twenty of them," said Edgar. He really was very fast, probably the best worker Mr. Ratikan had.

"Fine," said Mr. Ratikan, lowering the stick away from Edgar's face. "Tomorrow you can go back and do thirty more."

Edgar handed him a small wooden cup, and Mr. Ratikan dipped it carefully into a pail of water that sat on the porch. He handed the cup back to Edgar along with a bit of something that looked like dough and a slice of dry, overcooked mutton, which was the only way Mr. Ratikan ever prepared it. Nine meals out of ten it was tasteless mutton Edgar ate for dinner. The tenth was often no meat at all.

Edgar sat down under a tree away from the others, as was his habit. The dough was the best part of the meal and Edgar savored it, tearing small pieces off and eating them bit by bit with his dirty hands. The dough — as with so many other important items in Tabletop — came from the fig trees in the grove. If the trees were cut down after the third harvest and split open, a spongy, orange core could be easily pulled out from the inside. Mixing the substance with a little water turned it into dough that tasted like sweet cocoa.

When the last bite of dough was gone, Edgar sipped what remained in his wooden cup and quietly snuck away from Mr. Ratikan's house.

Once he was out of sight of the others, Edgar reached down into a large pocket on the front of his shirt and pulled out a fig. It was no ordinary fig, though — it was a dead one that had fallen off a tree. Such figs were slick, black, and heavy, about the size of his palm. Most of them were collected and used for fires, for they burned hot and long in the cool evenings and didn't create much smoke. Some of the children liked to make up games with them, but Edgar had his own ideas about what to do with the dead figs.

Next from his shirt pocket Edgar took out a sling made from long, thin strands of twisted bark from the second-year trees, attached to either side of a square of rabbit skin in the middle. He doubted that Mr. Ratikan would allow him to have a sling, because Edgar wasn't supposed to peel tree bark. He had never shown it to anyone for fear that it would be taken away and he would be punished for using it.

Edgar looked around to make certain no one was near. Then he chose a tree trunk in the distance as a target, loaded the black fig into the sling, and knelt down in the grove. He swung the heavy ball over his head. As it went faster and faster it made a terrific whirring sound until — *snap!* — he let go of one end of the string. The black fig flew through the grove, hit the tree where he'd aimed, and ricocheted out of sight.

Edgar ran to the tree and examined the mark he'd left there, hiding the sling back in his pocket as he went. He found the black fig and put it in the side pocket of his pants, for though he had a dozen more hidden in the grove, most of the fallen figs were taken by those in the village.

Edgar sometimes thought he'd like to demonstrate his target shooting with the other boys who worked in the grove, but he didn't spend a lot of time with them. The others had families in the village, and when the work was finished, they were quick to go, leaving Edgar by himself when night fell on the grove. After a while it was as though Edgar had become invisible to the people around him. He would have liked to make more friends, but he worried that what he did at night would be discovered.

An hour later Edgar had crossed through the grove to the other side, making his way alone to a very remote area of the cliff wall separating Tabletop from the Highlands. It was a quiet place away from the grove, the village, and the waterfall. The hour was getting late, and Edgar walked, touching the wall of the cliff as he went, his calloused hand sliding along the uneven surface in jumps and starts. For years Edgar had been coming here to practice with his sling while nobody was watching. Night after night, *every* night, Edgar had come here for another reason as well. He was searching for an object — one that was hidden — and finding it meant climbing the cliff wall, something he was forbidden to do.

At this hour in Atherton the cliffs were hidden in a cloak of grey light. It would last for many hours, this nearly night, and it would conceal Edgar as he went about his business. Guards walked near the foot of the cliff at night and looked for mischief, but Edgar was an expert at moving about unnoticed. The people of the Highlands had strictly prohibited climbing — especially near the waterfalls — and there would be terrible trouble if Edgar's secret were found out. Rumors floated around that if anyone were caught climbing, both legs would be broken, or the culprit would be thrown off the edge of the world into the Flatlands.

It didn't take long for Edgar to move fifty feet up the wall, scurrying like a spider across route after route high above the ground. The cliff was perfectly vertical, but it was filled with crags that were not difficult for Edgar to hold. He was helped by the dull light of evening, which allowed Edgar to see the stone surface before him. Light crept around the edges of the world of Atherton as it turned away from the sun, and total darkness came only briefly in the deepest part of the night.

Edgar climbed higher still, his body perched a hundred feet above the ground and no rope to catch him if he fell. He moved across to an area he'd never been to, and he tried to remember.

Edgar was raised as an orchard boy, but he hadn't always been alone in the world. He had a fractured memory of an earlier time, a time before the grove. He had a father, this much he knew. But Edgar was eleven now, and each year the memories grew fainter. All of what remained in his memory was focused on one exchange with a man. He had been here — at the cliffs — as a little boy of three or four when the words were spoken. The man was on one knee looking into Edgar's eyes. There was no face in Edgar's memory — only the soft hazel eyes, a smell of embers in the air, and the words he wouldn't let go:

> *"Do you see this rock wall, little Edgar?"*
> *"I see it."*
> *"Remember this place, won't you?"*
> *"I will."*
> *"I've hidden something way up there, in the rocks, where no one can find it."*
> *"Way up there?"*
> *"Yes, Edgar, way up there."*
> *"What did you hide?"*
> *"It will come to you, if you wait for it. Look for Atherton."*
> *"But what did you hide?"*

Every year Edgar remembered a little less even as he played the scene again and again in his mind. One thing he was sure of — it was shortly after this memory that Edgar found himself in the care of Mr. Ratikan.

It will come to you, if you wait for it. Look for Atherton. For years he'd pondered the meaning of that statement as he moved about on the face of the cliff. The older he grew, the more confusing the words became, and he began to wonder if he'd remembered it right. *Look for Atherton.* He was *in* Atherton — or so he thought — and he could only take its meaning to be that he should look everywhere. It was not a useful bit of instruction.

But we come upon Edgar's story at this moment with good

reason. On that very night Edgar climbed higher then he'd climbed before to places he'd never been. He climbed desperately, for trouble with Mr. Ratikan was growing more frequent, and the boy wondered if he might soon be caught. His fingers pried into every crack and crevice in the rocks as he went, until finally, a thousand nights of searching gone by, it happened.

Two hundred feet above the ground with darkness closing in around him, Edgar found something.

CHAPTER
3
RULES MADE FOR BREAKING

Deep night was approaching and only a hush of light remained. Climbing down would be even more treacherous than usual. Edgar was shaking — not with fright or cold but with excitement. He had always been a steady boy, and it was unsettling to feel his legs tremble.

Edgar had found a tiny, cavelike opening the size of his own outstretched hand. At first he had veered away from it, fearing that some unknown creature would dart out, grab him by the arm, and never let go. But even in the dim light Edgar could see that he had found what he'd been looking for.

Just below the hole there was a symbol etched in the rock, as if someone had come with a sharp object and hastily carved the marking into the cliff. Edgar supposed that if he could stand outside of Atherton and look at it from a distance, it would look

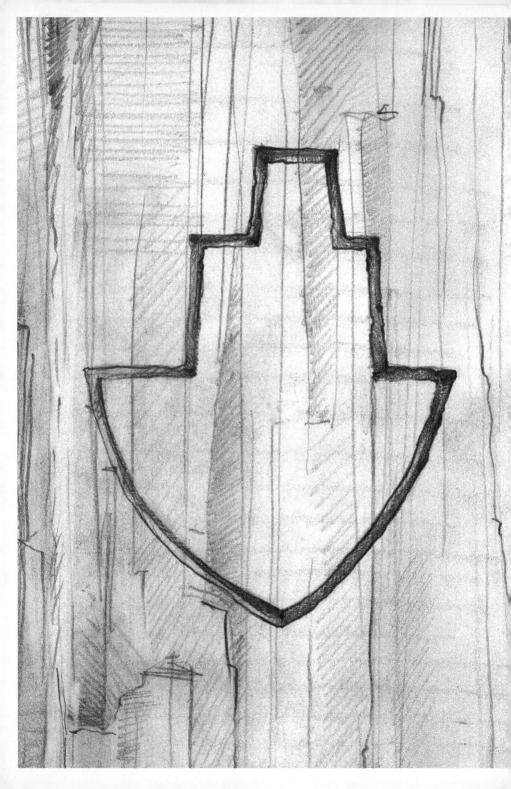

very much like the symbol before him. *Look for Atherton.* At last he had found what the man in his memory had left for him. He shivered with anticipation.

Edgar put his hand inside the hole and found that it wasn't very deep. His arm was only in to the elbow and already he touched rough stone. He felt all around, holding on with his other arm so he wouldn't fall, and he found that the space curved downward.

A chill ran through him as he thought once more about something alive in the hole. Just because a secret had been left there didn't mean it couldn't be used as a home for a boy-eating monster. Something with sharp teeth and claws. He felt around cautiously, slowly moving his hand from side to side, but there was nothing.

He shifted, and with an extra thrust of his shoulder, managed to maneuver his arm all the way into the space. Now the tip of his fingers touched something different. It was not stone; it was softer. As he fidgeted with his fingers the object moved back and forth under his touch. He hoped it wasn't alive. Edgar fumbled for what seemed like an eternity as he tried to get his fingers around the hidden item.

He risked letting go of the cliff with his other hand and rose up on his toes, forcing his arm into the hole until his cheek smashed up against the cliff. This turned out to be far enough. At last he had a grip on the mysterious thing he'd been hunting for for years, and pulled it out.

He was at once overjoyed and completely devastated. It was a beautiful item, leathery and brown with paper inside. It was a book. The book didn't have very many pages, but it was full of words that broke Edgar's heart, not for the things they said of honesty or nostalgia or sadness. The words broke his heart because Edgar could not read, and neither could anyone else who lived in Tabletop.

Weeks passed and Edgar did not return to the cliff. It was the first time he could remember staying away for more than a day or two. But he could not be consoled. Though he was young, it seemed to him that his life's work — the work of learning to climb and finding what was left for him — had come to a crashing and painful end.

Day after day he brooded over the book he'd found. At night when everyone was gone from the grove he would flip through the pages in the waning light, trying to understand. Not only was the book full of nothing but words, but they were written in a messy hand. Whoever had written it was either in a hurry or hadn't learned to write very well.

How could this man have left something so useless? Edgar had worked so hard and taken such risks, only to find an awful truth in the end — the treasure he sought was out of reach in a way that no amount of climbing could overcome.

Edgar fretted endlessly over what to do with the book. The rules of Tabletop were clear, and Edgar had heard them many times:

1: IF YOU SEND FOOD TO THE HIGHLANDS, THEY WILL SEND YOU WATER.

2: DON'T WASTE WATER.

3: IT IS FORBIDDEN TO CLIMB OR GO NEAR THE CLIFFS.

4: IF YOU FIND A BOOK, GIVE IT TO ONE OF THE GUARDS TO SEND IT UP TO THE HIGHLANDS IMMEDIATELY. DON'T BURN IT OR DESTROY IT AND DON'T KEEP IT. DON'T LOOK AT ITS PAGES. THERE ARE PEOPLE IN TABLETOP WHO WILL TELL US IF YOU DO.

Edgar had often wondered about the last rule. How would a book arrive in Tabletop to begin with? Nobody in the world of Atherton could read, apart from the people who lived in the Highlands. It made him wonder if he had been the only person looking for the book he'd found hidden in the cliff. He supposed, on thinking it through, that someone might walk along the edge of the Highlands above and accidentally drop one into the sky, where it would flutter and fall like a bird with a broken wing, the pages ripping as it came. Or, for reasons Edgar could only guess at, perhaps someone would smuggle a book down in one of the baskets.

For as long as Edgar could remember, there had been ropes and baskets hanging down from the Highlands at intervals around the cliffs. The people of Tabletop filled the baskets with figs, mutton, rabbit, and wool. The guards signaled the Highlands by tugging on a rope, and the baskets were pulled into the air. But why would anyone from above hide a book in the cliff?

Edgar finally decided to hide the book in the grove. First he counted the trees along one row until he had gone through every finger and every toe. He dug a narrow hole, wrapped the book in leaves, and dropped it inside. Then he covered the opening with a rock he could barely lift. The next day he would do the same, counting fingers and toes as he passed trees in another direction until he arrived at the base of a tree and buried the book once more. He was so very frightened of losing the book or of someone finding it that he thought of nothing else.

"Quit your sulking, you foolish boy!" Mr. Ratikan roared whenever he saw Edgar deep in thought, moving listlessly through the grove. As a rule Edgar produced more work in an hour than almost anyone else could achieve in two, but now he had turned sluggish and inattentive, unable to focus on the tasks put before him. A good worker gone bad enraged Mr. Ratikan, and he constantly criticized the boy's effort, fearing retribution from Lord Phineus if work in the grove moved too slowly.

Once in a great while, when the rulers of the Highlands were not pleased with the goods they'd been sent, someone from the Highlands — often Lord Phineus himself — would visit in one of the large baskets. Lord Phineus wouldn't come all the way down, but he did come far enough that everyone who gathered around could hear his grim voice, and usually what he came to say wasn't very nice: "You're not working fast enough!" or "Not enough rabbit!" or "Where are the figs you promised us?" In every case the punishment was the same: "There will be less water for a while, until things improve."

Edgar wondered if he might meet Lord Phineus someday,

and it was this thought one evening that finally broke Edgar's dark mood. He sat up and looked at the book in his hand, and his thoughts became words in the grove.

"If I took this little book to the Highlands, I wonder if I could find someone who would read it to me?"

It was an outrageous thought, and yet Edgar stewed on it. The baskets weren't a realistic option, since they were guarded night and day. But why couldn't he climb all the way to the top? It would be ten times higher than he'd ever climbed before, but that didn't mean he couldn't do it. If he were caught, they would probably throw him over the edge of the world. But wasn't there a chance that someone up there would help him? He didn't care if they locked him up or turned him into a slave or threw him to his death. He would be happy to give up his life in the grove in order to hear just a few of the words from this treasure he had spent his life looking for.

He buried the book once more, then sat with his back against a fig tree, staring off into the grove. Edgar's mind drifted to the cliffs, and he wondered if he possessed enough skill to climb all the way to the top, to a place he was forbidden to enter.

CHAPTER

4

CHANGE BEGINS

The next morning Edgar began work early in a part of the grove where the trees were beginning to sprout figs. His day would be spent pulling together the tiny vines that drooped from the limbs and tying them into bundles where they would hang heavily from the tree like clusters of tiny green eggs. A few weeks after the figs were tied together Edgar would return and pull the hard, black figs from their vines, releasing the rest from the string.

The monotony of tying bundles of figs together helped Edgar think clearly, for his mind was sharper when his hands were busy at repetitive tasks. He would need to find a way to leave the grove early in order to make his escape to the Highlands, and this would mean missing dinner. But there was only one way he could miss dinner without stirring up suspicion about where he'd gone: He would need to get into some trouble so that Mr.

Ratikan would take his dinner away from him. For once Edgar wanted to get caught doing something he shouldn't be doing.

He rolled this idea over in his mind most of the day as he pulled string after string from his belt and tied the green figs into bundles. By the time Edgar pulled the last string from his belt, he had decided what to do.

It was mid-afternoon and he walked the short distance to the old grove where the dying trees were stripped and gutted before turning poisonous. This was an odd place, not like the rest of the grove, in which trees had come to the very end of their short lives. Many of the trees still stood awaiting their doom, but plenty of limbs had already been torn off and trunks uprooted. The place had a chilling sense of bones in a field strewn everywhere while the remaining trees sadly looked on, unable to run away.

Mr. Ratikan was there, off at the far end, waving his walking stick and speaking to a group of workers who stood around a fallen tree. Edgar was supposed to meet Mr. Ratikan here when he'd finished with the tying so that more work could be assigned, but instead Edgar picked up the largest fallen limb he could carry and set his plan in motion.

He spied two old trees still standing near one another, climbed up one of them while dragging the limb behind him, and then dropped the long limb across to the other tree where it stuck firmly in the branches. The limb was about six feet off the ground. It didn't take very long for Mr. Ratikan to notice Edgar in the tree, getting ready to walk across the limb.

"What are you doing there, boy?" Mr. Ratikan screamed,

FIG TREE
3RD YEAR GROWTH

WHOLE FIG
(INSIDE VIEW)

WHOLE FIG
(OUTSIDE VIEW)

NEW HYBRID FIG

SAGO PALM
CYCAS REVOLUTA

PANACHÉE
+
SAN PIETRO
+
ISCHIA BLACK

THE GROVE
(TOP VIEW)

MR RATIKAN'S
HOUSE

FIGS ON
BRANCH

DR. HARDING

marching toward Edgar, his pinched face turning red. "Get out of that tree!"

He turned to the other workers, who were curiously watching the commotion. "Get back to work gutting those limbs!"

Edgar could see that Mr. Ratikan was in an even fouler mood than usual, and began to wonder if maybe this hadn't been such a good idea after all. It crossed his mind to jump out of the tree and run for his life, but Mr. Ratikan would have everyone looking for him if he did. And so as Mr. Ratikan approached, Edgar took a deep breath, smiled, and placed one foot on the limb he'd set between the trees.

"I just want to see if I can walk across it," said Edgar. "It won't take long."

"Get down from there, you idiot!"

Edgar took another step out onto the limb.

"What about a wager?" asked Edgar.

"You *stupid* boy!" screamed Mr. Ratikan. He could see Edgar had gotten his spirit back, and it infuriated him.

"If I fall, you can keep my dinner tonight," said Edgar.

"You'll be getting no dinner either way if you stay up there any longer."

It was about ten feet to the other side. Edgar wasn't entirely sure he could make it all the way across. He moved out onto the unsteady limb and felt it bow beneath his weight. Though it wobbled back and forth, Edgar walked steadily to the middle. Mr. Ratikan jabbed the limb with his walking stick, and it swayed violently. When Edgar still didn't fall, Mr. Ratikan started swinging the stick at his shins. But Edgar nimbly jumped and dodged his way across, and Mr. Ratikan never did get a clean blow at his feet.

Once Edgar reached the other side, he came down from the tree and stood grinning in the grass.

"I told you I could do it!"

Mr. Ratikan was not amused. "No dinner, *and* no water until morning. If I see you near my house begging for food, you can skip breakfast as well! How does that suit you?"

Mr. Ratikan had turned to go when the ground began to shake as it had before. It was more pronounced this time, or so it seemed within the confines of the old part of the grove. The trees were not healthy, and several toppled loudly to the ground. When the rumbling stopped, Edgar looked at Mr. Ratikan as though he thought maybe the man knew why the ground shook so.

"What are you looking at? Get back to the field and tie bundles until dark. And don't come near my house until tomorrow!"

Mr. Ratikan stumbled hastily away toward the workers, ordering them to meet him at the fallen trees and begin cutting them open. Though nothing was said, there was a sense that many of the workers were frightened by the trembling of the ground and the newly fallen trees. But Mr. Ratikan was in a tirade and would not let them talk amongst themselves.

Edgar had a mixed-up feeling in his stomach as he went back in the direction from which he'd come. He was hungry and thirsty with a promise of fulfilling neither before him. It made him wonder if he would have enough energy to climb all the way to the top of the cliff. And why did the ground keep shaking as it did? It seemed to be getting worse. Edgar was anxious as he thought of what might happen if the movement returned while he was climbing as far into the sky as the eye could see.

"This can't be right," muttered Edgar.

Early evening had come, and he had arrived at the cliff while everyone else was busy with dinner. It was lighter than when he'd come in the past, and at first he wondered if maybe that was why things seemed different.

He put his hands on the deep red and brown surface before him. Then he went about climbing up the first few feet, keeping a close eye out in case anyone appeared unexpectedly. With the added light he would need to be more cautious. He dropped down to the ground, moved to his left about ten steps, and put his hands on the cliff once more. He stood looking at the face of the cliff shaking his head, wondering what it could mean. The wall, it seemed, was lower then it had been three weeks before; about two inches lower. All of Edgar's holds — the places where he had countless times before set his hands and feet — were lower to the ground.

Could it be that he'd grown so much in the three weeks since he'd last been here? He'd never heard of such a thing. He stretched out his arms thinking maybe they'd grown longer, but they looked the same as before. Still, he was certain: the holds were lower than they'd been all his life. Something was altered.

"I must try to get more sleep," said Edgar, certain he must be making things up in his head. He tried to put whatever had changed out of his mind and fidgeted nervously with his fingers at the pocket on the side of his pants. He held two black figs and the sling there and hoped he wouldn't need them.

Edgar took a last deep breath, rubbed his hands together, and began climbing. Once he found his familiar holds again, his mind was focused and he moved swiftly along the rock face.

He thought about what the man who'd left the book might have been like. *If you could see me now, I suppose you'd send me to bed with no pudding.* He laughed at his own remark. Edgar hadn't enjoyed the luxury of fig pudding before bed in all his life.

Edgar looked up and reflected on the distance to the Highlands above. He'd thought about it many times in the previous few days, and he was aware once again that he would be doing most of the climb in the dead of night, something he had never done. But the time to turn back had come and gone, so there would be no gain from doubting himself now.

After he was a hundred yards up he looked down for the first time. Tabletop lay beneath him — his flat home of groves, pastures, and small villages. If a person walked along the far edge of Tabletop, it would take a week to travel all the way around. Walking near the Highland cliffs cut the time to a few days, and the distance between villages could be walked in half a day or less at a brisk pace. Mr. Ratikan had never given Edgar the opportunity to explore the world beyond the grove, so Edgar knew these things only from what others had told him.

As he held tight, catching his breath with the cool air of approaching night, he caught a glimpse of the world beyond Tabletop. Far below — miles it seemed — was another land, a vast and gloomy place. The Flatlands, much bigger than Tabletop, were a sprawling, dark mystery that few understood and no one spoke of. From where Edgar clutched the rocks he could see only a little of the Flatlands. The view had been much better when he had snuck out of the grove one afternoon and lay down at the very edge of Tabletop, where a sheer cliff face led to the Flatlands below. He'd stuck his head out over the edge only once and had never gone back. Could there be people living in such a wasteland? Or was there something else — something not human? Edgar wasn't sure he wanted to know.

Edgar began climbing once more, this time with more force. He had spent a long day in the groves, and it would seem that he should have grown tired quickly. But Edgar had extraordinary skill and stamina. It was as though the cliff had been laid flat and he was merely crawling on all fours as fast as his feet and hands would carry him. And then, suddenly, he stopped.

He felt a strange sensation start in his feet and move up through his body. He was halfway to the top, which was farther up the wall than he'd ever gone, when the cliff began shaking in his hands. Edgar tightened his grip and wondered if he'd made a disastrous mistake trying to climb up to the Highlands. The tremor built in power, showering Edgar with bits of dust and rock.

ROUTE TO
THE HIGHLANDS

Edgar was hanging like a broken limb from a dried-out tree. He was scaling unknown places, and the rock face was only a shadow as he went. Far below him on Tabletop, the first fires of evening were beginning to burn. What little he could see of the vertical rise above him was steep rock with few holds.

As the faint smell of smoke from the fires below drifted up around him, Edgar's foot slipped, spraying pebbles out into the night air. The thought of falling entered his mind for the first time. With a shudder, Edgar began to doubt if he would ever return home again.

CHAPTER
5
SAMUEL

The time that passed after dinner and before nightfall were quiet if you were a child living in the Highlands, for parents were very strict about keeping their children away from the perilous cliffs in the long, grey light of evening. But Samuel was a boy living within the House of Power — a palatial complex of courtyards, hallways, stairs, and passages perfect for exploration — and his life was different.

Samuel was very happy to spend entire days — sometimes entire weeks — doing nothing but reading books. This gave the boy a rather pasty complexion, as though he were always just leaving the bakery and his face and arms had been covered in a thin dusting of flour. Samuel was every bit as skinny as Edgar, but for entirely different reasons. His mother worked in the kitchen of the House of Power, and this provided him access to plenty of food, but Samuel's appetite had always been meager, and his interest in food was focused primarily on anything that tasted sweet.

His mother worked day and night and usually did not return to their room off the courtyard until very late. During the evening, Samuel often wandered the halls of the House of Power after he'd grown tired of lying on his bed reading. The main floor of the House of Power felt as if it were inside and outside all at once. Some of the halls were laid out under arches surrounding the courtyards where vines twisted endlessly around small trees. The abundant greenery of the courtyards spilled uncontrolled onto the stone walls and cobbled floors, as if it were trying to tear everything down and take over. The place had an unnatural quiet that made people want to speak in a whisper.

Sometimes Samuel would visit his mother after roaming the halls and ask for a treat or a cup of tea, and often she would respond by giving him some errand instead. We find Samuel on just such a night, a night of walking round and round down echoing corridors. He climbed the narrow staircase near his room until it ended at a door he always found locked. Back down the stairs and through the halls he continued until he couldn't stand going without a treat any longer.

"Maybe she will give me a cup of sweet milk if I offer a little help," Samuel said out loud. He heard the echo of footsteps coming toward him from a long way off. Not wanting to talk with anyone, he made his way through a rounded archway, out into the open courtyard. When he arrived at the kitchen, he was not certain he wanted to go in for fear of being given too much work to do, so he peeked around the corner of the door to see what his mother was doing.

She was frail but lovely to look at, though it was immediately clear when Samuel saw her that something was troubling his mother. She was dashing back and forth between the cupboards looking for something, her dark hair unwound partway out of a bun and dancing around the room behind her as she went. Her eye caught sight of Samuel hiding in the doorway.

"Figs and toast wanted in the main chamber," she said in a breathless voice. Whenever Samuel's mother became anxious, a red blotch appeared below her lip and would not go away for several hours. She rubbed the red mark nervously, searching for something behind the kneading table where she did most of her work.

"Why must they ask for things they know we don't have?" she went on. "I can't make figs appear out of the air, and we've been out for weeks. Yet they keep asking for them, every night, only to torment me."

Samuel's mother kept rubbing the red blotch of skin below her lip until Samuel walked into the room and stood beside her.

"It's not going to go away if you keep touching it like that."

Samuel felt some pity for his mother, but only a little, for he knew what was coming next.

"Will you run upstairs and tell them we have no figs, Samuel? I'll give you something you can take, something sweet. Can you do that for me?"

Samuel's mother hadn't always been so frail. There was a time when she'd enjoyed a higher station in life and demonstrated more poise, but then Samuel's father had passed away in a dreadful accident. When it happened, her thin outer shell of confidence was shaken and she seemed to crack into a thousand pieces all at once. Her station in the kitchen was the result of the loss of Samuel's father, for he had been a man of great importance before the accident. Without his authority, Samuel's mother had been relegated to a life of servitude.

"Can you put something sweet on the tray for me as well?" asked Samuel. His mother was already busy setting a tray of toast sprinkled with fig powder, along with some cups and a covered bowl of warm tea.

"I'll get you something when you return. Just be careful not to drop the tray or spill anything on the way." She held a round tray out to Samuel with a concerned look. "Can you manage it?"

The tray wasn't very big or heavy, but Samuel groaned all the same when he took it from her. "Yes, mother, I can manage it just fine."

Samuel made his way through the courtyard and into the House of Power. The pathway leading up to the entrance was made of a great many stones. There were openings throughout the pathway where small trees shot up out of the ground, their trunks covered in vines. The pathway ended at an archway with no door. On the other side there was a round room leading in three directions: a wide hall to the right, another to the left, and a steep stairway up the middle.

Samuel took the tray up the stairs and when he reached the top, there was a man standing before him with round cheeks and bushy grey eyebrows. He didn't have any hair on top of his head.

"What have you got there, Samuel?"

It was Horace, whose job was to keep people away from Lord Phineus when he didn't want to be disturbed. The Lord didn't *ever* want to be disturbed, so Horace was a near permanent fixture at the top of the stairs.

"Some treats for the main chamber," answered Samuel.

Horace peered closely at the tray and snatched one of the toasts away.

"You may pass," he said, then devoured the toast in one bite and swept his arm open in a grand gesture of invitation toward the main chamber. Samuel smiled, for though they had little occasion to see one another, he liked Horace and his theatrical ways.

Samuel hurried into the cool of the upper hall toward the enormous door at the end, eager to finish his errand and return for his promised dessert. He set the tray on the floor and knocked on the door. As he stood back up, the door opened, and Sir Philip stood towering over Samuel in a red robe like the one his father used to wear.

Sir Philip glared at the tray on the floor. "Did Horace take the figs from you or have we yet to see more production from the grove?"

As he stooped to pick up the tray, Samuel wished he hadn't gone to visit his mother.

"I'm afraid there are still no figs to speak of, sir. The harvest has yet to come."

Samuel's hands were shaking as he held the tray, and the

cups began to rattle. Past the doorway he saw a wide table inside the room, behind which sat Lord Phineus. He also wore a red robe, darker than Sir Philip's and with a wide, black band trimming its sleeves and hood.

"Let the boy through, Sir Philip. It's not his fault we have to wait for the things we want. A harvest comes when it's ready, not when we demand it."

Samuel hesitated at the door. There was a dark presence about Lord Phineus, and it crossed Samuel's mind to set down the tray right where he was standing and run back to his room.

"Come on, then, let's see what you have there before whatever it is gets cold."

Samuel crept into the room and set the tray down on the table. He looked to his right and saw there was another man gazing out one of the windows where vines crept in, covering some of the walls and floor. It was Sir Emerik, the last of the three men who controlled almost everything in the Highlands and Tabletop below. Not long ago his own father, Sir William, had been the fourth of these powerful men.

To his left, Samuel noticed a single column of white stone, which stood as tall as he was. On its top sat the carved stone head of a man.

"I see you are intrigued by Mead's head," said Lord Phineus. Samuel jerked his head back to focus his attention on Lord Phineus.

"I was only looking."

Lord Phineus smiled and beckoned the boy closer.

"It's a favorite thing of mine. Best you don't touch it."

Sir Emerik crossed over to the table and leaned down, whispering something to Lord Phineus in a voice that sounded like crumpling paper. Lord Phineus didn't seem very interested. He absently took the cover off the tea, and a puff of sweet-smelling steam rose into the cool air.

"We still miss having your father on the board of elders," said Sir Emerik in a raspy voice that made Samuel want to cover his ears. "He was very knowledgeable, but we're trying our best to manage."

"Let me ask you something, Samuel," said Lord Phineus, reaching across the table and taking a piece of toast. "Do you miss having your father around? I mean, were the two of you close, or are you more of a mother's boy?"

Samuel's face flushed and he looked down at his feet. He wanted only to leave the room and run back to the kitchen to yell at his mother for making him bring the tray. Lord Phineus set down his toast and reached his hand out over the table. He put his finger under the boy's chin, lifting it up, and Samuel tried to look away but couldn't.

Lord Phineus had a cruel look on his face, as though he'd knowingly hurt the boy by mentioning his father. "Be a gem and tell your mother to bring me some fig butter in the morning with my bread, won't you?"

"But there are no figs, Lord."

"I know. Ask her anyway. When I see her in the courtyard, I'll be amused by that little red spot under her lip."

Lord Phineus picked up the toast he'd set aside and examined it, considering whether or not he wanted to take a bite.

"You may go, Samuel."

Samuel turned to leave and found Sir Philip standing in front of him. He came to an abrupt stop and wouldn't look up. The familiar red robe was all Samuel could see, and it made him wish his father were there to scare all the cruelty out of the room.

"Step aside, Philip," said Lord Phineus. "Soon enough we'll put him to work, and I'm quite sure we can provide him with labor that will make a man out of him yet."

When Samuel was on the other side of the door, he ran down the hall, passed Horace without saying a word, and stumbled down the stairs toward the courtyard.

Samuel was out of breath by the time he stopped running. He looked back and saw how far he was from the House of Power, out in the open fields that lay before the edge of the Highlands. It wasn't a terribly long run, but Samuel was not in the habit of running or climbing. He passed through the field into a meadow of green grass that reached as high as his chest, and continued through a thicket of twisting trees.

Finally he reached a place where the grass turned to earth and rock and the trees fell away. Here he could see in the grey of night that there was a line where the ground turned to black: the edge of the Highlands. It was a dangerous place. A sudden stumble or a tiny push from behind and that would be the end of Samuel.

He lay down on the ground and hung his head out over the edge of the Highlands, lost in the memories of his past life, a life when his father was still alive and his mother was a different person. Down below he saw firelight and smelled a faint but rich aroma of burning wood and black figs. He was above the grove and to the side of the nearest waterfall, which ran close to the House of Power. As he lay there he wondered what the people of Tabletop did at the end of a day of working in the grove. He stayed at the edge thinking for a long time, until he felt tired and began to drift off to sleep. It was a dangerous thing to do at the edge of the world.

Samuel wasn't sure how long he'd been asleep when he heard a sound that startled him awake. At first he couldn't figure out where the noise was coming from, but as he sat up and rubbed the sleep from his eyes he understood. The sound was coming from beneath him. Samuel leaned his head slowly over the edge of the Highlands, peering into the darkness below. And there, to his astonishment, he saw something no one in the Highlands had ever seen before.

Someone was climbing up the cliff.

CHAPTER

6

A BOOK OF SECRET THINGS

It was nearing the darkest part of night, and Samuel began to wonder if he had only dreamed that someone was climbing up the side of the cliff. He was certain whatever it was had arms and a head, but it seemed as though it were smaller than it ought to have been for how close it was. Maybe it wasn't a person at all, but a creature of some kind, come to grab hold of little children and pull them over the edge into a cavern on the cliff somewhere below.

Samuel glanced urgently over his shoulder toward the House of Power and wondered if he ought to alert everyone to a possible invasion. But then Samuel heard coughing and a small voice mumbling to itself, and he turned back, looking down at the approaching figure. He realized that it wasn't a monster at all, but a boy. A *boy*. Could it really be?

Getting to his feet, Samuel walked in silence along the edge of the cliff until he was right over the ascending boy, and then he lay down once more. Looking over the edge, he began to ponder his options. Surely Lord Phineus and the others in the House of Power would want to know there was a person invading the Highlands. There might even be a reward for Samuel's valiant effort.

But Samuel worried about leaving the climbing figure. Maybe it would be gone when he came back. If that happened, Lord Phineus would be angry. The longer Samuel waited, the more certain he became that he needed to stay.

A boy my own age climbing into the Highlands. How can that be? Samuel felt his own scrawny arms and was embarrassed — no, jealous, really — of the boy who was now only twenty feet below him. How was it that a boy could climb so high — and why was he risking his life to do it? *How dare he.*

"You there! I see you coming up the cliff!" Samuel blurted out in his most threatening voice.

After a brief moment of acute fear, Edgar looked up and saw Samuel's little head poking over the edge in the night sky. The voice surely had not belonged to an adult, and the size of Samuel's head was a comforting reinforcement.

"How did you come to be here at such a late hour? It's almost as if you were waiting for me," asked Edgar in his friendliest voice.

Samuel thought for a moment, trying to figure out how to answer. What sort of boy was this?

"You can't just come crawling up here," said Samuel. "It's not normal. And anyway, it's *forbidden.* Didn't your parents tell you that?" But Samuel was having trouble hiding his curiosity, and for all his attempts to bully this boy invading his world, he really only wanted to know more about him.

"I haven't any parents to speak of," said Edgar. He had arrived only a few feet below the Highlands, and the two boys could see each other now in the faint light. Edgar smiled and put a hand up where Samuel could take it, but instead Samuel reeled back on his elbows and loose dirt cascaded down on Edgar's head. Samuel hadn't realized how uncertain he was of this stranger until his hand had come so close. He had been trained to view those from below as dirty and unsafe.

"Does everyone in the Highlands have such manners?" asked Edgar. There was good humor in his voice, and this calmed Samuel as he returned to gaze over the cliff's edge.

"Come on, then," continued Edgar. "Can't you give me a hand?"

"What's your name?"

"I'm Edgar."

A moment passed in the quiet of the night, and the two boys looked off nervously, wondering what the other was thinking.

"I hope I don't regret this," said Samuel, finally coming around. After a good deal of hesitation he reached his arm down. Edgar took Samuel's hand and found it to be small and frail. There was no strength in it, and Edgar was sure the two of them would go tumbling off the edge. To Samuel's relief, Edgar let go of his hand and quickly scaled what remained of the cliff on his own. Once at the top, he moved away from the edge, allowing himself a sigh of pleasure at feeling the solid ground beneath his feet.

Samuel shared his name with Edgar but could think of nothing else to say.

"So this is the Highlands," Edgar observed, drawing in a big breath of fresh air. "It smells good up here." Edgar looked around and wished he could see the new world he'd arrived in, but found only the shadows of trees in the distance.

"I live in a grove like that one back home," said Edgar, pointing toward the shapes of clustered trees he could make out in the dark.

"That's not a grove, it's just a bunch of trees. They don't produce anything. They just sit there and hide what's behind them."

"What's behind them?" asked Edgar, so curious that he began walking toward the trees.

"No! Don't! You'll be seen . . . and they won't be happy you've come. You'll get into trouble." Edgar came back and sat down next to Samuel.

The two boys were at the edge of the Highlands, and neither of them knew what to say or do. Samuel had been told all his life that people like Edgar were good for only one thing: providing for the needs of the Highlands. For his part, Edgar knew only that the people of the Highlands controlled everything in his home, and that they took whatever they wanted. Edgar was awfully short on time, but he wasn't at all sure he could trust this boy of the Highlands. The two had been trained to dislike one another, even though they'd never had the occasion to meet until now.

"Why have you come here?" asked Samuel. There was no accusation in his voice, only genuine curiosity.

Now that he was sitting down after hours of rigorous climbing, Edgar realized how tired and hungry he was. It was almost impossible to imagine that soon he would have to go back down, and he didn't know when he would be able to return.

"I don't know if I can trust you," Edgar began. "But I don't have a lot of time, either. I have to be getting back to the grove or I'll be missed, and then Mr. Ratikan will punish me."

"You're not armed and you don't look like a threat to me," said Samuel. "I don't see what I would gain by turning you in. Nobody needs to know we've seen one another."

Edgar sensed Samuel's concern and curiosity. "I don't know," he said. "I *want* to trust you, but I've only just met you."

Samuel thought a moment before trying once again to convince a boy from Tabletop that a boy from the Highlands could be trusted.

"It's not what you think," said Samuel. "Here in the Highlands. I don't like it here. I don't *want* to tell anyone you've come, don't you see? I want it to be our secret."

Edgar continued to ponder the matter. It might be that this boy would betray him in the end, but Edgar had come to have the book read to him, and he'd found someone who might be able to do it — someone who appeared trustworthy.

With some hesitation, Edgar told Samuel about the man he thought might be his father, about the many years of climbing by himself, and about the thing he had been looking for but could not find (although he didn't yet say exactly what it was).

Samuel listened carefully to everything Edgar said before making his reply.

"So you've spent your whole life secretly breaking the rules and putting your life in danger, all so that you might find this thing that someone left for you?"

Edgar nodded enthusiastically.

"But why did you come all this way?" asked Samuel.

Edgar didn't answer right away. Could he really trust this scrawny boy who wouldn't last a day in Mr. Ratikan's grove? He couldn't be sure, but he knew he had been very lucky to be discovered by another boy nearly his own age rather than a guard. He decided it was a risk he was willing to take.

"I found what was left for me," revealed Edgar. He reached his hand into the large pocket sewn onto the front of his shirt, but then waited another moment.

"You don't have to show me if you don't want to," said Samuel. He was curious, but he didn't want to scare Edgar away. "If you go back, I'll pretend I never saw you."

Edgar pulled the book out of the pocket and held it close in the night air. Samuel was immediately enthralled at the sight of it. He loved books, and this one looked different than any he'd seen before. It wasn't like those in the Highlands, which were all large, heavy, and bound in hard casings. This one was small and leathery. It looked old and worn.

"Where did you get that?" asked Samuel, his voice betraying his excitement. But when he took his eyes off the book and looked at Edgar's face, he suddenly remembered the rules.

"You can't read," said Samuel. "That's why you've come, to find someone who might read it to you."

Edgar didn't respond. He looked away into the darkness with a wounded expression on his face.

"It's nothing to be ashamed of," said Samuel. "It's not your fault."

Edgar was unconvinced. "You don't know how lucky you are, living up here. It must be paradise."

"It isn't like that," said Samuel. He hesitated, then added, "I'll tell you a secret of my own and you'll see."

Samuel pointed to somewhere in the distance, down the line of the cliff.

"Down that way, about a year ago, my father fell off the edge. Since then my mother hasn't been the same." Samuel rubbed a spot below his lip, feeling an itch somewhere beneath the surface of his skin. "Now I spend a lot of time in my room by myself. I don't like to go out."

This was an important moment for Edgar, for he realized something that he had never thought of before: He was lonely. Sleeping alone in the grove, protecting his secrets, staying away from the other children. He'd had a certain feeling all along but somehow never understood what it was. And there was something more. Edgar understood, for the first time, that there were two kinds of loneliness. One happened because you chose it, and it was all right for a time. The other chose you, and it was never all right. Samuel was living with the second kind, and Edgar felt sad for him.

And yet, there was something in Samuel's story that didn't quite make sense to Edgar. He wondered if Samuel were trying to trick him.

"That's odd," Edgar mused.

Samuel was taken aback by Edgar's choice of words. He thought it more tragic than odd that his father had fallen to his death.

"Is everyone in Tabletop so kindhearted as you?" Samuel said bitterly. He lashed out easily when his feelings were hurt.

"It's just — well — to be honest, the story is a little hard to believe."

"What do you mean?"

"I mean if someone were to fall out of the sky into Tabletop, I think I would have heard about it. Everyone talks. It's not the sort of thing that wouldn't get around."

This took Samuel by surprise and he thought on it a moment. Could it be the story had been false? Who would invent such a horrible tale? Samuel didn't know what to say.

"I really am sorry about your father," said Edgar, shaking Samuel from his daze.

Samuel tried to put the stirring new thoughts out of his mind. "Shall we have a look at that book?"

This time Edgar didn't hesitate. He held it out, and Samuel took it from him.

"There isn't much time," said Edgar as Samuel examined the cover. "I work in Mr. Ratikan's grove — right down there — and he'll be looking for me in the morning. He'll have my hide if I'm not there come first light." Edgar looked wearily toward the edge of the cliff. "And it will take me a long while to get down."

"This is a strange book, Edgar."

"Why do you say that? Does it look different than the other books you've seen?"

Samuel tried to think of how to put it. "The paper is so thin and white. All of the books in the Highlands have thick, yellowing pages and hard covers. I've never seen anything like it in the Highlands. I wonder where it came from."

Samuel opened to the first page and discovered handwriting inside that was so sloppy he could hardly make out what it said.

"What does it say?" asked Edgar.

"I'm not sure," answered Samuel.

"You can read, can't you?" There was a panic in Edgar's voice.

"Of course I can read!" Samuel retorted. "It's just the writing is so terrible and there's hardly any light. I can barely make out the words on the page."

Samuel had an unfriendly thought — *Who does this boy from Tabletop think he's talking to?* — followed by a better one: *I may have found a friend and I shouldn't think of him that way.*

"The first line is the only one that's written clearly," said Samuel. "It says, 'A book of secret things — for Edgar.'"

A shiver of thrill and delight ran up Edgar's spine. The book was for him. For *him*. Those words alone were worth all the trouble it had been to get here.

"What else does it say? Just the first page — can you read the first few pages?"

For the next twenty minutes Samuel pored over the words on the first page and tried desperately to piece them together. His reading came in fits and starts, and waiting for the next words to come drove Edgar mad. But in essence what Samuel read to Edgar that night was very close to the following:

I am in a hurry and must write quickly. I have only tonight to leave for you what I can and to hide it well. I don't know if this will ever be found, but it is a good precaution, and so I'll take the time to write it. Using the basket to hide this book of secret things up high will be another challenge, but I believe I can do it without anyone catching me. We shall see.

Edgar — I'm leaving this for you knowing that most of what I write you won't be able to understand. If by some miracle you do stumble upon this message, I don't think you'll be able to read it (unless an unexpected change occurs). I think you'll be eleven years old — that's when this little book would come to you, if it comes at all. My hope is that you'll hide it until you can find someone who will read it to you. DO NOT give the book to someone in the Highlands without making sure you can *trust them. There are many in that part of the world who would do you harm.*

My name is Luther. Some call me Dr. Kincaid. I brought you here, Edgar. Of this I will tell you more if there is time — just know I did what I thought was best for you.

This is the first thing you must know and it is a hard thing to explain: Atherton is not what you think it is. I will try to tell you the truth in the few pages that follow. . . .

Both boys sat dumbstruck. A moment of silence passed at the edge of the Highlands. Deep night had come in the reading of the first few pages, and the very last of the grey light had passed. Total darkness had arrived, and suddenly Edgar was aware of the hour.

"I must go."

"Are you sure you can climb down in the night?"

Edgar leaned out over the edge and saw there were only four or five orange dots from the few remaining fires below. *I've stayed too long.* He looked back at Samuel and held out his hand.

"Deep night will only last an hour, then the light will slowly return until morning comes. If I leave now, I think I can make it," said Edgar. "Give me the book."

Samuel drew the book closer and tightened his grip. It would be hard to let it go.

"Why not leave the book here with me? I can figure out what it says, then I can tell you everything when you come back."

Edgar knew that Samuel could not outrun him or over-power him. It would not be difficult to take the book and go.

"Samuel," Edgar said. "I trust you. I know the book says I shouldn't, but I do. It's not that. . . ."

There was an awkward pause while Edgar tried to explain.

"I can't leave it here, Samuel. I just can't. This is the only thing in the world that truly belongs to me. Let's read it to-gether. I'll come faster next time, to the same spot, and we'll spend a good long time going through it."

Samuel wanted to keep the book so badly he almost tore off into the trees with it. But Edgar was the closest thing he had to a friend, and a friend was something he really needed. Samuel held the book out to Edgar.

"Here's what we'll do," said Edgar, putting the book back in the front pocket of his shirt. "You keep helping me read this book of secret things, and I'll see what I can find out about what happened to your father. If he did fall from the sky, someone in Tabletop will know about it."

Edgar was over the edge of the Highlands, his feet searching blindly for holds in the dark. He was tired, and it would be an even more dangerous trip down than the climb up, but he was determined and anxious to return to the grove before daylight.

"When will you come back?" asked Samuel.

Edgar looked up one last time.

"I'll need some time to rest." Edgar seemed to ponder how long it would take to regain his strength for another climb to the Highlands. "Seven nights from now, that's when I'll come again. Look for me!"

And so a pact was made: Samuel would help Edgar read his book, and Edgar would help Samuel find out about his father. The fact that they'd met would be their secret.

A few moments after they parted, Samuel lost sight of Edgar on the cliff far below. He wanted to call out to him — to say goodbye once more — but he was afraid someone might hear. He returned to his room and spent a sleepless night thinking about his new friend, his father, and all the strange things he'd read in the book at the edge of the world.

CHAPTER

7

A SPY WITH A SLING

The grey of night had passed and morning light was in the air as Edgar dropped the book of secret things back into its original hiding place on the way down the cliff. He had never been this high up on the wall with daylight upon him, and for a moment he stayed very still, surveying the waking world beneath him.

From where he clung motionless to the wall, Edgar could see everywhere he'd been in his short life. He had rarely traveled beyond the grove, the small village, and the pastures in between. From above it was a rich blanket of gold and green. There were several people milling around in the village already. Before long it would be completely light, and the world would be alive and watching. Edgar had no protectors — no parents or family — and if danger came he would have no one to depend on but himself.

It was hard for him to imagine a worse kind of trouble than being caught in the light of day in such a forbidden place.

Edgar turned to the wall and began moving once more, slowly but with purpose. Like a droplet of water he slipped smoothly down in silence. It seemed as though he belonged on the cliffs; a person would have to look very carefully to realize he was not somehow part of the rocks themselves. Edgar was one with Atherton.

When he reached the bottom, he moved swiftly across the dusty expanse to the trees in the distance. But it was already late, and even his best effort was not enough to keep him from returning to the grove an hour after he was due among the saplings.

Edgar crept quietly toward the younger trees, twigs crunching as he went, a bright sun turning the leaves transparent overhead. It was a peaceful time of day in the grove. The air was cool but not freezing, and Edgar could almost taste his breath. He ran his fingers over limbs and leaves as he went, and the sound of the leaves softly stirring made him feel sleepy.

"Why aren't you in with the saplings?" The tranquil moment in the grove was broken by Mr. Ratikan's sharp question. He had a maddening way of emerging out of nowhere when least expected. Mr. Ratikan's hair was matted and his old pants were wrinkled, as though he'd crawled right out of bed and into the grove.

"I asked you a question, boy." He swung the walking stick at Edgar's shins, and Edgar didn't move, thinking a little cruelty might soften Mr. Ratikan's mood. It didn't. "Where have you been hiding this morning?" he demanded.

Edgar wasn't sure how to answer. He hadn't slept or eaten in a long while and he couldn't think clearly.

"All right, if that's the way you want it," said Mr. Ratikan. "There'll be no water and no food until you tell me. And don't think of lying about it — I've asked around and I know where you *haven't* been. I want to know where you *have* been."

Mr. Ratikan poked Edgar in the chest with the walking stick and almost knocked him off his feet, but the boy stayed quiet. Edgar could think of no lie to cover his tracks, and he certainly couldn't tell Mr. Ratikan the truth of where he'd been.

"Now get to those saplings and don't stop until you've finished the rest of them! I suspect a little hard work and hunger will open that closed mouth of yours."

As he silently watched Mr. Ratikan walk away, stooping under low-hanging limbs, Edgar realized "the rest of them" meant over fifty saplings. To trim each one would take until late afternoon even if he worked fast. It would be a long day with no water and no food.

Edgar went to the sapling field and started to trim the first of many small trees. These were the babies — the future of the grove — and they stood only a little taller than he was. The bark was thin like paper. A gentle breath on the tiny green leaves would make them dance all around, but not let go.

The trees were only a year old and they would grow quickly. By the time they were two they would produce a crop of figs,

and when they were three they would produce one more crop —
known as the third-year harvest — and then be cut down, the
insides scooped out for dough. The trees were a miracle of production: figs, dough, paper, wood for building and burning —
nearly every part was put to use.

But the trees in the grove had problems as well. They consumed
enormous amounts of water, which meant Tabletop could grow
only a few hundred at a time, leaving even less water for the
residents of the village. Two hundred saplings, just a hundred
second-years (for the saplings were delicate, and half were dead
by the second year), a hundred more third years — this was all
the grove could handle and still provide enough water for the
village. The best of the trees produced less than a hundred us-
able figs a year, while many of the fragile trees produced nothing but hard black balls.

The greatest danger from the fig trees came if they were left
in the ground more than a few weeks after the third-year harvest.
The leaves became toxic to the touch, and the bark transformed
into a bright orange moss that dried out and turned to dust. If
the dust caught in the air, many in the grove suffered an agoniz-
ing cough that lasted for weeks. This, Edgar suspected, was one
of the most important reasons Mr. Ratikan was so strict about
the fig harvesting schedule. There was little room for error.

Edgar tried to work fast all day, but more than once found
he was sleeping right where he stood. He went from tree to tree,
trimming and pruning, entirely lost in his own world as the day
slowly passed into the dinner hour. As he neared the end of the

last row of saplings, Edgar snapped out of his reverie when he heard a *crack* and something shot just a hair past his head. He ducked and instantly reached for his sling.

"I saw you."

Edgar spun around and saw Isabel standing about ten paces away, reloading from a little bag full of black figs hanging around her waist. She began swinging the sling once more, and Edgar froze. She let one end of the string go with a *pop*, and another black fig flew a few inches over Edgar's head.

"You've gone mad!" he screamed, fumbling in his side pocket to seize his own weapon. But Isabel had already reloaded and was swirling another black fig over her head. She was unbelievably swift in her movements.

"I followed you before dinner last night," she said. "I saw what you did."

"I don't know what you're talking about," said Edgar, loading his sling. "Put that thing down!"

"I know where you went and what you were doing."

She let go of the string once more with a *snap*, and this time the black fig nearly grazed the right side of Edgar's head.

"I've always known."

Always known? Could it be true? And when had she made the sling? Edgar didn't think anyone else had thought to make one, and certainly not *Isabel*. It was clear she had mastered its use. She could aim it and throw with force.

"We can't talk if you keep throwing those things at me," said Edgar.

"I wasn't going to hit you," she said. "I've better aim than you and I can throw a black fig farther. Do you want to know why? Because I spend my time *practicing* while you climb around trying to get yourself killed!"

Now Edgar was angry. Who did this nine-year-old girl think she was, following him around and spying on him day and night? He would show her how wrong she was.

Edgar loaded a black fig into his sling and began swinging it over his head.

"Do you see that second-year tree down the line, the one on the very end?"

Isabel nodded. It was a long way off down a narrow path through the trees. Edgar's black fig whizzed through the air down the path and glanced off the trunk. Not a direct hit, but a hit nonetheless on a target so far away Isabel could never hit it.

"I don't know what it is you're doing climbing around up there," she said, fishing around for a fig in her little bag. "It's dangerous! And it's against the rules — I mean the really big rules, the ones you can't break or they take you away."

"Why must you always sneak around?" said Edgar. His secret was known by someone — and not just any someone. It was Isabel!

She stepped closer to Edgar and began swinging the black fig in a wide circle over her head. Edgar realized for the first time that her sling was longer than his, quite a bit longer. Around and around it went, gaining speed and force. When Isabel let it go, Edgar was astounded to see that it plainly traveled much faster than Edgar's had. And not only that, but it hit the very center of the second-year tree that his had only glanced.

It was true. Isabel was a better shot than he was. And she probably could hurl a black fig farther than he could, too.

"A long time ago I watched you make a sling, so I made one, too."

Edgar didn't know what to think. He showed no emotion — only a blank stare — which wasn't surprising, having had no sleep or water or food for so long.

Isabel stood before him, her anger having turned to concern. "Last night, when you didn't return for so very long —" Isabel broke off, embarrassed, and tried to find the right words. "I thought you were never coming back."

Edgar was finally beginning to understand that he'd spent so much energy trying to keep people away for such a long time — to remain hidden — that he hadn't realized Isabel's true intentions. She wanted only to be his friend. And yet he was still angry.

"I don't trust anyone," said Edgar. "And I'm afraid you'll tell someone."

Isabel turned and scampered off into the trees a short distance away. When she returned, she held out a handful of dough and a cup of water to Edgar. Isabel had come to him at his weakest, and he couldn't resist reaching for it.

"Why must you climb the cliffs when you know it's forbidden?" Isabel asked, pulling the dough and the water back so Edgar couldn't reach it.

"I can't tell you."

The two were at a standoff. They were like two lonely saplings standing near one another, rooted to the ground, unable to come any closer.

"I have my reasons for climbing the cliffs," said Edgar. "I can't tell you what they are, only that they are very important."

Isabel's dark eyebrows were her most expressive feature, and they moved up just a little, which told Edgar she wished he would go on. When Edgar had nothing more to offer, Isabel relented and handed over the dough and water.

"I won't tell anyone what you're doing, I promise I won't. And we'll never be friends if I keep sneaking around trying to understand you, so I won't do it anymore."

Edgar gulped some water and swallowed a hunk of the dough, barely chewing it. He'd always been alone, but now found himself with Isabel *and* Samuel — two allies where before he'd had none. The speed at which things were moving made him nervous, and yet the idea of having companions he could trust captivated him.

"There's been a lot of talk in the grove these past few days," said Isabel.

Edgar looked up nervously, wondering if word of his climbing had gotten out.

"Oh, no — they don't know anything about the climbing," Isabel reassured him, as if reading his mind.

"What, then?"

"Remember when the ground shook yesterday and the day before that?"

Edgar nodded.

"People are scared. The adults gathered in the village last night, but I couldn't get close enough to hear them. They're preparing for something. And that man, do you remember him, the one who was sick at dinner the other night?"

Edgar nodded again.

"Well, he's still sick. From what I've overheard, he hasn't eaten or been back to work. He just lies in bed moaning. People are nervous about it. They think maybe it was something in the grove that caused it."

"You mean something he ate?"

Isabel shrugged. "I don't know."

"Well, it doesn't have anything to do with us," Edgar said, changing the subject. The water and food were clearing his head, and there was a little more energy in his legs. "In a couple of nights I have to go somewhere. Do you think you could do something for me?"

Isabel's eyebrows darted up. Maybe he had decided to trust her after all.

"Tomorrow night, if I'm up to it, I'll be traveling to the Village of Rabbits on an important errand. I could use some food and water for the journey. Do you think you could get anything for me?"

"I can always get more than I need."

Her reply made Edgar realize once again that he had long underestimated the cleverness of this girl of the grove.

"You know where I usually sleep, on the far side of the main grove?"

Isabel nodded.

"Can you meet me there in the morning with something to eat, and again after dinner?"

"I can."

Edgar ate the last of the dough and drank what was left in the cup, then handed the cup back to Isabel. The two of them parted ways. Isabel walked toward Mr. Ratikan's house and Edgar went the other way, to the place where he slept.

Not long after, Edgar heard the snap of a sling and ducked down in the grove. A black fig slammed into a tree beside him and bounced along the ground at Edgar's feet. When he looked back there was no one, only the trees of the grove and the sound of a girl laughing in the distance.

CHAPTER
8

THE VILLAGE OF RABBITS

True to her word, Isabel brought food to Edgar the next day and night. They talked, but only a little, and Isabel was careful not to ask too many questions. Edgar was surprised to see how much food she was able to bring, and he was especially pleased by the water, which was much harder to attain. She was really quite resourceful.

Edgar had enjoyed a good night of sleep in the soft undergrowth of the grove and an easy day of work almost entirely free of encounters with Mr. Ratikan. As he stood in the early evening light, ready to embark on his journey, a chill of excitement ran through him. This would be Edgar's first exploration in Tabletop away from the grove.

"Do you need any black figs?" asked Isabel. "I've got some."

Edgar shook his head, for he already had two of his own. He was in the habit of traveling light.

"I could make you one of these little bags that tie around your waist. Mine holds ten black figs. You could bury the bag like I do and only take it out when you need it."

Edgar had to admit it seemed like a good idea for the future, because he'd never felt quite so vulnerable before. He'd broken two of the rules of Tabletop, and planned to continue doing it. Carrying around more black figs seemed a good idea.

"Be careful," said Isabel, and she was off, racing through the grove to the village on the other side.

There were three villages in Tabletop, and each produced something different — rabbits in one, fig trees in another, and sheep in the third. The farms and villages were near the water-falls, and Edgar had to stay wide of them to avoid being seen. Later, when he was well clear of the grove, he could veer back and walk along the cliffs.

Tabletop turned dry and dusty as he moved farther away from the water. After a while Edgar bent down and touched the ground. It was hard and infertile, completely devoid of life. As he stood in the silence, feeling a little cold and alone, the ground began to move. It was slow at first, but a moment later the wave of movement became stronger and shook dust into the air. Edgar knelt down on the ground, waiting and wondering. It didn't last very long, and when it was over, Edgar got up and began to run until he was able to put the strange occurrence out of his mind.

Edgar had brought with him a single dried fig — a rare

treasure that had been secretly hidden away since the last harvest. This was not a black fig, but rather one that had once been fresh and chewy. If these were saved long enough, they turned hard and crumbly, but they tasted magnificent. This was not true of black figs, which were entirely inedible. The farther Edgar got away from the grove, he knew, the more the little treasure would be worth. Edgar thought that in the Village of Rabbits, he could probably get ten rabbits for the dried fig in his pocket, though rabbits were beside the point. What he sought was information about Samuel's father.

It may have crossed your mind by now to ask why figs were such a coveted item on Atherton, and a long, dull walk across a lifeless plain seems as good a time as any to tell you. There were no candies or chocolate on Atherton, no sugar or sweets to speak of. Unless of course a person happened to have a fig, in which case *everything* could be made sweeter, whether the fig was fresh off the tree, churned into butter, or dried and ground into powder. In Tabletop figs were truly a treasure because the Highlands wanted them all. Of the thousands of figs harvested, only a tenth remained in Tabletop, and those were often plucked in secret during the harvest, taken out one by one and stashed in a hat or a pocket.

When Edgar came upon the Village of Rabbits, it was late and he was cautious as he crept into town. It was a young place. The oldest person in the village was forty, and about three hundred people lived there. They didn't have a burial ground because nobody who lived in the Village of Rabbits had ever died.

Edgar hoped he might find someone he could talk to, someone who wouldn't ask too many questions but might be able to answer a few of his. He made his way down the dusty main street and entered the one public establishment that was open — an old inn with a kitchen that served rabbit, rabbit, and more rabbit. They also offered small servings of water, but it was far too expensive for most passing through.

When Edgar entered, he caught the smell of meat cooking. A woman was sweeping a hard dirt floor with a broom. The room was poorly lit by a fire in the middle, where a man was turning three whole rabbits skewered on a stick. It smelled awfully good.

One of the three small tables in the room was occupied by a man and a woman, and the other two were empty. Edgar strolled past the fire and sat at one of the open tables.

"It's a bit late for a stranger to be out." It was the woman sitting at the table. "What's a young boy like you doing away from home at such a late hour?"

Edgar had expected questions and he'd concocted a story. "I work in the big grove. Well, actually, I live in the big grove." He paused and put on a face of embarrassment, hoping they would see him for the orphan he was. "My caretaker sent me to get rabbits for a celebration, and I got a late start. We're very busy in the grove."

"Mr. Ratikan? I've heard he's quite a hard man to work for," remarked the fellow who sat with the woman. He had a beard that grew in patches on his face, as though he weren't quite old enough to make it work but was determined to try.

"I hope he's not expecting you to work tomorrow," added

the woman. "You'll be walking most of the night to get back by morning."

Edgar nodded somberly before he answered.

"It will be a long walk back and a busy day in the grove tomorrow. He does make us work long hours, but I don't mind, really I don't."

"You see there? Mr. Ratikan is a hard man, I've heard that before," said the man, pleased that he had been right.

They told Edgar their names — Morris and Amanda — and Edgar told them his. Edgar thought they seemed the type who might stay and sit at the table for hours on end talking idly about nothing in particular to whomever passed through. He looked to the fire in the middle of the room and watched as the man poked one of the rabbits with a sharp stick, and watery blood dripped out. The coals hissed and smoked.

"How do you expect to pay for these rabbits you seek?" said the man at the fire. He had black hair that looked like dark water and a solemn face reflecting orange and yellow light.

Edgar fished around in his pocket for the dried fig and set it on the table, which produced an abrupt change in Morris and Amanda's leisurely tone. The two were overcome with a sudden interest, and the man turning the rabbits licked his lips, thinking of a taste he hadn't enjoyed in quite a while.

"Mr. Ratikan wants ten rabbits for it," said Edgar. "That's what he told me to ask for."

Edgar had needed a reason to make his visit to the inn plausible, but now that it was out of his mouth he began to wonder what he would do with ten rabbits if he actually got them. On quickly considering the matter, he determined he could leave them secretly on the doorsteps of those who had been kindest to him in the grove. No one would need to know where they came from.

Morris and Amanda looked at one another for a long, silent moment and then nodded. "We've got ten rabbits at home we can have here in no time," said Morris, and he was out of his seat and heading for the door.

"Now hold on a minute!" said the man cooking the rabbits, whose name was Briney. "This is my place and if there is business to be had it's going to include me."

Edgar sat quietly and let the sparks fly between the people in the room. The woman with the broom stopped her work and came over to join the conversation. Edgar gathered that her name was Maude and she was the wife of Briney, the cook. What ensued was a long and heated exchange that drove up the price of the fig. When all was said and done, the terms of the deal were as follows:

» Morris and Amanda would buy the fig and pay ten rabbits to Edgar and one rabbit to the cook. They were to retrieve the rabbits immediately.

» As the proprietor of the establishment, Briney would take a corner of the fig, ground it up into powder, and use it to season the three rabbits hanging over the fire. Morris and Amanda would get the rest of the fig to do with as they pleased.

» When the couple returned with the eleven rabbits, they
would be given one perfectly seasoned and cooked rabbit
along with a small cup of water. Edgar would get a cup
of water and a whole seasoned rabbit for his dinner, and
Briney and Maude would enjoy the remaining rabbit.

The longer Edgar stayed quiet, the better the arrangement became for him. This would be a mouthwatering feast to which he
was unaccustomed, for Edgar had only enjoyed rabbit twice
before — both times prepared by Mr. Ratikan — and both
times it was dry as a bone. Morris, Amanda, and Maude hov-
ered over Briney as he carefully broke off a corner of the dried
fig, debating over whether the portions were fair. Shortly after
they reached an agreement, the couple went to get the rabbits,
leaving Edgar alone with the cook and his wife.

"Can I ask you a question?" Edgar said, leaning in closer to
the rabbits on the stick and wondering what the crisp skin would
taste like. Briney mumbled and nodded and seemed agreeable,
though his real attention was on the piece of fig he was grinding
up. It was altogether possible he hadn't even heard Edgar.

"Have you ever heard of people falling out of the sky?"

Briney had finished grinding up the fig and was carefully
sprinkling it on the rabbits while turning the stick with his other
hand. He didn't say a word until all the coarse powder was gone
from his hand and the rabbits sizzled with flavor.

"That's a very odd question, young man," said Briney. He
never took his eyes off the rabbits. They were almost ready.
"Why would you ask such a strange thing?"

Edgar hadn't thought of an answer to this question, and he was suddenly aware that it *was* a very odd question, especially from an eleven-year-old boy wandering around in the middle of the night buying rabbits.

"Those rabbits really do smell good," Edgar said, trying to change course. He sighed with delight over the aroma.

Briney at last turned to face Edgar directly. "If ever someone did fall out of the sky, I can practically guarantee that I would know about it. Everyone comes through here on the way to somewhere, and they've all got a tale to tell. People falling out of the sky hasn't been one of them, and I've never heard of anyone seeing a dead body at the foot of the cliffs." He looked uncomfortable with the thought of a dead person, as though he found the idea hard to comprehend.

Edgar was relieved to hear the news. It certainly didn't sound like Samuel's father had fallen out of the Highlands, just as he had suspected.

"However," Briney continued, moving the rabbits off the fire and onto the unused table. "There was once a man who came in here talking endlessly of a huge four-legged animal that fell from the sky. He heard it bouncing against the cliffs on the way down and only just got out of its way when it landed — or so he says." Briney rolled his eyes and made a motion with his hand as if to say the person who told the story was probably crazy, then he pushed the rabbits off the stick, and they lay steaming on the table.

Just then the door flew open and in charged Morris and Amanda, each of them carrying armloads of rabbits. To Edgar's surprise, the rabbits were still alive. He had assumed they would be wrapped and ready to go. Morris closed the door to the inn and dropped the rabbits onto the floor. The rabbits bounced in every direction, and Edgar began laughing, but everyone else in the room acted as though eleven rabbits hopping around the place was a completely normal occurrence.

"How will I get them home?" said Edgar. He imagined himself walking back to the grove with ten rabbits on a string. He might never make it back.

"Not to worry, Edgar," said Maude, who had been sweeping. She had just finished putting all the cooked rabbits on wooden plates. As she approached Edgar's table with his meal, he observed that she had a rather round face and big red lips. She seemed like the kind of person who would be plump if given the chance. Maude set the rabbit on Edgar's table, grabbed hold of two of the legs, and tore them off with a snap.

"That's too much rabbit for such a small boy," she said. "I'll trade you these legs for a bunny sack."

Edgar nodded, and Maude started eating the rabbit leg in her left hand as she walked away. A moment later she returned with a cup of water, then sat with Briney and enjoyed what remained of her own meal.

The next half an hour was one of the best of Edgar's young life. Everyone seemed to invite Edgar into their lives, if only for an evening, nearly giddy from the unexpected treat of fig-encrusted rabbit. They told a fable about gigantic child-eating rabbits and another about a man who wished so long and hard to be a rabbit himself that one day he hopped out of the village and never came back. Everyone was kind to him, they all laughed, and the dinner tasted very good. When there were only bones on his plate and an empty water cup in his hand, Edgar was content and cheerful.

After the meal was finished and all the stories had been told, Morris gathered up the rabbits in the bunny sack, a useful item made of rabbit skins tied together with little holes everywhere so the rabbits can breathe.

"You'd better be getting on if you must," Morris said. "You've got a long walk ahead of you and ten rabbits weigh a little something. Are you sure you have to be back? You could stay the night with us if you like."

Edgar was about to answer when Morris put his hand on the boy's shoulder and stopped him.

"Be cautious, Edgar. All that shaking of the ground, there's a reason for it. Things aren't safe, at least not for long."

"Morris!" hollered Briney from where he stood at the fire. Morris looked at him helplessly, but Briney shook his head with a stern look on his face. Morris turned back to Edgar.

"Just be careful, all right? Get back to the grove and stay put for a while. No more night errands."

"Let the boy go, Morris," said Briney.

"Is there something I should know?" asked Edgar.

Briney gazed into the fire and didn't look up when he answered.

"You're welcome back here anytime if you find yourself with no place to go, but for now you need to go back home."

Edgar didn't quite know how to thank his new friends, for

thanks was something he had had little occasion to give. Hoping they would understand, he nodded to the cook, picked up his bunny sack, and walked out of the inn.

Before long Edgar was out of the village with a squirming bag of rabbits on his back. Even if he traveled fast, he would only get a couple of hours sleep in the grove before light. He changed course this time, walking close along the edge of the cliffs reaching up to the Highlands. This late at night he didn't expect to see anyone so far away from the waterfalls. He could see the cliff and liked to run his hand along its surface as he walked. It was a habit he'd grown accustomed to, as though the rocks were his companions.

Edgar's mind drifted to Samuel and the Highlands above, and he imagined his new friend alone in his room reading books. It would be a good bit of news that his father hadn't fallen, or at least that no one in the Village of Rabbits ever saw falling people or bodies lying near the cliffs. But Samuel would have to wait a few more days to hear the news.

Edgar doubted that he would also need to travel to the Village of Sheep to continue his investigation. He felt sure he would get the same answer there as he'd gotten at the inn. In the Village of Sheep there were more people — about five hundred — and they traveled to the Village of Rabbits frequently. Surely someone would have made mention to Briney at the inn if they'd seen something so noteworthy.

Edgar walked for a long time with the weight of the rabbits on his back, listening to his feet crunching on the ground. Then he heard a strange noise he couldn't quite place. At first he thought it might be the sound of the rabbits squirming in the bag, but when he stopped, the rabbits sounded as if they'd gone to sleep. The sound persisted, like rocks scraping and sparking against each other.

Edgar set the bunny sack on the ground and watched it flatten. The top of the sack was cinched tight with a string, holding the rabbits in as they hopped back and forth inside. The holes throughout the bunny sack were about as big as the tip of Edgar's thumb, and quite a few sniffing rabbits poked their noses through the openings.

Edgar listened deeply, placing his hands flat against the cliff. He could feel a vibration in the stones that made him jump back. Why was the wall shaking? It sounded to Edgar like the sound was coming from the rocks themselves. But the origin of the sound was lower. Edgar got down on his knees and examined the base of the cliffs. And there he saw the source of the strange sound in the dim light.

At first he couldn't believe his eyes. But then he put his hand on the thin layer of dust where the cliff met with Tabletop. He could see *and* feel what was happening. The cliff was slowly moving down, scraping against the earth of Tabletop and disappearing into the ground.

Edgar understood then why his holds had been off when he'd climbed to the Highlands. He understood why the ground had been trembling.

The Highlands were sinking.

The rest of the way home Edgar watched and listened to the cliffs. He saw in that hour of night the cliffs descend twice the length of his hand. And then — as though he had been dreaming what he'd seen — the sound stopped. The cliff sat still and quiet and didn't move again for the rest of the journey back.

An hour later Edgar was standing in the village by the grove with dawn rapidly approaching. If the bag were opened, all the rabbits would hop away. He couldn't very well leave them on doorsteps, so he walked into the grove, dropping a live rabbit here and there along the way. When he finally lay sleeping under the trees, there were ten busy rabbits making mischief in the grove.

CHAPTER

9

DANGER IN THE GROVE

A little more than two hours later, Edgar was jolted awake by the sound of Isabel's voice.

"Get up, Edgar! Get up!" She tugged his arm, trying to get Edgar into a sitting position. Edgar jumped up and steadied himself with his hand against a tree.

"Mr. Ratikan is fuming! Someone let rabbits loose in the grove and they've chewed up some of the saplings. I've never seen him so angry."

She looked at Edgar and saw immediately in his expression that the orphan boy of the grove was in big trouble.

"*You* did it?"

She had been hoping Mr. Ratikan was only blaming it on Edgar, but that Edgar hadn't actually done it.

"But *why*, Edgar?"

Edgar was having some trouble coming to grips with the situation. Two hours' rest had left him with a dizzy buzz in his head.

"I thought they'd be cooked when they gave them to me," said Edgar, which made Isabel think he was still asleep and dreaming.

"Wake up, Edgar! This is serious! Mr. Ratikan is *really* angry this time. I don't know what he'll do if he finds you here."

He had finally come fully awake and realized the stupidity of his actions the night before. If Mr. Ratikan was coming toward them, then he had very little time.

"Listen to me, Isabel." Edgar motioned for her to join him behind the tree where he stood.

"It might be getting too dangerous for me to stay here. If he comes for me, I'm going to have to leave."

Isabel couldn't imagine the grove without Edgar in it.

"I want you to do one more thing for me," continued Edgar. "Everything is changing, Isabel. I don't understand why or exactly how, but there's a place I can go where I might find some answers. If I'm gone when you try to find me again, I need you to put your sneaking and spying to good use, do you understand?"

Isabel nodded. She was beginning to have a sense of where Edgar was going, and it sounded like a terrible idea.

"You can't go to the Highlands, Edgar. They won't help you. They'll punish you for going up there."

Edgar peered around the tree to see if anyone were coming and found no one, then turned back to Isabel.

"Keep an eye on Mr. Ratikan like you never have before. Listen to what the people in the village are talking about. Find out whatever you can. I'll come back, I promise I will."

"Take this with you." Isabel untied the bag of black figs from around her waist. "There's a little dough in there with the figs, and my sling. I can make another."

Isabel wanted to say more — to persuade him not to climb to the Highlands — but she was forced to stop when the sound of a man's voice came barreling through the trees.

"*Edgaaaaaaaaaaar!*" It was Mr. Ratikan.

Isabel said, "You'd better run, Edgar — we'd both better run."

Mr. Ratikan had come into view, his walking stick in one hand and a squirming brown rabbit in the other. Isabel was gone in a flash before Mr. Ratikan could see her, but Edgar remained a moment longer, tying the bag of black figs around his waist.

Mr. Ratikan spotted Edgar hiding behind the tree. He pointed his walking stick toward the tree and wished he were close enough to knock the boy down.

"I know you did this. I just *know* it! Do you dare try and deny it?"

Edgar thought of his options: He could confess, lie, or blame someone else. Whichever he chose, Edgar was sure he'd get no food and a frightful beating. Mr. Ratikan knew, and there was no getting out of it. So Edgar turned from mean Mr. Ratikan and sprinted away from the grove faster than he'd ever gone before.

"EDGAAAAAAR!" Mr. Ratikan screamed, his anger boiling into a rage as he started after the boy. But Edgar just kept running, sure of where his legs would take him. Atherton was changing, and Edgar needed to find more answers than the grove had to offer. He needed to get the book and find Samuel.

Edgar hid all day in the village between a stack of wood and a house. It was a tight squeeze, but once there he was able to lie down and fall asleep. When darkness came, the village was still alive with activity and it was difficult to find a moment in which he could make his escape. He had to lie there for a long time until finally things began to settle down and he was able to sneak quietly away to the cliffs.

As he scaled the rock face, he stopped to retrieve the book of secret things. Sometime after that he felt the cliff's slight vibration under his hands. Was it going up or down? Could it be that the Highlands were always rising and falling, like a deep breath in the night when no one was awake to notice?

Night passed and early morning came as Edgar climbed. His late start would bring him into the Highlands in the light of day. When he reached the very top of the cliffs, the trembling stopped and everything was still once more. It was as if the rocks themselves knew Edgar was about to climb over the edge, to see the Highlands for the first time, and they had paused to pay respect to his visit.

Edgar's excitement was momentarily tempered by a sudden dread. His stomach rumbled as his head came even with the edge, for he'd long ago eaten the small bit of dough from the bag. He had no other food or water and no idea what he would encounter in the Highlands. He was a visitor to a hostile place with four days to fill before his only friend would come looking for him.

The trees he'd only seen in the dark on his last visit were close by. They were different than those in the grove, much taller and more majestic, with milky white bark. He couldn't see beyond them. Before the trees there was a sea of tall green grass that looked soft and inviting. It would make a good place to hide.

Edgar rolled into the Highlands and darted toward the line of green. When he reached the grass, he found that it came as high as his waist, but it moved out of his way like water as he pushed it from side to side. He broke some off in his hand, sniffed it, then tried to eat it. It tasted bitter and Edgar spit it out, wishing more than anything for a cup of water.

He was soon to be distracted from his thirst. Edgar was an inquisitive boy to begin with, but access to an entirely new world he'd never seen made his head hum with excitement. Edgar ducked down into the meadow and crawled until he reached the end of the field and parted the grass.

The trees before him were thick with golden leaves that drooped down in every direction. He walked out among them and put his hands on the smooth, white bark. He touched the golden leaves and was momentarily lost in the idea of climbing through the branches and jumping from one limb to another, feeling the wide leaves brush past his face as he flew.

On the other side of the trees, obscured through dangling leaves, Edgar spotted more grass — only this time it was yellow.

Curious what it might feel like, he walked toward it, but when he was a few steps away, he was startled by a noise. It sounded like Mr. Ratikan sneezing, all the wet juices flying out of his mouth, but it was much, much louder. When the sound came again, Edgar sprinted forward, diving headfirst into the yellow grass on the other side of the trees.

After a lingering silence that seemed to last forever, Edgar slowly rose onto his feet until his two eyes peered out over the field of yellow. He looked toward the trees, but there was nothing; then he turned the other way, and there he saw what had made the noise.

They were large animals, ten times the size of a sheep, a hundred times the size of a rabbit, with enormous noses protruding from long necks. They were fenced in, eating the yellow grass only a short distance away. One looked up and made the wet, sneezy noise again. It looked at Edgar but seemed indifferent to his presence.

The animals were stunning to look at, and yet they only held Edgar's gaze for a moment, for behind them lay the entire Highlands in full view. Edgar's wildest imagination could not have prepared him for what he saw.

The Highlands looked alive, as if the very land itself were breathing. There were fields of deep green and gold rolling uncontained as far as Edgar could see. Scattered between them were small groves of the trees with the milky white trunks. Bright blue streams meandered in sharp curves back and forth, cutting the land into pieces. The deep green and gold meadows turned pale at the streams' edge, as though their color had been washed away by the power of water. Edgar followed the nearest stream with his eyes — back and forth through the grass — until he couldn't be sure where one blue band of water ended and another began.

His eyes settled on the very center of the Highlands where the twisting streams found their beginning. There was a wide hill with a slow rise, and on the very top was a white stone formation surrounded by an even whiter stone wall. The water, it seemed, was coming from somewhere atop the hill, within the white structure.

Edgar felt the dry roof of his mouth with an equally dry tongue and wanted nothing more than to walk to the nearest channel of water and quench his thirst. But there were small groups of homes in every direction along the streams, and he was afraid he might be seen. The giant animals moved off in a group, and he could feel them pounding the earth with their feet. Could it be they that had made the Highlands move?

The animals had been spooked by someone entering the fenced area. It was a man wearing grey-blue trousers and a long, cream-colored shirt. Another man followed behind the first, and the two began talking as they worked with the animals. Edgar became nervous and shuffled along on his knees in the grass until he reached the large trees. There he saw no one and decided to run low along the tall grass in search of water. If he could stay out of sight and keep moving through the line of trees, he would eventually arrive at one of the three streams.

The curving blue stream he'd seen was moving so slowly and quietly, Edgar couldn't hear it. He listened for the sound of a waterfall, but suddenly realized that the sound of water falling off the edge of the Highlands would be very different than the roar of water hitting Tabletop. He ran, hunched over next to the grass, until his mouth was so dry he wasn't sure he could swallow anymore.

Edgar began to think that coming to the Highlands had been a mistake. If he'd stayed in the grove, Isabel would have brought water and food. But he couldn't make it back down now on what little strength he had left. He wasn't even sure he could survive the day all alone and confused. What if one of those beasts came after him? What if he were discovered by a guard and thrown off the cliff as punishment?

Looking for some scrap of comfort, Edgar took the book he'd been carrying out of the pocket on the front of his shirt. *His* book. He opened it and looked at the words he couldn't read, wondering what they meant. *Atherton is not what you think it is.* Edgar gazed out along the trees and the grass and spoke with a dry, cracked whisper.

"I've got to find Samuel."

He put the book back in his pocket and continued searching desperately for a stream of cool, clear water that would save him.

CHAPTER
10

MR. RATIKAN'S EXPERIMENT

The path narrowed until Edgar couldn't run without brushing up against the trees and the tall grass as he went. When the trail disappeared entirely, he found himself walking through a sea of yellow grassland that stood well above his head. So it came as a shock when he suddenly broke free of the high meadow and fell face first into a crystal-clear stream.

Edgar had never felt the sting of icy water before, and when he came up for air he blubbered and coughed. He felt more awake than he ever had — cold and alive with water dripping down his face. This was a far cry from the warm, dirty pool he bathed in once a week in Tabletop.

The stream didn't even reach his knees, but it was so clear he could see the stone bottom of the channel streaked with green and gold. He'd never stood in water like this, and he wasn't sure what to do. It was like standing in a sea of figs with so much abundance all around him he couldn't think to take some of it and eat. He thought he might cry or laugh out loud, but instead he leaned down and put his callused hands in the water. Edgar was about raise his hands and drink when he was startled by a high, quiet voice.

"This is my spot. You can't play here." Edgar spun around and saw a wet-haired, shirtless child of three or four standing in the middle of the channel a little way off. The boy was pushing a floating wooden toy back and forth in the water between his hands.

"This is my spot," the boy repeated, but kept his attention on the toy and didn't look at Edgar. Behind the boy the channel curved to one side and out of sight. Edgar looked quickly the other way to get his bearing in case he needed to escape. He saw that the channel also curved not far ahead in the other direction and disappeared once more. He was in something of a wide pool with a slow current.

"Where is your mother?" Edgar asked. He hadn't drunk any of the water yet and his voice sounded harsh and full of air. The boy looked up.

"She's right there." He pointed up around the corner. As if to answer Edgar's question directly, the mother's voice came next, unseen but close.

"Don't go past the pool, David." It sounded like a command that had been made many times before.

"Mommy's washing," said the boy. "This is my spot."

Edgar sensed the danger of his situation. The mother might

come quickly around the corner and see a stranger — an invader from below — within snatching distance of her child. And yet he saw an opportunity he couldn't let slip away. Edgar cupped some water in his hands and drank while he thought of what to say. His chest and head filled with energy.

Turning to the boy, he said, "David, I'll leave your spot if you can help me with something."

The boy was suddenly alert, thinking it was a game.

"I'm looking for an older boy named Samuel — a boy about my age. Do you know where he lives?"

David smiled and took hold of his wooden toy, no longer interested in letting it float between his hands.

"Yes! I know him. He lives by the big house."

"Where by the big house?" asked Edgar.

"Da-vid . . ." The woman around the corner sang the name as mothers often do.

"I'm here, Mommy," said David. Edgar was afraid the boy would mention his new friend, but he did not. He felt sure the mother would come around the corner at any moment.

Edgar pressed the boy with a little more force in his voice: "David — where does Samuel live by the big house?"

"Next to the kitchen," he answered.

"And how do I find the big house?"

The boy pointed behind himself, toward the white wall and the white structure Edgar had seen from his hiding place in the grass. Edgar gulped more water and thanked the boy as he started to leave.

"I'll leave your spot now," he said. "Can you keep a secret?"

The boy was starting to like Edgar, and he nodded ear-nestly.

"Don't tell anyone you saw me, okay? I'll come see you again in a day or two or three, but only if you're quiet."

The boy nodded again. He went back to playing with the floating toy while Edgar disappeared into the tall yellow grass.

Samuel was the only child who lived in the House of Power, and this afforded him a certain view of things. In the beginning, he was put there because his father was appointed to the board of elders and he was the only elder with a child. As a child among adults, Samuel was universally ignored, and he found early on that he could move about without much notice if he wanted to, especially at night. He hadn't been very interested in what was going on in the main chamber for a long time, because it was a painful reminder of his father. But the humiliation he'd felt when delivering the toast to Lord Phineus and the visit from Edgar had set his mind on a different course. On the night after he'd met the boy from Tabletop, Samuel decided it was time to take a closer look around.

There were a great many twists and turns in the House of Power, along with all sorts of stone formations behind which to hide. Some of the structures held trees, others surrounded rows of flowering plants, and still others were simply decorative stones in odd shapes and sizes. They were not items of a size that would hide an adult, but for a child they made excellent coverage when unexpected people came around a corner. It was this recurring architecture of halls and objects that made the House of Power such a perfect place for a small child to explore unseen.

Night was coming on as Samuel made his way up the main stairs, managing to sidestep Horace in the shadows as the guard nodded off. He went down the dark hall to the door of the main chamber and listened but heard nothing. The door was too thick for Samuel to hear through, even if someone had been shouting behind it. Nearby was a stairway leading up to the bedchambers for Sir Emerik, Sir Philip, and Lord Phineus. Samuel crept up the steps until he reached a wide landing.

Off to one side was a stone window where faint light crept in from outside, and Samuel went to it. The slightest sound might give him away, for he stood just over the chamber where he'd delivered the tea and toast for his mother. There was not a lot of movement on the grounds of the House of Power, but he could hear voices from the chamber below.

"There is word from the grove. From Mr. Ratikan. It seems that our assumptions have been proven correct. His experimentation provided favorable results." It was Sir Emerik.

"Lord Phineus will want to know." This time it was Sir Philip, who sounded pleased with the news. There was some discussion of who would share the information, and then Samuel suddenly heard the door to the chamber open. Footsteps approached on the stairs and Samuel's heart raced as he realized whoever it was would be on the landing in no time at all. There was only a small leafy tree held within a stone pot behind which to hide, and Samuel dashed toward it as quickly as he could.

He was down on his knees when Sir Philip and Sir Emerik both arrived on the landing, but he had not made it all the way to the little tree. Samuel stayed perfectly still and watched. Though the light was dim, he was out in the open, and he felt sure he would be seen at any moment.

Sir Philip and Sir Emerik seemed to be in a rush as they turned to the left and rapped on Lord Phineus's door. This gave Samuel the chance he needed, and in a flash he was behind the leaves of the small tree, hidden from view. Lord Phineus's door opened.

"Sorry to disturb you, Lord," said Sir Emerik, always the one to take center stage if he could. "I have news from the grove, from Mr. Ratikan, and I am certain you will want to hear of it."

Lord Phineus put his hand up as if he wanted Sir Emerik to stop speaking, but Sir Emerik was not so easily silenced. "Shall we meet you in the chamber, after you've had a moment?"

Lord Phineus stood aside and invited the men into his room.

"There are ears all about the place. One cannot be too careful."

Lord Phineus peered down the hall and seemed to feel that something wasn't quite right. He sniffed the air as the two men came in, then reluctantly shut the door. When the door closed, Samuel jumped out from behind the tree and ran down the stairs toward the kitchen. As he hurried past, he saw Horace was still slumped in a chair with his chin on his chest.

When he arrived at the kitchen, his mother was absorbed in her work and couldn't stop to visit with him. She was pulling hand-sized baguettes of bread out of a stone oven when she glanced over her shoulder and saw her son standing there.

"Did you tire of reading already?"

Samuel shrugged. He'd come to the kitchen instinctively because his mother usually made him feel safe, but now he was suddenly afraid his mother might make him deliver bread to the main chamber.

"How about some bread?"

Samuel's mother pushed one of the warm baguettes across the table, and Samuel picked it up. With a quick word of thanks he headed for the door, determined to leave before his mother presented him with a night errand.

The path from the kitchen to his room had two sharp turns through the courtyard garden. As he made his way, only two questions were on his mind: *What sort of experiment had Mr. Ratikan performed, and why did Lord Phineus want to know about it?*

Samuel's room was exactly twenty-five steps from the kitchen door. He knew this because he enjoyed taking precisely that many steps to go between the two whenever he made the trip. He counted the steps as he went, hugging the bread to his chest so the smell would rise to his face. *One, two, three, four, five, six, seven* — he reached the first curve and the grouping of trees and vines — *eight, nine, ten* —

"Samuel — over here, Samuel," whispered a voice from the garden.

Samuel crouched down instinctively, frightened by the voice. It had been a perilous evening and his nerves were frayed. He gripped the bread tighter than he ought to have, and the crust crumbled onto his shirt.

"Who's there?"

Edgar stood up high enough for Samuel to see him — but only for a moment — then he stooped back down low in the garden. "It's me, Edgar."

"You're days early!" said Samuel, suddenly aware of the risk of the situation. If Edgar were found in the Highlands, there was no telling what Lord Phineus would do.

"Is there somewhere you can take me?" whispered Edgar. "A place where I can hide?"

Samuel looked all around and, seeing no one, motioned Edgar out from behind the bushes and onto the pathway.

"I'll take you to my room — it's just here, around the corner."

"What if your mother comes back?"

"She works very late, and there's a door between our adjoining rooms. It's all right, Edgar. Come on!"

The two of them walked quickly to the next corner on the path, where Samuel held Edgar back and peered around the bend. Nobody was there. Samuel picked up his count right where he'd left off — *twenty-two, twenty-three, twenty-four, twenty-five* — opened the door, and the two of them went inside.

CHAPTER
11

DR. KINCAID'S REVELATION

"We must be quiet," said Samuel. "No one can know you're here."

Edgar nodded as he peered into a room barely lit by the flicker of a small flame. The light sat on a table against the wall and cast a pale glow onto a large, open book. Samuel took a slender stick off the table and held it over the tiny flame. Walking around the room, he lit two more wicks, the first illuminating a bed with a round stool to one side, the second revealing a small pile of books sitting on a shelf. Samuel blew out the flame on the stick and waved his hand to disperse the smoke.

"I can't believe you're here, Edgar. How did you find me?"

Samuel was delighted to see his new friend, but he was harboring a fugitive from Tabletop, and logic told him it was a reckless thing to do. The two of them wouldn't be able to remain hidden for long.

"I'm sorry to come again so soon," said Edgar. "I had no place else to go." He told Samuel why he had to leave Tabletop, how he had come across the little boy named David, and then waited until dark to sneak into the courtyard.

"But there's only one gate to the House of Power, and it's guarded. How did you manage to get in?"

Edgar didn't have to answer. There was a towering wall all around the House of Power, and though it was flat and smooth, it was no match for Edgar.

"You climbed over the wall!" said Samuel, startled once again by Edgar's skill and boldness. "Nobody's ever done that before."

Edgar wasn't as impressed by his own accomplishments. "What have you got there?" he asked instead, finally overcome by his own hunger and curiosity. Samuel looked at his hand, which held the bread he'd forgotten about, the smell of which was growing stronger in the closed room.

"Why, it's bread," said Samuel, holding it out to Edgar. "You must be starving."

Edgar had never seen such a thing, and when he took it in his hand, he wasn't sure what to do with it. Was there something inside that might spill out if he took a bite?

"Go on, eat it. I don't need anything to eat. I'm not even hungry."

Edgar thought of the bitter green grass he'd eaten earlier in the day.

"What does it taste like?"

Samuel couldn't believe his ears. Could it really be that Tabletop had no bread? He was beginning to wonder what Tabletop *did* have.

"Trust me, Edgar. You'll like it. It will fill you up."

Edgar held the baguette close to his nose and smelled it, then took a small bite. He had never tasted anything so good.

"Wait here a moment," said Samuel. "I'll go and fetch some water and come right back."

Edgar ate all of the bread and choked it down with a dry throat before Samuel returned with the water. He drank the water in three big gulps and then burped louder than Samuel imagined anyone could. The two boys couldn't help laughing, although Samuel was aware of the danger that careless noises might bring.

"Don't do that again," said Samuel, trying his best to hold back a smile. "We really must try to keep quiet."

The two boys sat down in the chairs at the table, and Edgar was at once mesmerized by the sight of the large, open book.

"Are there many books in the Highlands?"

"Oh, yes. Thousands. Everyone has books, not just us." He was referring to the people who lived in the House of Power. "They've always been here, but there are never any new ones, so we take special care of them. That one is all about Poseidon."

"About who?" asked Edgar.

"It's mythology. He's the god of water, my favorite."

Edgar didn't understand what Samuel was talking about. Though he wanted to hear more about books, he was also feeling unexpectedly tired. The food had settled in his stomach, and all the events of the day and night had taken every ounce of energy he had. And yet there was so much to talk about. He had important news to share with Samuel.

"I have to tell you something. I've done some asking around, and I don't think your father fell."

Samuel appeared cautious, uncertain of how to react. "What do you think happened to him?"

"I don't know, but the only thing I've heard about that might have fallen out of the sky is a giant four-legged animal. I saw one today when I was hiding. One of those might have fallen once."

"It did!" Samuel said. "One of them did fall, I remember that. My parents were very concerned. The House of Power debated a great deal about what they should do."

"Samuel, what *are* those things?" Edgar was afraid of them, but didn't want to say so.

Samuel felt increasingly surprised by how different the worlds of Tabletop and the Highlands were.

"They're just horses, Edgar. They eat grass and carry people around. You don't need to be afraid of them."

Edgar breathed a sigh of relief.

"There's something I need to tell you as well," said Samuel. He leaned in a little closer to Edgar, somehow feeling the need to whisper what he was about to say. "Did you say the man who ran the grove was called Mr. Ratikan?"

Edgar nodded, immediately suspicious of his old caretaker.

"I overheard something tonight. He's done some sort of experiment, something Lord Phineus wanted him to do. Maybe you should look around if you go back."

"That's all you heard? Nothing more?"

"Lord Phineus and the others went behind a closed door after that, but there was a tone in their voices, like they were plotting something devious."

It was getting awfully late and there was so much to talk about, but Edgar was sensitive to the fact that nothing was as important as what he carried with him from the cliffs. The horses, books, and plots overheard would have to wait. He pulled the book of secret things out of his pocket and handed it to Samuel.

"I'm so tired," said Edgar, heaving a great sigh to try to rouse himself awake. "But I think this book might be even more important than we thought. Atherton is changing, and this book may be able to tell us why. Let's at least read a few pages while I can still keep my eyes open. Maybe it will go faster this time with the better light."

Samuel was ecstatic at the sight of the mysterious book. He took it from Edgar's outstretched hand and held it nearer to the light on his desk. The light came from a bowl filled with a clear liquid that had a wick in the center. The waxy substance was derived from the fat of animals and burned like fuel. The same kinds of lights were used in Tabletop, so Edgar was not surprised to see them, though he'd never seen so many in one little room before. Fuel, water, and food were scarce in Tabletop and were regarded as precious. Edgar didn't sense that people in the Highlands felt the same way.

Samuel turned to the page where he and Edgar had stopped two nights before, and he began to read. He was growing accustomed to deciphering the scribbles on the page, and the added light helped Samuel pick up his pace. He spent the next twenty minutes reading the following entry out loud:

As time is my enemy, this very short telling of events will have to do. I will try to explain this in simple terms that a boy can understand.

Atherton is a made world, Edgar — a place created by men at a time when almost every part of the known world was used up. In the beginning, we farmed and gathered food and resources, and in doing so we wiped out a great many trees and animals. Many years later we developed machines to do our work for us. Do you know what a machine is? I suppose not. Machines made life easier — or so it seemed — as they ripped and tore at the earth and sky in ways we hardly understood. These first two developments — farming and the making of machines to do our work for us — should have taught us to care for the world, but they did not. We only learned to destroy it with more efficiency.

Near the end, we made thinking machines, and these were our undoing. They became so very powerful that we used them to make places to live, food sources, almost everything. These machines finished off what was left of the forests and wild animals. I have utterly lost you, have I not? But I am a scientist, and I don't know how to make it simpler. I will move on to something altogether different.

There was a boy who came of age when the world was unraveling. I found him when he was very young, in a park filled with nothing but dirt and metal, a place where only poor children played. When he was ten he already understood science, math, and the world itself in ways that I couldn't quite grasp. When he was twenty he showed me a glass tube set on its side with no openings. The tube contained a world of its own — bugs, earth, plants. With shaking hands he told me the tube had been empty but for a spot of dirt a week before. He had put all his knowledge of biology and science and machines to bear on the smallest strands of earth and built himself a world within a tube. It had grown from a speck of dirt into a tiny habitat teeming with life.

This was the first experiment that, many years later, would lead to the making of Atherton, the place you call home. Atherton is full of mysteries even I don't understand. It is a living world all its own, but it is unstable, and catastrophic changes are afoot. Atherton is not as ready for people as we once thought. The man who built it is not well. He has kept things from us, awful things that only a mad scientist could conceive of. He may have lost his mind in the making of Atherton.

*I will tell you as much as I can about how
your world was made, why it was made, and by
whom it was made — but first I must warn you
of something. Edgar, if you have found this book,
then it has come to you and the world has begun
to change. How else would you find it? You must
be on your guard. Trust only those you can be
absolutely sure of. There are bigger changes ahead
that will bring destruction, maybe even war.
Do you know what war is, Edgar? I wonder
if you do. . . .*

Samuel stopped reading. He didn't understand how Atherton had been made, but he knew what the word *war* meant, and it scared him. He had read about wars between gods in his books. They had been exciting on the page, but he had no desire to experience the terror of a *real* war.

Samuel looked at Edgar and saw that his friend was only barely awake, trying with all his might to keep his eyes open.

"Wake up, Edgar! Don't you understand we have to keep reading? We have to know what's going to happen to us."

Edgar had heard everything Samuel said, but he didn't know the meaning of war. Even if he had known, he was so tired he wouldn't have been able to register surprise or concern. He had unwound so far he couldn't rile himself back up again.

"I have an idea," said Samuel. "You lie down under my bed and rest where no one can see you. I'll look through the rest of the book of secret things. When you wake up, I'll tell you what I've discovered."

Edgar wanted only to sleep, and for the first time he lost his will to protect the book. He stumbled over to the bed, slid underneath, and fell immediately into a deep slumber. Samuel struggled to put a blanket over Edgar and made sure he was well hidden, then returned to his desk.

Hours passed and the only sound in the room was the occasional flipping of an old ragged page. Sometime in the night there came the sound of ripping paper, and it stirred Edgar for a moment, though he never came fully awake.

"Why is your light on at such a late hour?"

Edgar heard the voice from where he lay under the bed, loud and shrill in the night.

"What have you got there? What's that you're reading?"

The voice was that of a grown man. Disoriented, Edgar turned his head so that he could see out from under the bed, and then he remembered — he was in Samuel's room. Edgar could see the light dancing on the floor, stirred by the door being shut. The man walked across the room with heavy steps and stopped where Edgar could see his boots.

"Where did you get this book? WHERE DID YOU GET IT?" the man screamed at Samuel, but the boy wouldn't answer. "Lord Phineus is going to be very interested to see this," said the man. "*And* you."

Samuel was pulled out of his chair, and now Edgar could see all four feet moving for the door. He listened as Samuel was hauled out of the room and the door slammed shut.

Edgar was alone. Samuel was gone, and the book had been taken by what sounded like a cruel man. Where had he taken Samuel, and what would he do to him? Edgar was surprised to find that he cared more about what happened to his friend than he did the book, his only true possession. He felt responsible for putting Samuel in danger. A new feeling of dread settled into his stomach that he'd never known before. *I should never have come here.*

After his racing heart slowed, Edgar crept out from under the bed. He looked all around the small room, then sat down in Samuel's chair and leaned forward over the table. He was startled by a crinkling noise, as if something were in the front pocket of his shirt. Edgar sat up straight, reached into the pocket, and pulled out a piece of paper, ripped and crumpled at the edges. The size and handwriting were familiar. It was a page from the book of secret things.

But how had it come to be in Edgar's pocket? And more importantly, what did it say? And then he had an awful thought that sent his heart racing once more.

They will be looking for this page, and the first place they'll come is here. I must get out.

Edgar quietly opened the door, looked all around, and ventured out into the night.

Lord Phineus stood at an open window in a private chamber at the top of the House of Power, surveying the world below. He was a tall man with a long face and short black hair that came to a widow's peak high on his forehead. It was a haircut that heightened the severity of his face — the cold eyes, the bony nose.

There was no higher place in the world than the window where he stood, and it pleased Lord Phineus to stand above it all, relishing the power he had attained. He alone controlled the water flow in Atherton. He lived in a mighty fortress of stone, and he had an army of Highlanders to protect him should the need arise. He had carefully built an inner circle of devoted allies in Sir Philip, Sir Emerik, and Mr. Ratikan. They were all indebted to him and motivated to do his bidding. He'd gotten rid of those who questioned his authority.

And yet, as Lord Phineus stood at the window, he couldn't help thinking about what would happen if ever the people in Tabletop were to revolt and try to find a way into the Highlands, and this thought wiped the wicked smile from his face. He had weapons and horses, which Tabletop didn't have. The cliffs had always protected him, and he could never be reached by an army from below. Still, the idea of invasion troubled his dark mind as he looked out over the sleeping world. His entire army comprised just one hundred twenty men and horses. There were many more people below, over a thousand, and all of them serving the few in the Highlands.

His anxiety had increased when people started reporting that the horses were restless. And there was something else, something more peculiar still. He had woken in the night several times and thought he'd felt a trembling. It was a deep, quiet movement he did not understand. In recent days the trembling had occurred during the day, and it had gotten stronger. Others had felt it, too. Could it be the water moving faster out of the spring below the House of Power? Or maybe it was the horses themselves — agitated by a force unknown — pounding across the fields with a fury?

As Lord Phineus sat brooding over these developments, he felt it again. The soft and steady rumble went on for a time before he left his room in search of where it came from. He had only one thought on his mind now: *What is that strange trembling?*

While Edgar was making his escape from the Highlands, a rabbit found a hole in his pen and slipped out of the Village of Rabbits. He hopped past the inn where Briney was busy tending the fire and his wife was sweeping the floor. After a time, the rabbit arrived at the cliffs leading up to the Highlands. He sniffed all around as the rock wall in front of him moved down.

The rabbit hopped back and forth as he watched. He had spied a small bit of green grass growing out of the cliff five feet above and wished he could have it.

He didn't have to wait very long.

*Learn from me, if not by my precepts, at least by my example,
how dangerous is the acquirement of knowledge, and how
much happier that a man is who believes his native town
is the world, than he who aspires to become greater than
his nature will allow.*

DR. FRANKENSTEIN
FRANKENSTEIN, 1818
MARY SHELLEY

PART
TWO

"How could you let this happen? You knew he was unstable and you let him go anyway."

Dr. Kincaid didn't know what to tell them. He was every bit as devastated as they were.

"We always knew this could happen. As brilliant as he is, we knew there was a risk we'd lose him. A risk we'd lose everything."

"Not acceptable! There has to be a way to get it back. YOU have to get it back."

Dr. Luther Kincaid knew what they were asking was impossible. If Dr. Harding did not want to be found, he would get his wish, and there was nothing anyone could do about it.

"Do you remember when I found him? He was playing in the dirt at the edge of the park. Even then I knew there were risks. He was smashing the ants with a rock. He knew the power of Earth."

"What in God's name are you talking about, Luther? You're as mad as he is!"

But Luther knew this wasn't true. Even at seventy-eight years old he was in remarkably good health. Dr. Luther Kincaid knew himself well enough to know he hadn't lost his mind.

"There is yet a chance."

"What do you mean to say?"

Luther clicked off the device and smiled vaguely, thinking of another time, another place.

CHAPTER

12

A TREMBLING WORLD

Sir Emerik was a man who was always trying to figure out how he might increase his own authority and put those around him on a lower footing. Such a man has a mind full of suspicious thoughts, forever on the prowl for someone to strip of power so that he might increase his own. It was just such a thought that led him to Samuel.

That boy is sneaking around too much. He's up to no good. I shall keep an eye on him.

A few days after this thought emerged in Sir Emerik's mind, he passed through the courtyard at night and saw the light under Samuel's door. He wondered what the boy was doing so late in the evening and, hearing nothing, he banged on the door and barged in without invitation. What a magnificent surprise it was to find Samuel in possession of a secret document, one that held information sure to interest Lord Phineus.

Sir Emerik grabbed Samuel by the arm and hauled him out of the room. As they went past Horace at the top of the main stairs, Samuel tried to speak, but Sir Emerik silenced him with an icy stare. They continued on until they reached a narrow stairway that was steeper than all the rest. Sir Emerik pushed Samuel onto the twisting case of stairs and followed him up. At the top was a door, which Sir Emerik unlocked and opened. He threw Samuel inside, and the boy tumbled onto the stone floor. It was cold and dark inside, with an eerie sense of emptiness.

"I'll be back," he said, "*with* Lord Phineus. I hope you're ready to do some explaining."

After locking Samuel in the room, Sir Emerik made his way to Lord Phineus's chamber, but stopped short just as he was about to knock on his master's door. *I really ought to read this book before I hand it over. Lord Phineus will keep it from me and I will miss my chance.*

He stood there a moment, clutching the book and considering his options, then he decided to retreat to his own room. When he turned to go, Lord Phineus was standing before him. Sir Emerik jumped with fright and tried to hide the book behind his back.

"You startled me, Lord Phineus."

The lord of the House of Power was in a foul mood and he spoke with venom.

"Is there something I can do for you, Sir Emerik?"

"No, nothing — I was just turning in for the night. I had a question, but it can wait." Sir Emerik was instantly sorry he'd said it.

"What can wait?" said Lord Phineus. He was blocking the way to Sir Emerik's room.

"Ahhhh . . ." Sir Emerik hesitated.

"Could it be about whatever you're hiding behind your back?"

Sir Emerik knew better than to try to trick Lord Phineus. He was caught. With some hesitation, he pulled the book out from behind his back.

"I thought you might be asleep and I didn't want to wake you, but now that I see you're up — well — I caught the boy, Samuel, with this book. I've never seen it before, have you?"

Lord Phineus took the book from him, his mood growing darker still. His brows set low over his eyes as he looked down at the thing in his hand.

"How long have you had this in your possession?" His voice had deepened to a cold, raspy whisper. It was not a book he recognized, but there was something about it that made him anxious, as though he *had* seen it before but couldn't remember when or where.

"Oh, not long — not long at all," stammered Sir Emerik. "I locked the boy upstairs and came directly here."

Lord Phineus looked down at the book, the tip of his black widow's peak pointing to the floor. When his gaze returned to Sir Emerik, there was suspicion in his eyes.

"Get Sir Philip and meet me in the main chamber."

A thought crossed Lord Phineus's mind, and he changed the order just before leaving.

"Give me an hour with it alone; then you may come."

When Lord Phineus was gone, Sir Emerik felt his temple. A cold sweat clung to his skin, and his hands were shaking. *I wonder what it is I've found.*

The main chamber of the House of Power was a sterile, private place of stone and wood. There were round bowls on the center table full of oily fuel with long wicks aflame in the open air. The statue of Mead's Head seemed almost alive in the dancing shadows of the night. An hour had passed in which Lord Phineus scoured the pages of the book. Sir Philip and Sir Emerik had arrived outside the door, wondering if they ought to go in.

"You should be aware," said Sir Emerik. "He's in a foul mood."

"When is he not in a foul mood?" asked Sir Philip. He had a crooked front tooth that seemed to want out of his mouth, for it was always pushing on his upper lip and making him perform a sort of half-smile, which he was doing just now.

Sir Emerik knocked on the door, and the two went in. When Lord Phineus looked up from the book, there was a mysterious, cold look on the man's face. Without a word of introduction, Lord Phineus turned a few pages back and began to read aloud. He read to them the parts that Samuel and Edgar had already read, and soon he was reading sections that Edgar hadn't had the opportunity to hear.

. . . There were volunteers, people who had a great deal of wealth or position, and had the means to finance this chance for escape. There were also those who were starved for adventure, for something natural and beautiful they couldn't find any longer in their own world. And there was a way — a way that would put you to sleep and give you a kind of new memory. It didn't stop you from being yourself; it only changed what you remembered about certain things. When people woke up, they were on Atherton — you were on Atherton, Edgar — and you were new like Atherton was new. I don't know how else to explain it so that you will understand. I sent you to Atherton to save you, not to harm you.

The words had a chilling effect on Sir Emerik and Sir Philip, but they seemed to have no effect on Lord Phineus. The wheels in his mind turned on how he might use the information, but he betrayed no outward emotion. There was a stretch of seven or eight pages in which the words had smeared over time. Whole sections were nearly impossible to read. Toward the end, the words became legible again, as though the inside of the book had somehow gotten wet throughout the years and the outside, near the leather cover, had remained safe and dry.

As they came to the last of the little book, Lord Phineus saw that a page — the final page — had been ripped out. He ran his fingers over the tattered edge where the page had been, and a great curiosity grew within him. These were the final words the three men found:

Edgar — you must understand that I am an intelligent man, but my thoughts are simple compared to Dr. Harding's. I and the others helped him, but he was the architect of Atherton, and I fear he kept many things from us. As I leave you here on Tabletop and make my escape, I feel certain we've brought you and the others here too soon. But it's too late. You are here, the others are here, and Atherton is not what it seemed when we began. We thought it was fully formed, stable, ready to popu-late. It's what he told us, but I've discovered a part of his hidden plan and it speaks of something more. If you have found this little book it can only mean that it came to you, that what I feared has come to pass. The Highlands have fallen into Tabletop. It's the only way you could have this book, the only way it could come to you. Time is short and there is only one thing more I must tell you. It is this. . . .

And then Lord Phineus understood what the soft trembling was. He knew, and his mind was aflame with the thought of it. *The Highlands are sinking.*

"What this Dr. Harding said to Dr. Kincaid is true," he told them in an even voice. "He's made a game of it, don't you see? All the things we have and all the things they don't. . . ."

"How can this be?" asked Sir Philip, his face awash in fear. He received no reply, only a look of bewilderment from Sir Emerik and something more from Lord Phineus — something odd. It was a cold resolve.

"He's a madman — *was* a madman," said Sir Emerik. "Could this really be true?"

"If it is true," said Sir Philip, "we must act quickly and with great care." He was the most military-minded of the three and understood immediately the peril of a fallen world.

Sir Emerik felt the world trembling under his feet again and wondered aloud, "What will become of us?"

Lord Phineus said nothing, for his mind was preoccupied with only one thing: What sort of man had *Lord Phineus* been before reaching Atherton? If this Dr. Harding had planned to put him to this kind of test, then Lord Phineus must have been a powerful man indeed. *Well, Dr. Harding — I suppose the game is afoot, now, isn't it? We shall see if things go as you expected.*

Lord Phineus closed the small book and pushed it slowly across the table, then centered his gaze on Sir Emerik.

"Bring me the boy."

It didn't take long for Sir Emerik to return and push Samuel into the room, where he fell to his knees. Samuel raised his head meekly from the floor and saw the eerie face of Lord Phineus, liquid in the orange glow of flames.

"Have you read this book, Samuel?"

Lord Phineus took a drink from a cup on the table. He seemed not to notice as trickles of water spilled from the corners of his lips and down his chin.

"I didn't read it," said Samuel.

Lord Phineus picked up the book and held it to his nose for a moment, then he reached across the table and forced the book into Samuel's face. Samuel tried to retreat, but Sir Emerik held him firmly in place.

"Do you smell that, Samuel? It smells like fuel, don't you think?" Lord Phineus pulled the book away from Samuel's face. "I don't suppose you tried to destroy the pages of this book, did you, Samuel? Maybe you were smearing the pages when Sir Emerik arrived and stopped you from finishing the job. Were you going to burn the book, was that it?"

Samuel struggled to free himself from Sir Emerik. He was gripping the boy's arms forcefully, and it was beginning to hurt.

"You do realize, Samuel, that we have quite a problem on our hands." Lord Phineus was serious and direct in the face of a changing world.

"I barely touched the book," said Samuel. "I only glanced at it and couldn't read it. How could anyone read it?"

Lord Phineus stood and advanced toward the boy. He bent down so that his face was very near Samuel's.

"So you don't know that the Highlands are sinking and that

soon we will find that our city on a hill has come even with the world beneath us?"

"What do you mean?" Samuel was trying his best to hide what he knew.

"I'm not here to answer your questions — you're here to answer mine," said Lord Phineus. "There are a few things I need to know, Samuel — and until I know them, I'm afraid I can't allow you to leave this room."

Lord Phineus took hold of Samuel's wrist and turned it around until it felt like a tight spring in his hand. Samuel screamed.

It didn't take long to break poor Samuel's will. He was a smart boy, but his strength and will were thin as paper. Soon enough Lord Phineus knew who Edgar was and where he had come from. Samuel managed one convincing lie, and it was one he was determined to hold onto even if Lord Phineus broke his arm in two.

"I don't know anything about the missing page. I didn't see it was gone. I tell you I don't know!"

Samuel's heroic effort hid the whereabouts of the final words of the book, but he could only hope that somehow Edgar would find a way to read the page before it was too late.

Lord Phineus hauled Samuel to his feet by the arm, then thought better of the idea and swept his foot across the boy's skinny legs, sending him tumbling to the floor.

He took two steps toward Mead's head, the white stone statue on the pedestal, and he touched the stone face. He put his thumb over the stone eye and was lost in his own thoughts. It soothed his mind to touch Mead's head, to wonder about it. The moment passed in silence, and then Lord Phineus commanded Sir Philip with an order.

"Ready the men and the horses. The Highlands have been trembling for weeks, and now we know why. There's not going to be much time to prepare, and we may soon have use of your little army." Lord Phineus picked up the book once more. "The people from below must be kept out of the Highlands."

Sir Philip's crooked tooth slowly emerged, and a grave smile overtook his face. His chance had come to show his worth. He wasted no time leaving the room, and soon the sound of his boots echoing through the stone stairway was gone. Lord Phineus aimed his piercing eyes at Samuel.

"He's got more on his little mind than he's telling, but there's no time to get it out of him now." Lord Phineus moved his gaze to Sir Emerik. "Lock him up with no food or water and come right back. I have an important errand for you."

Sir Emerik had been angry when Lord Phineus gave so much responsibility to Sir Philip, but now he beamed. He had been the one to find the book, and now Lord Phineus would surely reward him with a grand role in protecting the Highlands that would be worthy of his position. He commanded the boy to get up, took him by the arm, and pulled him out the door.

CHAPTER
13

BLACK FIGS AND BLISTERS

It took only half as long for Edgar to get down to Tabletop as it had taken him the first time. He was feeling proud of himself as night turned to morning and he arrived at the bottom. When he looked up, he understood why his descent had been so easy, and his satisfaction turned to surprise. The distance to the top was only half as far as it had been when he'd gone up.

There was a constant, gravelly sound seeping from the guts of the world, and it alarmed Edgar. He saw the cliff slowly but steadily disappearing into the earth. If this kept up, it wouldn't be long until the Highlands were no more — it would be one with Tabletop in a matter of days.

Edgar crept across the expanse in front of the grove until he was within a few feet of the first trees. People would already be at work, and he had to hide quickly. He chose the first large tree he encountered and climbed up into its thick branches, surrounded by leaves and tiny green balls that would soon grow into figs. He took the page out of his front pocket and looked at it once more, wishing he could read the words. As he retraced the messy lines and loops and dots on the page, he felt secure, hidden in the branches of the tree — but he was wrong to assume that no one had seen him enter the grove.

He heard the snap of a sling, then the sound of a black fig hitting the trunk of the tree he was hiding in.

"You're back awfully soon." Isabel's voice came through the trees.

"And you've made a new sling."

She arrived under the tree and peered up through the branches. Edgar jumped down and stared off uneasily toward the center of the grove.

"Everyone is working in the third-years today. It's the farthest from the cliffs, and Mr. Ratikan is trying to keep them focused on the work. There's been nothing but talk since you left."

"Talk of what?" asked Edgar.

Isabel glanced nervously toward the third-year portion of the grove before answering. When she returned her gaze to Edgar, she spoke quickly.

"Everyone in the village knows the Highlands are moving down. It's all they've been talking about. And someone else has become ill in the grove."

Edgar couldn't believe his ears. What was becoming of the grove, the only home he'd ever known?

"I'm worried, Edgar," she said. "Everyone is asking whether

or not the Highlands will keep falling and if there will be enough water. Already the pool beneath the waterfall is half what it was a day ago. Mr. Ratikan says the Highlands will stop sinking, that everyone in the grove needs to keep harvesting or they'll slow the water supply even more. But he's having a hard time keeping everyone working. They want to talk about what's happening. They want to know if the water will keep coming. If the Highlands come down much farther, I think everyone might stop working. People are scared. They don't know what to do."

Edgar thought about everything she'd said. He spotted the black fig Isabel had hurled a few feet off and picked it up.

"So everyone is in with the third-year trees right now?"

Isabel nodded as Edgar handed her the fig.

"Even Mr. Ratikan?"

"*Especially* Mr. Ratikan. He's doing everything he can to keep them busy and away from the cliffs."

"Do you think we could get into his house without being seen?"

As Edgar started for the center of the grove, Isabel wondered what anyone could possibly want from Mr. Ratikan's house. Edgar whispered while they zigzagged between the trees.

"I have a friend in the Highlands — a boy my age named Samuel. He heard something that makes me even more suspicious of Mr. Ratikan. If there's anything to be found, it will be in that house of his."

Isabel wanted to know everything about Samuel and the Highlands. It was a struggle for Edgar to describe something so different from Tabletop, but he tried his best to share what he'd seen with her. Isabel thought it sounded very green and gold, full of water and exotic animals. Her imagination was running wild as they approached the clearing in the trees where Mr. Ratikan's house sat. The two of them became more solemn.

There was no one about the place, not even the sound of someone in the distance. Edgar went first, followed by Isabel, but when they reached the three steps to the porch, both of them felt paralyzed. It had always been a forbidden place.

"The door is going to be locked," said Isabel, breaking the silence between them. "Let's go around the back and see if we can find another way in."

They tiptoed all the way around to the back side of the house. At the top corner of the pitched roof there was a single window covered with wooden shutters.

"That's our best chance," said Edgar. "I'll climb up and try to push it open. You go back to the front and make sure the door is actually locked." He started up without waiting for Isabel's reply. Edgar didn't want to go on the porch and hoped Isabel would find the courage to do it for him. She nodded hesitantly and dashed off toward the other side of the house.

When Edgar reached the shutters, he found them locked from the inside. He shook them back and forth — and even tried punching one of them — but they wouldn't come open. Then he heard a whirling sound from below.

"I can fix that." Isabel had found the front door locked and had come back around. She was swinging a very long sling around in circles over her head, and it was gaining speed.

"Move aside a little more," she said.

Edgar leaned into the small space on the side of one shutter and waited until he heard the *pop!* of the sling and, to his great surprise, felt the fig hit him in the shoulder. It stung more than anything he'd ever felt, like someone had taken a sharp stick and jammed it into his flesh until it came out the other side on his chest. Edgar tried as hard as he could to hold in the howl of pain that was building in his throat, but he couldn't contain it.

Isabel said she was sorry eleven times before Edgar could get any coherent words to come out of his mouth. He shook his arm back and forth, holding on with one hand, and the sting in his shoulder turned to a tingling ache.

"This is our only chance, Isabel," Edgar finally said, his voice cracking as he tried not to cry from the pain. "You'll have to try again. Someone is sure to have heard me shout and will come to find us."

"I can't control it! I've made it too long."

"I trust you," answered Edgar. "Just try again. If you can hit the shutter, it'll go right through."

Isabel fumbled in her pocket for a black fig and placed it in the sling. Her hands were shaking. *I'm going to knock him off the house or hit him in the head and kill him. I can't do this.*

"Hurry, Isabel. Someone will be here!"

She swung the fig around and around and never took her eye off the shutter farthest from where Edgar was hanging. When she let it go with a snap, she closed her eyes and heard a loud *thud.* Either she'd hit Edgar in the head and quite possibly killed him or she'd managed to connect with the shutter. When she looked, there was a hole in the shutter where one hadn't been before, and Edgar was putting his hand through it.

"I got it! I got it, Isabel."

The shutters flew open, and Edgar climbed inside, closing them behind him. He was hanging from a high windowsill near the ceiling in a dark corner of the house. A thick shaft of light poured in from the hole in the shutter as he looked at the room beneath him. A chair sat against one wall, a bed, a round tub of . . . what was that? *Water.* Enough water to take a bath in if he'd wanted to. Cups and spoons were piled up in one corner, and a large basket with a lid in another. The room smelled like sweaty clothes, warm and stale. A ladder stood against the far wall, and Edgar took this to be how Mr. Ratikan opened the shutters.

"Isabel! Why aren't you at work with the others?" It was the sound of a voice from outside. Just as they had dreaded, Mr. Ratikan had heard Edgar's cry of pain.

"Get to the grove and don't bother showing up in the dinner line tonight! Maybe that will cure you of your snooping around."

Edgar heard Isabel run off and felt sure she'd stayed out in the open only to deflect Mr. Ratikan's attention away from the house. But now Mr. Ratikan was coming up onto the porch: a step, then the thump of his walking stick striking wood, then a step. He was in front of his door.

Edgar heard the big key turn and watched the latch flip over, wondering just how horrible it would be to find himself locked in a small room with Mr. Ratikan and a swinging walking stick.

Just as the door was swinging open, Edgar realized the shaft of light was still shooting through the hole Isabel had made in the shutter, and he reached out a hand to cover the opening.

Mr. Ratikan left the door open, and light streamed into the room. He walked purposefully to the basket in the corner of the room and opened it up, peering inside and touching something with his hand that Edgar could not see. He shut the basket once more.

As he made his way back to the door, Mr. Ratikan's foot slipped out from underneath him and he nearly fell before regaining his balance on the walking stick. With a frown he picked something up off the floor. It was the black fig that had put the hole in the shutter.

"Someone's been in here," he said under his breath. *"Isabel."*

He bolted for the door with the black fig in hand and slammed it shut, locking it tight before racing down the steps, yelling Isabel's name through the grove.

Edgar instantly descended to the floor and made haste for the door, but stopped short just as he was about to leave. He looked back at the basket in the corner of the room. *What is Mr. Ratikan hiding in there?*

Inside the basket Edgar found a sack made of sheepskin with a drawn string at the top. It felt like a heavy bag of dirt, but why would Mr. Ratikan hide such a thing? Maybe there were figs hidden inside, a secret stash he ate when no one was around.

Untying the top, Edgar discovered that it was filled with dirt, just as he'd imagined it would be. He put his hand inside, rubbing some of it between his fingers. There had to be something special about it — or something hidden in the middle of it — that Edgar couldn't see.

The sheepskin bag was a common item used all over the grove to carry figs during harvest. Edgar scanned the room for an empty bag. He was in the house of the man who ran the grove, and as such there ought to have been any number of fig bags stored somewhere. He was about to give up when he looked under a table and found a box with a dozen or more fig bags stuffed inside. He took one of the bags, unlocked the door, and ran outside — keenly aware that Mr. Ratikan could return at any moment.

Edgar filled the bag with dirt from the grove as fast as he could and returned it to the basket in Mr. Ratikan's house. When he had set the original bag he'd found on the front porch and locked the door from the inside, Edgar climbed back up to the shutters and let himself out, locking the shutters behind him.

As he climbed down the outside of the house, he began to feel an itching on the fingers of one hand, and he rubbed the feeling away on his pant leg. But it returned with a vengeance as he ran to the front of the house, picked up the heavy bag, and headed into the grove.

By the time he'd made it back to the tree where he'd hidden earlier in the morning, his hand was burning and covered with blisters. It was the hand he had put into the bag.

Isabel wasn't sure how to react when she heard Mr. Ratikan yelling her name as he approached the third-year line of trees where she stood. She tried to look busy near her mother and father, who were spending as much time looking nervously over their shoulders at the Highlands as they were tying figs in clusters.

When Mr. Ratikan saw Isabel, he marched directly to her mother and thrust the black fig toward her with an accusing gleam in his eye.

"Your daughter broke into my house!"

Isabel's father, Charles, came over, along with some of the other workers from the grove. A crowd was gathering.

"Get back to work — this doesn't concern the whole lot of you!" screamed Mr. Ratikan, but nobody moved. Isabel took the sling out of her pocket and held it out.

"I was just playing with my toy when I shot that fig through one of your shutters. I didn't mean to do it."

"Give me that ridiculous thing," snapped Mr. Ratikan, reaching out his hand and snatching the sling away from Isabel.

"Leave the girl alone," said Isabel's father. "She was only playing."

Mr. Ratikan raised his walking stick threateningly toward Isabel's father, and the crowd lurched forward. He stepped back, for a fleeting moment unsure of his authority in the grove. But the feeling quickly passed, and he set his scowl on the group before him.

"Are you set to rise up against me, is that it?" said Mr. Ratikan. "We have been lucky to have the Highlands so far off, but now they come near. If they find you've fallen behind in the grove, their punishments will be swifter and harsher than you've ever experienced before."

"What will keep us from walking right in if it comes all the way down?" asked Charles, emboldened by the men at his side. "Are you going to stop us?"

Mr. Ratikan looked hard at Isabel's father and answered without the slightest fear in his voice.

"They have many ways of keeping you out, ways of violence that you should not test."

This seemed to weaken the group's hostile stance, and they mumbled amongst one another.

"Get back to work!"

Mr. Ratikan turned his gaze down at Isabel.

"And you!" He waved the sling in the air before her. "Don't ever make another of these if you care to eat at my house again."

The crowd dispersed. When Mr. Ratikan had moved far enough off into the grove, Isabel's father knelt down beside her, whispering softly.

"Can you show me how to make one of those slings?"

Isabel couldn't believe her ears.

"I can."

"And does it throw a black fig very far and very fast?"

"It does."

Isabel's father stood up again and stared at the towering cliffs.

"Then you'll have to show me how to use it, won't you?"

She looked up at her father with apprehension. They were a gentle people, and Isabel had her doubts about this sudden turn to violent thoughts. She wasn't sure she understood her father's intentions.

"What will happen if the Highlands fall all the way down?"

Isabel's father hesitated. He was a hardworking man unaccustomed to such intimate conversations.

"If they come with cruelty, I must help protect the families. I must protect *you*, Isabel."

He looked at her with strength and determination, as though he were a shield that would protect her.

"I'll show you how to use a sling if you think it will help," she said.

Her father nodded, and they both went back to work, each of them imagining what was to come.

CHAPTER
14

DRIED LEAVES AND ORANGE DUST

For all his ranting, Mr. Ratikan knew that most of the children in the grove were of little use with the third-year trees. They were too short to tie the figs and too weak to carry off the trees that had been pulled down. He had no patience for babysitting, and soon Isabel was sneaking away once more to find Edgar.

When she arrived at the tree where she'd found him earlier in the morning, it was not the same Edgar whom she had left. He flopped down out of the limbs and sat at the base of the trunk, holding the bag he had taken from Mr. Ratikan's house. One of his eyes was swollen shut and his hand was teeming with blisters.

"I found what Mr. Ratikan was hiding," said Edgar, trying with all his might to put on a good face.

Isabel had seen sores like the ones on Edgar's hand before.

"It can't be!" she cried in disbelief. These were the symptoms experienced when one made contact with the leaves of a tree that had been left too long in the grove.

"I figured out that this bag is filled with dried, crumbled leaves, but it's mixed in with a lot of orange dust —"

Isabel broke in, "The dust that catches in the air off the old trees."

"Exactly," Edgar agreed. "And I made the mistake of rubbing my eye." He was sure that if he put his head in the bag, his lungs would tighten and he would cough violently for days and days.

"Now I think I know what Mr. Ratikan was experimenting with," he continued. "I wonder what would happen if I put some of what's in this bag into a cup of water and drank it? Do you think my insides would look like my hand and my eye? I imagine I'd throw up a lot — or worse."

"The two sick people in the grove!"

Edgar nodded. Isabel slumped under the tree with Edgar and they both stared at the bag. The idea of such an inhuman act was hard for both Edgar and Isabel to grasp, and yet it was equally difficult to turn away from the facts.

"That's a lot of poison. What do you think they were going to do with it?" asked Isabel.

Edgar faltered, unsure if he should say what he thought, for fear of scaring Isabel.

"I don't know, but I think we have information that needs to be shared. People need to know this bag of dust and leaves exists — and who made it."

Edgar scratched at his hand and it burned. He had only

touched a tiny bit of the dust from the bag, and he hoped it
wouldn't get any worse.

"You look like I hit you in the face with a black fig," said Isabel. Edgar pulled his shirt down over his shoulder and revealed a swollen, black-and-blue shoulder that was almost as dreadful-looking as his face. Isabel gasped.

"The pain in my shoulder helps me forget the burning in my hand. You did me a favor."

The two of them laughed under the tree, but Isabel still felt terrible.

"It all looks a lot worse than it feels," he offered. "Just a little itching and soreness, nothing I can't handle."

Isabel explained what had happened in the grove. They agreed that Edgar would take the bag to the inn at the Village of Rabbits. He had friends there who needed to know the truth. Maybe they would even help him find someone who could read the page in his pocket. Isabel would stay in the grove, helping the villagers make slings and teaching them how to use them. She would also tell them what Edgar had found.

The grinding sound of the Highlands descending toward their homeland swept over Isabel and Edgar as they started off in different directions, wondering if they would ever see one another again.

A few hours before Edgar made his escape from the grove, a group of men stood in the Highlands before a large basket that hung from the cliffs. The basket was extended out over the edge on a wide, fallen tree trunk and lowered with thick and leathery braided ropes. It was large enough to hold a great many bags of figs or mutton or rabbit on the way up to the Highlands. The basket was broad and curved with a V-shaped bottom, which made it challenging to stand in it. It was particularly difficult for Sir Emerik, who hadn't been inside one very often. He was seated in the basket where he couldn't see over the edge.

"Get up, you fool!" Lord Phineus couldn't stand the sight of cowardice — especially in someone so near his gaze. Sir Emerik struggled to his feet. The basket was lifted off the ground by a rope and pulley, whereupon it swung like a pendulum and settled over the open air. The two men who maneuvered the basket were amused when Sir Emerik's face turned bone white as he looked out over the edge.

"When you get to the town with all the rabbits, I want you to investigate how people are reacting," Lord Phineus said. "Find out if they are frightened, confused, and most important, *organized*. And ask about the boy. When you've finished with this task, come and find me in the grove at Mr. Ratikan's house. I'll be there just before nightfall on an errand of my own."

Lord Phineus stood perilously close to the edge and looked down once more. He was alarmed at just how far the Highlands had fallen without his knowledge. It had been two days since any of the baskets had been used, a common lapse in transferring goods given the time of year. There being nothing to move, not even the men who lowered the baskets had been near the

THE BASKETS

Heavy Rope
(Multi-Braided).

FRONT VIEW

Top View

WOOD BEAM

FOOTINGS
SUPPORT
SUB STRUCTURE

HOLDS UP TO
500 lbs.

CLIFF FACE

edge. It was a dangerous place, avoided by everyone, and no one went there unless they had to.

Lord Phineus turned his gaze on Sir Emerik and found that he had sat down in the basket again.

"Lower him double time!" he yelled to the two men holding the wheel. They started letting out rope, and the basket began its quick descent to the bottom.

Sir Emerik enjoyed a smooth ride until the basket met with Tabletop, where it tipped on its side and he tumbled onto the ground like a sack full of rabbits. Brushing himself off, he looked toward the empty grove. *Where is everyone? That Mr. Ratikan must have them leashed to the trees.*

Hours later, Sir Emerik approached the Village of Rabbits in a bad temper. He wished he had been in charge of the horses and the trained men, as Sir Philip was. Sir Emerik felt as though he were on a fool's errand, wasting his time while Sir Philip taunted him with glorious pursuits of horses and weapons. Tired and hungry, he could hardly believe he was expected to return to the grove later that same day. It was outrageous, and he planned to tell Lord Phineus as much when they met once more.

With a sleepless night and a morning of wretched walking behind him, Sir Emerik's thoughts were on the food and rest he might find in the village. He had been to the inn once before and eaten the cooked rabbits, and he was overtaken by a desire to fill his stomach. *There can't be much expected of me without at least something to eat. And besides, the inn will be a good place to start digging for information about this boy Edgar. How could such an important book, holding the secrets of Atherton, be written for a mere child in Tabletop?*

It was with these thoughts that Sir Emerik arrived at the inn in the Village of Rabbits with a large appetite and droopy eyes in search of food, rest, and — if it happened his way — some useful information.

CHAPTER

15

SIR EMERIK'S INTERROGATION

Edgar's mouth began to water when he opened the door to the inn and smelled the familiar aroma of rabbits cooking. Outside the world was changing, but in the warmth of the inn, everything had remained the same. Maude was cleaning a table and Briney was tending the fire and roasting a sizzling rabbit on a stick. The rabbit crackled as Briney looked up to see who'd come in.

"What's happened to you?" he asked with some concern, setting his work aside and waving Maude to join him. They were unusually quiet as they approached Edgar, and Maude pointed toward the back wall of the inn. There was another man — quiet and alone — sitting in the dark corner of the room. His hood was pulled up and his head was on the table.

Maude took Edgar by the arm, looked him in the eye the way a doctor might, and hauled him into the back room. It was darker than the main room of the inn, where an orange glow came from flames in bowls of fatty fuel sitting on every table. Maude knelt before Edgar, and then Briney arrived with a leg torn from the rabbit he'd been cooking.

"Here, eat this," said Briney, staring at Edgar's swollen eye. "You look terrible."

Edgar's eye was swollen almost shut, and he was having some trouble seeing in the darkened room. Maude offered a tiny bit of water, and Edgar thanked them as he devoured the small meal.

"Did Mr. Ratikan hit you?" asked Maude, her voice rising in anger. "I'll bring my broom to the grove and have his head off with it!"

"It's not what you think," answered Edgar. He nodded his head toward the door to the front room. "Who is that man in there?"

Maude sighed and whispered back, "It's the strangest thing. He came in looking exhausted and starving, dropped one of the biggest figs I've ever seen on the table, and asked for a cup of water and two full rabbits."

"He's from the Highlands, you know," she continued. "I hear that's the way the important ones dress up there, with those cloaks and hoods."

"What do you suppose he's doing here?" asked Edgar, trying not to betray his fear. He'd suspected they would look for him, but hadn't imagined they could find him so quickly.

"Well, I don't exactly know. He devoured the rabbits and fell right to sleep. He must have been awfully tired, that one. He hasn't stirred."

Edgar ate the last of the rabbit leg and set the bone on the table.

"What's that you have there?" asked Briney, pointing to the bag Edgar had carried from the grove. The two adults then noticed the swollen sores on Edgar's hand.

"What have you gotten yourself into, Edgar?" asked Maude, concern rising in her voice.

Edgar wasn't sure how to begin. There was so much to say, but he hadn't anticipated a sleeping man from the Highlands sitting in the inn who might wake at any moment.

"The Highlands are sinking," said Edgar. "You do know that, don't you?"

The tone in the little room changed all at once. Briney peered around the corner into the front room and saw that the man was still asleep.

"We know, Edgar. Everyone in the village knows. There's been a lot of talk about what will happen if it reaches the bottom. People are talking about going in. About *forcing* their way in. They talk about the water mostly, about how the Highlands won't be able to keep it from us any longer."

Edgar rubbed his inflamed hand against his pant leg, then he quickly told them what was in the bag, where it had come from, and what he thought the Highlands had planned to do with it.

"I wish you'd left that outside," said Maude when he'd finished, leaning away from the bag and eyeing Edgar's infected hand. "They intend to do us harm, that much we can say for sure."

"What shall we do with it?" asked Edgar.

"Leave it with me," said Briney. "With the Highlands falling, we've got people traveling between the grove, the Village of Sheep, and us. Everyone is trying to decide what to do and when. We'll figure out what should be done with it."

Edgar was surprised to hear that the different villages in Tabletop were in communication. Were they organizing, preparing for — what did the book of secret things say? *A war?*

Edgar got up and glanced at the sleeping man.

"Can you go outside and leave me alone with him?" asked Edgar. It was an odd request.

"I suppose we could, but why?" asked Maude, baffled.

"I have some questions I'd like to ask him that only he can answer, but I don't want him to think you had anything to do with it. I don't want to endanger you or your plans."

Edgar saw they were both puzzled by what he wanted to do.

"Someone is bound to come into the inn soon, and my chance will be lost," said Edgar. "Please trust me, won't you? It will only take a moment to get what I need, but you can't be involved. He'll know you're against them. *They'll* know." Edgar raised his head in a gesture toward the Highlands.

Struck by the determination on Edgar's face, Briney and Maude conceded. They started for the front room to lock the door to the inn, but Edgar stopped them.

"Do you suppose I could get you to help me tie him up?" said Edgar. "I can't have him reaching across the table or trying to escape."

He scratched his eye, and the two adults looked at one another. They didn't say anything, but instead seemed to read each other's mind and know without asking what the other had decided.

"We'll need a good long bit of rope," said Briney.

"I know just the place," continued Maude, moving to the very back of the darkened room.

Edgar had achieved one small victory, but it was yet to be seen if the man would read the page hidden in Edgar's pocket.

When Sir Emerik woke up, he didn't open his eyes immediately. First he sat up and tried to stretch his arms over his head, which was something he was in the habit of doing whenever he got out of bed in his room in the House of Power. He was still sleepy, and it felt like he was trapped in a dream in which he couldn't move. He was so very tired that he thought it best to go back to sleep for just a little longer. *Another hour won't hurt. Then I'll go about the village and make the long walk to the grove. Such a long walk.*

He was about to drift back into a dreamy world when he felt something hot near his face, which forced him to open his eyes.

The room was dark, and it took Sir Emerik a moment to see much of anything other than a glowing orange object near his right cheek. He blinked furiously and wished he could wipe the mush out of his eyes, but he was still immobile. As he became more conscious, he was able to make out the figure of a boy sitting in a chair across the table from him.

"Don't move," Edgar said. "You wouldn't want to get burned."

Edgar had a flaming torch in his hand, the fire dancing just to the side of Sir Emerik's head. The room was otherwise empty. Briney and Maude had gone outside to keep anyone from coming in.

Sir Emerik was fully awake now and became aware that he had been tied to a chair. The grime in his eyes had moved off to the corners, and he could see Edgar clearly. He saw that the boy had been hit in the face and wondered if Mr. Ratikan had belted him with his walking stick.

"You better know what you're doing, boy," Sir Emerik said in his most threatening tone. "This is a dangerous game you're playing."

Edgar remained undeterred. He put the page down on the table where the open flame of the torch illuminated the words.

"Read that to me. Read it quickly or I'll set your hair on fire."

Sir Emerik could hardly believe what was happening. He was at once enraged at the audacity of the boy before him and overjoyed at the prospect of having found Edgar and the missing page. *If only I'd stayed awake, I'd have them both in my grasp. There must be a way to bring things under my control.*

"You've been to the Highlands, haven't you?"

Edgar only looked at Sir Emerik and waited.

"How else would you have gotten that page from Samuel?"

He paused, letting the boy think on what he'd said; then he turned very serious.

"There are very harsh consequences for climbing around on the cliffs — you know this. And there are even harsher punishments for having a page of writing in your possession. You're in quite a lot of trouble, aren't you, *Edgar*?"

Edgar reeled back slightly on his chair when he heard his name called out. Samuel must have told them.

"Oh, yes, we know all about young Edgar. We have our ways." Sir Emerik leaned forward as much as the ropes would allow. *Now, finish this miserable lad for good.*

"If you're caught, they'll break your legs. They'll make sure you never go climbing around again. There's no place to hide, Edgar. Even if you escape the inn, we'll find you, and then you'll pay." Sir Emerik was beginning to feel very confident — despite the fact that he was still tied up, and Edgar hadn't even flinched with discomfort at his words.

"I can help you, Edgar. I *will* help you. Just untie me and I'll get you out of the trouble you're in."

Sir Emerik leaned back on his chair with a smug look on his face, certain that he was about to be untied.

Edgar moved the flame of the torch closer to Sir Emerik's head. Then, with a quick flick of his wrist, he set the man's hair on fire. Sir Emerik hadn't even thought to prepare himself for the attack. The hair flamed up orange on one side with a burst of black smoke and bright light. Sir Emerik started to scream.

Edgar tossed a bunny sack on Sir Emerik's head, putting the flame out as fast as he had started it. When he pulled the sack from Sir Emerik's head, a plume of smoke escaped, and Sir Emerik coughed and bellowed. The burnt hair smelled awful.

"You've gone mad!" Sir Emerik shouted. Most of the hair on the right side of his head was gone. What remained was a glob of black goo that stuck to his scalp.

"Read the page," demanded Edgar. "Quickly now — time is short and I must be getting on."

"You're a little madman, that's what you are. A wee little madman!"

Edgar put the torch in his other hand and held it next to the opposite side of Sir Emerik's head.

"Please, just read the page. It's not that hard."

Sir Emerik looked down. Though it was written in a sloppy hand, it was a short message, and he was able to read the few words written there without too much difficulty. Part of what he read was quite a shock. But when he had regained his composure, Sir Emerik realized he could tell the boy part of what he'd read, but not all. How would Edgar know the difference? Sir Emerik relished this moment of bliss as he looked up at Edgar.

"It won't do you any good, what that page says," Sir Emerik said. "It's useless."

Edgar noticed that Sir Emerik's face seemed somehow askew with all of the missing hair on one side, and he had to stop himself from setting the other side on fire to even things up. The poor man looked terrible.

"I'll decide that for myself. What does the page say?"

Sir Emerik didn't like the fact that this child was bossing him around. Flame or no flame, he couldn't help looking at the boy with contempt. This was a mistake, for the moment he did so, Edgar set the other side of his head on fire.

When the bunny sack was again thrown over Sir Emerik's head and removed, and the acrid smoke had cleared, Sir Emerik looked symmetrical again, although there was a tuft of hair sticking up on top that Edgar was tempted to set ablaze.

Edgar held the flame under Sir Emerik's nose and asked once more if he would please just read the page. Exasperated and afraid, Sir Emerik finally relented.

"It says there is a second book of secret things in Atherton."

Edgar wasn't sure how to take the news. It was awful knowing that even if such a book existed, he wouldn't be able to read it. He was forever having to rely on other people to get the information he needed.

"What else does it say? Does it say where the book is?"

"That's just it," cried Sir Emerik with a sinister laugh, his fear overcome by a chance to dash the boy's hopes. "The only way to find it is to go below, to the Flatlands. That's what the page says. How do you like that, Edgar?"

Sir Emerik was very pleased with himself because, to his knowledge, there was only one way to get down to the Flatlands: to climb. He could think of no better means to get rid of the boy than to send him on a quest that could end only in disaster. This foolhardy child would believe him and make a go of it, leaving only him — Sir Emerik — with the truth of what the page had actually revealed.

"I've told you what you wanted to know, however useless it may be. Now set me free, you little monster!"

But Edgar merely rose from his seat, took the page in his hand, and walked toward the door.

"You can't just leave me tied up like this, Edgar. You must let me go," Sir Emerik insisted, still speaking in a condescending tone. It took all of Edgar's will not to return to the table and burn off the last of the man's hair. Instead, he dropped the torch into the fire, casually picked up the rest of the rabbit with the missing leg from the skiff, and departed without even a last glance at his captive.

He could hear Sir Emerik shouting with indignation when he got outside, where he was greeted by Maude and Briney.

"What did you do to that man? He sounds as though he's going to kill someone!"

"He's all right, just angry." Edgar decided not to mention the burned hair. Instead, he held out the cooked rabbit. "I know it's asking a lot, but could I have this to take with me?"

Briney waved his approval. "Of course you can have the rabbit. But what did he tell you? Where are you going?"

There was no one else on Atherton who would even consider trying what he was about to do.

"I'm going down to the Flatlands."

Maude and Briney both gasped at once.

"What in the world are you talking about?" said Maude. "That's not possible!"

"I've already climbed up there," said Edgar, pointing to the Highlands. "*Twice.*"

"How could you have gotten all the way up there?"

Edgar shrugged. "I'm a good climber. A *very* good climber."

"Well, I should say so," said Briney. He ran his fingers through his coarse beard and gazed with stunned amazement at the cliffs and the boy before him.

"You've been very kind," Edgar said with genuine gratitude. "But I really must go."

Edgar started to move off, but Maude told him to wait a moment more. She ran around the back of the inn, and when she returned she had a small sack made of rabbit skin in her hand.

"It's water — the last we've got for today, but you can have it."

Edgar thanked them both, and then he was gone, making his way to the edge of the world.

Briney and Maude opened the door to the inn with a look of astonishment at the sight of Sir Emerik's charred head. When they got him free, they were surprised to find Sir Emerik smiling, for what he had read on the paper was a magnificent secret full of potential uses. He would save it for Lord Phineus when he got himself out of the mess he was in.

CHAPTER

16

HORACE LEAVES HIS POST

As morning turned to afternoon in the Highlands, word began to spread of the strange descent into Tabletop. Rumors were mounting of armed men from below preparing to loot and burn their Highland paradise. Fear flooded in liquid strides through delicate stone houses and along glistening streams, darkening the mood of all the families of the Highlands. Every man of the Highlands was bombarded with desperate questions as he left in the morning on orders from Sir Philip.

"What shall we do if they come for our children? What if they come with torches to burn down the house? Will you ever return?"

As the men gathered in a large open field with sharp wooden spears and horses, they wondered if the catastrophe called *war* that all of them had read about in books had finally found its way to Atherton.

As Sir Philip went about the business of arming and instructing his men, Horace sat at the top of the stairs in his usual spot, pondering what he'd seen and heard the night before in the House of Power. He was back on duty after a morning of rest, and he looked down the hallway toward the main chamber, trying to imagine why Samuel had not returned. He was a good boy whose father had been taken from him. Why would Lord Phineus and the others want to torment the poor child by locking him in a room?

"Horace?"

He was jolted from his thoughts by Samuel's mother, who had quietly crept up the stairs behind him. Anxiously rubbing the red blotch beneath her lip, she held a small loaf of bread out to him.

"I came in late last night and Samuel wasn't in his room. I've asked everyone in the courtyard and the kitchen, even Sir Emerik and Lord Phineus. Nobody seems to know where he's gone."

Horace was embarrassed to accept the bread in exchange for information, but he was also very hungry. With all of the bustle in the House of Power, he hadn't had a moment to eat. He took the bread and thanked Samuel's mother.

"You don't look like you've slept," said Horace.

"I haven't. I've been all over the Highlands searching for him. And with Tabletop coming so near and the rumors of what they might do . . ." Her voice trailed off and she dropped her head, rubbing the red spot once more. When she looked up, there was heartbreak in her voice.

"Have you seen my boy, Horace?"

Horace paused. Lord Phineus and his two men were gone, leaving their rooms and the chambers above empty and still. "I have an idea where he might be, but I'm not certain," he said. "I'll tell him to get on home if I see him."

"Did you see him during your shift last night?"

Horace didn't want to appear overly confident about the whereabouts of the boy. "The House of Power is in a bit of chaos, as you might have noticed. But I'll look around as my duties allow. There are a few places I can check where he may have run off to."

"Thank you, Horace!" Samuel's mother touched Horace on the shoulder awkwardly and took a few steps back down the stairs. "I'm already late for the kitchen. If you find him, send him there, won't you?"

Horace nodded and shooed her away. After taking a few bites of bread, he began his search. He knew the boy wouldn't be in the main chamber or any of the three private rooms on the floor above that. He would be hidden at the top of the narrow, winding stairs if he were anywhere near this part of the House of Power.

When he arrived at the door to the room where Samuel was locked away, he knocked on it and waited. Thinking he heard a stirring on the other side, he unlocked and opened the door. Samuel was crouching against the back wall, looking at Horace like a trapped animal.

"Have you come to take me to the main chamber?" asked Samuel, certain he was being summoned for more questioning.

"I'm here to take you to your mother, who's worried sick about you," said Horace. "You shouldn't scare her like that. Hiding in here all night. Have you lost your mind?" He was pretending not to know the truth of Samuel's imprisonment. Should Lord Phineus ask, it would be best to act as though he'd found Samuel and let him out, thinking he'd been locked in by accident while playing where he shouldn't have been.

"These doors have a way of locking on their own," he went on. "Remember that the next time you go sneaking around!"

Samuel was ready to dash out of the room until he remembered that one of his captors might be around any corner.

"Nobody's here, Samuel," Horace reassured him. "Go see your mother in the kitchen."

Samuel grinned from ear to ear, free at last, and bolted for the stairs.

"And tell your mother to bring me another loaf of bread," Horace called after him. "I'm fit to die of hunger."

When Samuel reached the courtyard, he immediately sensed something had changed in the Highlands during the short time he'd been locked away. Baskets of food were carried past, men with tools and weapons raced from place to place. It seemed as though everyone was in a rush to get somewhere. The walls around the House of Power were guarded with a heavy presence of somber men, the likes of which he hadn't seen before.

Samuel's mother beamed when he arrived in the kitchen, then she cried softly as they embraced. Samuel kept to Horace's story and told her he'd locked himself in a room by accident. As he recounted his tale, she brought him a small baguette and a cup with water.

"You must stop your sneaking around the House of Power," she said, then knelt down so she could see Samuel's expression. "Samuel, do you know what is happening in the Highlands?" she questioned. His blank stare indicated that he did not, and so she told him only what she felt was absolutely necessary. "The Highlands are falling. Our land has shifted toward Tabletop, but we don't know what it means. It's no matter, though — you're safe in the House of Power. Stay inside and everything will be fine."

It was really happening! Samuel couldn't stop thinking of Edgar and the grove and how he must find his friend. There were things Edgar didn't understand, things he couldn't know without reading the last page of the book of secrets.

"Now," said Samuel's mother, "I have much bread to bake." As if to confirm what she'd said, a guard entered the kitchen and took the large basket of bread away, leaving an empty one in its place. She rubbed her nose with the back of her hand and stood up. "Stay in your room unless I tell you to come out, all right?"

Samuel nodded and followed the man with the basket out the kitchen door into the courtyard.

"Excuse me, sir," he said, after he was far enough away from the kitchen that his mother couldn't hear.

The man glanced down at the boy with some irritation.

"What do you want?"

"How far down have the Highlands sunk?"

The man began walking away from Samuel again, but said something over his shoulder.

"Farther than you can imagine."

Thinking quickly, Samuel headed back to the kitchen and begged his mother for two more loaves of bread and some water, which she hesitated to give. He couldn't understand her uncertainty, for there had never been a shortage of food or drink, and Samuel had always enjoyed whatever he wanted. Though the demands on the kitchen were greater than ever, eventually Samuel's mother relented, sending him off with the items he had asked for.

Back in his room, Samuel transferred the water from the cup into a leather container and sealed the top with a string. He put it and the two baguettes inside a sack retrieved from under his table. Tying the bundle around his waist, he made his way to the main gate.

A bustle of activity surrounded the entryway to the House of Power. Men on horses were let through and given supplies to take out to the field. When a large group of men heaving baskets and bags proceeded through the gate, Samuel skirted around and between them. One of the men saw him and laughed, thinking the boy was looking for adventure, and didn't want to spoil his fun.

"Where are you off to?" he asked curiously.

"I just want to see what everyone is doing."

"Then you'll want to come this way," said the man. He called to his comrades. "We have ourselves a little soldier!"

Though the men were dreading the confrontation that might occur, they were also proud and oddly excited and willing to give a future mate a look at what all the fuss was about. Samuel tagged along, asking questions while planning to sneak away to the cliffs when they weren't watching him. He desperately hoped he could discover a way down, and that he would find his friend waiting in the grove.

All the while the ground trembled on, drawing Samuel closer to a world he'd previously known only from a distance.

CHAPTER

17

QUAKES AND TREMORS

When Sir Emerik arrived in the grove, he tried to put his hood on to hide the hair that had gone missing, but it stuck to his head with a burning and itching he couldn't stand. As he made his way through the trees, some of the workers stared curiously. When he finally stood at the front steps of Mr. Ratikan's house, he was trying to think of a lie that would disguise the absurdity of what had actually happened. He didn't knock on the door until he was satisfied with his own telling of things.

"Lord Phineus, are you in there?"

Mr. Ratikan opened the door, and Sir Emerik found Lord Phineus sitting in a chair waiting for him.

"What happened to you?" scoffed Mr. Ratikan, who stood behind Sir Emerik, gazing at what remained of the man's hair.

"Oh, shut up!"

Sir Emerik was just about to tell Lord Phineus of the battle he'd had with the rebellious villagers when the floor of the house began to shake. It started softly, then grew into a violent heaving. The cups and spoons on Mr. Ratikan's table rattled furiously and began falling to the floor in groups of three or four. The three men raced outside, and Sir Emerik fell to his knees as Lord Phineus and Mr. Ratikan steadied themselves against a swaying tree. The house was beginning to collapse into itself.

"My house!" screamed Mr. Ratikan. "My beautiful house!"

But Lord Phineus wasn't looking at Mr. Ratikan's home as it fell to pieces. His eyes were fixed upon his own home in the Highlands, in awe as it sunk into the ground, faster than he'd thought possible in his wildest imagining.

"Look there," he said with a surprising calmness, pointing to the cliffs that plummeted with such fury. A brutal crunching noise rippled across the land as it made its way down. Lord Phineus estimated that at this rate, it might take only a few hours to crash into Tabletop.

And then — as quickly as it had begun — the quaking settled down to a low hum, and the descent of the Highlands slowed. Lord Phineus could hear it churning, grinding the earth as it slowly continued its march. *We are but a day away, if that. I must move quickly.*

Sir Emerik raised himself off the ground, fallen leaves stuck to the side of his head. "Every soul in Atherton knows now, of that we can be sure."

Mr. Ratikan was in a state of shock as he stood before what was once his home. All that remained were the three steps leading to a pile of rubble.

"What's happening, Lord Phineus? What have you done?" asked Mr. Ratikan, rage brewing in his eyes. He was looking at Lord Phineus as though the ruler of the Highlands could move mountains.

Lord Phineus took hold of Mr. Ratikan's walking stick and tore it from his hand. Then he stepped back and swung it at the master of the grove, just missing his head as he ducked and tumbled to the ground.

"I would prefer it if you didn't use that tone with me, Mr. Ratikan."

There was nothing Sir Emerik liked more than to watch as someone of importance was beaten down. He had always hated Mr. Ratikan for his lack of cleverness, and he was sure the man was in the habit of hoarding figs from the grove that should have been sent up to the Highlands. *He's finally getting his due,* thought Sir Emerik.

Lord Phineus continued, holding the end of the stick only an inch from Mr. Ratikan's face. "I'm glad one of us had the presence of mind to bring this out of the house." In his other hand he clenched the bag of dirt from the basket. "Can you imagine the grove with *this* released freely into the air?"

Sir Emerik began to ask about the curious bag in his master's hand.

"Silence!" Lord Phineus screamed, pointing the walking

stick at his companion. Mr. Ratikan tried to stand up, but the stick was back in his face before he could escape.

"Keep the people under your charge in control until I return. If there is an uprising in the grove, it is you who will pay." Lord Phineus raised his gaze to the Highlands once more, then tossed the walking stick aside. "We must go, but I suspect we'll be back sooner than you think."

Lord Phineus was not in a chatty mood as they walked under the canopy of trees. Sir Emerik had grown to understand that there were times in which speaking would not be to his advantage, and so he kept his mouth shut. Neither of them liked to be in the grove, for the trees forced them into uncomfortable ducking and weaving, which annoyed both men. When they finally came free of the trees and stood upright, Sir Emerik could feel the question coming from his quiet companion even before it was in the air.

"What happened to your head?" asked Lord Phineus. They were moving toward the cliffs now, and Sir Emerik had other concerns on his mind.

"Do you really think it wise to try and go back? What if there is more shaking and the basket loosens? We'll be killed." The Highlands moved slowly now, but the two of them could still see and hear its determined progress.

"All right then, if you won't answer that question, then tell me how the people in the village are reacting to the Highlands' descent."

Sir Emerik thought, *By burning all of my hair off, you heartless madman!* Regaining his composure, he told the story he'd concocted on the way back from the Village of Rabbits.

"There was a great deal of questioning and hostility. The townsfolk had me cornered at the inn — a place we should seriously think about closing down — and they weren't going to let me go. When I struggled to escape, the monsters tried to torch me! I think we should be prepared for the worst, Lord Phineus."

Lord Phineus smiled cruelly.

"I do believe you're right, Sir Emerik. We will do well to anticipate them, don't you agree?"

Sir Emerik nodded. "Always better to be on the offensive," he said, though he had not an ounce of military knowledge to back his assertion.

"And there was no sign of the boy?" asked Lord Phineus.

"No, I didn't see the boy. No one in the village knew who I was talking about." It would not be an overstatement to say that Sir Emerik was a magnificent liar, and it was impossible for Lord Phineus to tell that he'd just been told a big one.

Not another word passed between them as the two made their way to the cliff walls. A pair of guards were on duty at the basket when they arrived. The men were accustomed to watching the pool at the grove, but Lord Phineus had demanded they be moved earlier in the day. Things were unstable, he thought. What if someone from Tabletop tried to take control of the basket, leaving him stranded below?

"Everything still in one piece?" asked Sir Emerik, a hint of nervous energy in his voice.

"Yes, sir — everything works fine," said the taller of the two guards.

"Fine, then get back to your watch at the pool. The water supply might become . . . compromised."

Sir Emerik couldn't hide a certain amount of contempt when he spoke to these people. They couldn't read, and in his mind this made them stupid and only marginally useful. But Lord Phineus saw them differently. He had long taken comfort in knowing he could control things from afar. The guards at the basket were of the minority in Tabletop who could be bought with a price to maintain control. They worked for Lord Phineus and received special privileges for doing so, but it was hard to say where their allegiance would lie if a conflict arose. He wondered now if the Highlands could count on them.

"Gentlemen, you understand that the Highlands may collapse all the way and become even with Tabletop, don't you?" The guards nodded. "I shall put you to great use if this should come to pass. Understood?"

Both men said "yes," but neither was entirely sure on which side he would serve if ever relations between the two realms turned violent.

"Instructions will follow shortly." Lord Phineus carefully set the bag from Mr. Ratikan's house into the basket, then climbed in. Sir Emerik was not enthusiastic about following, but the alternative bothered him even more. He couldn't be left behind while Sir Philip and Lord Phineus plotted a war without him.

As if marking time, the mound of rope at Sir Emerik's feet was growing larger as the cliffs continued their descent.

"Get in, Sir Emerik. We haven't got all day," Lord Phineus snapped.

Sir Emerik sighed, grabbed hold of the edge of the basket, and jumped inside.

It was a strange sensation rising up while the cliff was coming down all at one time, but it was especially disorienting for Sir Emerik. He had endured a difficult day of being tied up, having his hair go up in flames, and trekking for miles between the grove and the village. Instead of watching the world below, he sat on the floor of the basket wondering about the purpose of the bag at Lord Phineus's feet. The basket pitched from side to side, and he felt his stomach swirl.

Lord Phineus glanced down at Sir Emerik and saw his ill expression. Along with his burnt head and hair, it was a revolting sight. He quickly turned away.

"If you're going to be sick, don't do it in here." Lord Phineus stepped away from Sir Emerik, who stood and leaned out over the edge of the basket. Out came the rabbits from the inn, the water he'd drunk there, and the baguette he'd eaten for breakfast. He remained sick for the rest of the trip, and when the basket reached the top, Lord Phineus hastily departed, leaving Sir Emerik to hobble back to the House of Power on his own.

Even in his misery, Sir Emerik could not help but notice the frenzied activity among the inhabitants of the Highlands. Horses and food were being moved, the courtyard gates were heavily guarded, and the children were being gathered and sheltered indoors. *Sir Philip's certainly gotten everyone worked up now, hasn't he? I wonder if he's in over his head.*

When Sir Emerik arrived at the door to the inner chamber, it was locked, and neither Lord Phineus nor Sir Philip could be found. The two of them were in there — Sir Emerik was sure of it — and it worried him that he'd not been able to return sooner. He didn't trust the two alone.

With great urgency, he knocked on the door, but was refused entry.

"Go away!"

"But sir, it's me, Sir Emerik."

"I'll call for you when I'm ready. You may rest awhile."

Sir Emerik thought he might try to listen, but what if they opened the door and saw him there? He hesitated, then started up the stairs toward his room. *The more I think of it, the happier I am that I've kept my secret well. Only I know the contents of the last page of the book. I must get Sir Philip alone to make the most of it.*

Mr. Ratikan had gathered all the men from the grove and in his haste and fury demanded that they stop what they were doing and go directly to work repairing his house. Thirty men were pulling up the walls and tearing out the fallen ceiling. They retrieved the furniture — most of which had been smashed — and then Mr. Ratikan called all the women and children from the grove to fix the broken bed and chairs and tables.

Everyone in the grove had fallen houses of their own that they were now unable to attend to. Some had a sheep or a box of rabbits at home — treasures, to be sure — and these animals were seen dashing through the grove, nibbling on the grass beneath the trees. Mr. Ratikan was strutting about the place, rapping knees and backs with his walking stick and hollering, "Stay away from the water!" and "Get busy there, you!"

And so it came to pass that the people of the grove began quietly whispering to one another that they would rise up and depart the grove as one and leave mean Mr. Ratikan to tend to his own house. Cruelty finally became Mr. Ratikan's undoing, for they tied him to a tree and left him alone, without food or water, in full view of his broken house. He wept and cursed all day, but mostly he wondered what would happen to him when Lord Phineus came back to find he'd lost control of the grove.

In the Village of Rabbits, some people were sifting through the rubble that had been made of their homes. Others were scurrying after thousands of rabbits that hopped down cobbled paths through the wreckage of the village, trying in vain to retrieve their property.

And there was something else, something very odd that put people on edge. Someone had died, and this had never happened in the Village of Rabbits before. It was a Mason — Gabriella Mason — who was crushed when one of the walls of her home collapsed upon her. There was no cemetery on Atherton, and no one knew what to do with the body. Eventually they moved it to the steps of the inn, where Maude cleaned it and covered it with bunny sacks.

After a time, the few hundred people of the village gathered around the first victim of the fall of the Highlands, and stood in silence. More than one rabbit hopped on Gabriella Mason's body and sniffed all around before continuing in search of something to eat.

CHAPTER
18

THE SOUND OF BREAKING BONES

The sun had moved off to the other side of Atherton, casting a cold shadow over the cliff, where Edgar sat gazing down at the Flatlands. The rocks were darker and smoother here, with long winding curves that were nearly impossible to grab. With his great agility and climbing skills, Edgar was able to slide through the seams of these enormous formations and move quickly.

But there was a problem he'd realized early on as he made his way down. It would be impossible — even for him — to climb back up again. Every inch he moved down was an inch to which he could never return, and he began to understand that the mysterious wasteland below would soon be his new home. There would be no escaping it once he arrived. It was a thought that haunted him in his descent to shadowy and unknown places.

He would miss the grove and the Village of Rabbits, but not

as much as the people he'd come to know — Isabel, Samuel, Briney, and Maude. Edgar hadn't thought it would be so hard to leave them, and he wondered if making friends had been a mistake after all.

Edgar was just coming to a ledge where he could rest when he shifted in a way that crushed the cooked rabbit in his pocket for what seemed like the hundredth time. He was trying to save the food for when he really needed it, but it was becoming wet and greasy against his skin, and the smell was starting to make him hungry. After carefully situating himself — legs dangling out over the edge — he pulled the roasted rabbit out of his shirt pocket.

"Better to put this in my stomach where it can be of some use," Edgar said out loud. He ate the three remaining legs first and flicked each of the bones into the open air as he gnawed them clean of every last bit of meat. He couldn't help leaning forward and watching as the bones slowly disappeared, well before they hit the Flatlands.

"I hope I'm not dropping these on someone's head." He chuckled to himself, but suddenly realized he didn't know who or what threat might be below him. He strained to see people moving or smoke rising from below, but there was nothing — only a barren swath of rocky ground beneath him. After that he stopped throwing the bones, placing the rest in a small crack in the rocks.

His hand was beginning to feel better. By now all of the blisters had burst and scabs were forming, and he could see out of his eye without forcing it open. Looking up, he was once again reminded of the almost immeasurable distance down to the Flatlands. He estimated that he'd come only about a third of the way in the same amount of time it had taken him to make a complete trip down from the Highlands, even with the speed of his descent.

Edgar was an impulsive boy of unusual determination, and he had set his mind to finding the second book of secret things without giving much thought to what he would do with the book once he found it. Even if he discovered the book in the vast openness of the Flatlands — which would be a feat in itself — he had no way of reading it and was unlikely to find someone in the Flatlands that could read it to him. He did not even know if there were another human being in the Flatlands.

Edgar quickly shut the horrible thought out of his mind. That would be a kind of loneliness he'd never experienced and would never choose for himself.

Edgar spent the rest of that first day climbing and sliding and almost falling too many times to count. The evening turned chillier than Edgar was accustomed to, and the lower he went, the colder the air enveloping him became. As night fell, he found a spot where he could lean back on the rock face. It wasn't a cave, but it was almost flat, and though he had trouble sleeping for a while for fear of falling, eventually he drifted into a sort of half-sleep that revived him.

When morning came, he saw that he was farther than half-way. He sipped at the precious water from the leather sack tied round his waist and nibbled at the few remaining bones in his pocket, and then he started off again.

It was midday when Edgar arrived at a place in which we are well suited to rejoin him: He was now near enough to the bottom that he was actually beginning to see the Flatlands for the first time.

Before we discover what Edgar saw, it is worth noting that Edgar was usually a careful climber, even when he was moving over easy routes he'd done a thousand times before. But every climber will say the same thing: being careful *most* of the time is precisely what will get you into the greatest trouble in the end. You might just as well be careful none of the time from the start and get your falling over with early, quit climbing altogether, and be rid of the habit with your limbs unbroken and your life intact. No, it most certainly is a boy just like Edgar who eventually gets into trouble of the most serious kind.

It is not surprising that Edgar was enthralled by what he saw in the Flatlands. Beneath him lay a desolate world of sharp stones, where darkness and light were split in two by shadows of every shape and size. Between the shadows the Flatlands were alive with a writhing movement the boy had never seen before. Edgar was so captivated that for an instant, he was careless with a foothold. This one careless act would cost him dearly.

As he looked down at the Flatlands in wonder, Edgar moved his left foot to a place that felt firm and fast. But the moment he put his full weight down on it, the footing broke loose, and his left foot dangled out into the air. He held firm for a moment with his hands, but soon he was clawing at the rocks, slipping quickly down the curved stone with nothing to hold.

Edgar's chin bounced on the rock as he went, and he scrambled with all his might to catch hold of something, anything, but his speed only increased.

Fortunately, Edgar's ample resourcefulness and climbing instinct kicked in, and he latched onto an idea. It would be painful, very painful, but he could do it. The rock face to his right was filled with crags, and if he could reach over and take one of them in his hand, he might just be able to slow or stop himself.

Bracing himself for the pain that was sure to come, Edgar scanned the face of the cliff wildly as it raced by. He shot his hand into a tiny crevice at precisely the right moment.

There was a violent jerk of his entire body and a searing pain, but he kept falling as his hand slipped free. Edgar tried once more, and, as luck would have it, his hand found a long, skinny crack in the rock that started wide and gradually narrowed. The gap clamped his arm until it was stuck in the rock and his shoulder popped.

Edgar came to a vicious stop, hanging limp and screaming. The same shoulder Isabel had nearly destroyed with a black fig was now firmly wedged into the side of the cliff.

Edgar's feet instinctively found new holds, and his wedged arm remained immobile. This was fortunate, because Edgar soon fell into shock and closed his eyes.

When he awoke some time later, Edgar was quite sure that he had pulled his shoulder out of its socket. The pain pulsing from his elbow to his neck was almost unbearable, but his hand had gone entirely numb, and for this small blessing he was thankful. That is, until he wrenched his hand free from the rock and saw how bloody it was, which at first troubled him because he'd never been cut so badly before. But when he realized why there had been so much blood to begin with, it was more hor-

rifying still. Edgar turned his hand around and saw that the
little finger at the end — his pinky — was missing.

He remembered how his body had jerked and continued to
fall, leaving the pinky behind. It had been a hidden blessing to
have his hand so utterly wedged between the cracks of the rock
when he'd finally come to a stop, because it had virtually cut off
his circulation and stopped the bleeding. This, combined with
the fact that he'd unintentionally held his hand up over his head
for an hour, had saved his life.

There were other problems. His shoulder would hold no
weight, and the hand with the missing finger dangled at his waist.
It was the same hand that he'd used to touch the dust in the bag,
and the scabs had been torn off. As the numbness wore off, his
hand began to throb mercilessly, and blood dripped slowly from
a thick scab forming at the stump where his pinky used to be.

Edgar was nearly dizzy with anger and frustration at himself for his carelessness. An already nearly impossible feat had
just been made even more difficult. He would have to make do
without the pinky the rest of the way down, and he wasn't quite
sure he could do it.

It wasn't until he looked down again at the Flatlands, his
hand and shoulder alive with roaring pain, that he remembered
what he'd seen before falling — and now he knew why it had
been such a shock.

Whatever was moving below him on the ground was not
human.

Dozens of glistening thin trails appeared against the shadows like a tangled mess of bright green threads and winding

ropes. Though he couldn't make out the features of the creatures — whatever they were — from where he stood high on
the cliff, he could see they moved fast. He counted seven beneath him, writhing across the landscape and occasionally slith-
ering into or over one another.

Beyond these strange beings Edgar could make out formations of jagged stone and a great deal of what could only be
described as nothing at all. It was haunting and silent in its vast-
ness, a blanket of rocks and dry earth with a primal power that
took Edgar's breath away.

The rest of the day was very slow going, as you might imagine, but Edgar made steady progress at about half the pace he'd
been going before. If it weren't for the pain he had to endure, he
might even have relished the challenge of trying to climb with
three rather than four limbs. He cursed himself for not trying it
sooner so that he might have become skilled at it.

Edgar was an injured boy of eleven who was all alone in the
world and took no comfort in food or water or tears of self-pity.
But there came a point when even he found himself thinking,
I won't make it another night up here. I'm too tired to hold on in
the dark. It was thoughts such as these that kept him moving in
the face of impossible odds. Life had granted him adversity at
every turn, and it had become his habit to find a way to keep
going. His humble past served him well as he made his final
descent into the unknown. And he would have completed it
without further trouble, too, if he hadn't been startled so dra-
matically near the very bottom of the cliff.

There were only twenty feet to go, and night had long since fallen on the Flatlands. Edgar didn't know for sure how close he was to the bottom — only that it was near enough for him to feel its closeness. He had been near the bottom of a cliff after nightfall before and had noticed the same certain smell, a change in temperature, and other subtleties that played on his senses.

Suddenly there came a tremendous noise Edgar had never heard before, like the sound of a thousand dry bones snapping at once. It was close, as if it were coming from right below him. Edgar turned and gasped — but he saw nothing, for when he shifted, the pain in his shoulder flared hot and he let go of the cliff. He tumbled toward the ground — bouncing here and there off smooth stone for twenty feet or more.

As he hit the ground, Edgar felt as though his body had shattered inside and his brains had exploded into tiny parts that careened inside of his head. He heard the horrible noise once again, even closer this time. Then Edgar closed his eyes and lay still in the Flatlands.

CHAPTER
19

THE SHEPHERD'S IDEA

Many of the houses in the Village at the Grove had toppled over, but some had weathered the quake surprisingly well, and the largest of these was buzzing with activity. Mr. Ratikan was tied to a tree and could do nothing as people from all three villages gathered in the night. There were two women and a man from the Village of Sheep, Briney and Maude from the Village of Rabbits, and an assortment of adults from the grove.

Isabel sat outside the door at a table weaving slings out of thin strands of tree bark with two other girls. She had become queen of all the children, guiding them in the duty of collecting black figs and storing them in bags at the back of the house. Now and then a child would approach her as one would an emperor and ask her a question. *It's getting dark, shall we keep go-*

ing? We've found all we can in the second-year trees, where should we go now? Will you show me how to throw a black fig as you do? Isabel's story had already become legend among the other children — her dangerous friendship with a climbing boy, her mastery of a sling. Some even whispered that Isabel alone had destroyed Mr. Ratikan's house and freed the grove.

The group in the house was arguing over what should be done with the bag of poison brought along by Briney and Maude when Wallace, a man hairy from head to toe who lived in the Village of Sheep, had heard enough.

"I believe we must go to him, if we are to know the whole truth of the matter."

They all knew of whom Wallace spoke and where this person could be found. The group of them nodded agreement, and a small party was assembled to visit Mr. Ratikan. The group consisted of Briney, Wallace, and Isabel's father, Charles.

"How are things coming along, Isabel?" her father asked on the way out the door.

"Very well! We have bags and bags of black figs and more are arriving by the hour. And these girls are exceptional weavers." She nodded at the two girls beside her, who beamed with pride. "We already have twenty slings and we're only getting faster."

"We're going to need a lot more than twenty," said her father. He looked concerned. "Why don't you show some of the adults how to make them?"

The girls scowled at Isabel's father, as if he'd slapped their heroine queen across the face, and then looked to Isabel for hope that their important duty would not be taken away by the adults in the village.

"We've got plenty of black figs," said Isabel, trying to save the glory for her loyal followers. "I'll move some of the others to making slings and see how we do. Give me an hour."

Leaving Isabel to her work, the three men made their way through the grove. They stopped at the pool and drank some water, for the guards had seen the error of their ways. Their loyalties to Tabletop ran deeper than the temporary delight of a few extra figs given for their work on behalf of Lord Phineus.

Charles filled a cup as they left and brought it with him through the grove. He and the other two men arrived at the tree where Mr. Ratikan had been tied. The poor man was sleeping where he stood, the ropes holding him upright, his head slumped over. Charles dipped his fingers in the cup and flicked water on Mr. Ratikan's head. When Mr. Ratikan continued snoring, Charles tried yelling the man's name — and then kicked him in the shin.

"Get back from my house, you wretched man!" Mr. Ratikan screamed. His throat was dry as dirt and he struggled to swallow. But then he noticed the cup in Charles's hand.

"What have you got there?" asked Mr. Ratikan, his voice cracking out of a raspy whisper. He'd screamed until his voice had become shredded, and he'd gone without water all day.

Charles ignored the question. "Did you poison two men from the grove?"

Mr. Ratikan was surprised, and it showed in his reaction. *How could they know?* He denied the accusation and demanded to be let go. Briney stepped forward, holding the bag.

"Do you know what's in this bag?" he asked.

"I haven't the slightest idea," said Mr. Ratikan, though the shape and size of the bag was very similar to what Lord Phineus had, he thought, taken back to the Highlands.

Briney opened the bag, taking care not to disturb its contents. He took a stick from the ground and dipped it in the cup, then into the bag. Mr. Ratikan gasped when he saw the stick was covered in an orange dust. Briney handed the stick to Charles and tied the bag once more.

"You act as though you might be thirsty," said Charles. He slurped from the cup and smacked his wet lips together. "Can I offer you some water?"

Mr. Ratikan thought for a moment that his thirst might finally be quenched after a long, dry day against the tree.

"I haven't had a drop all day," he said.

Charles dipped the end of the stick in the water, the orange dust swirling in the cup, then he held the cup under Mr. Ratikan's chin, where he could reach it with his mouth.

"Get that away from me! I won't drink it! I won't!" It had become clear to Mr. Ratikan that these men were in possession of the leaves and dust from the grove. They knew what he had done. *How did Lord Phineus allow the bag to find its way into the hands of grove workers?*

"I'm going to ask you once more," said Charles, holding the

cup a few inches from Mr. Ratikan's face. "Did you poison two men from the grove?"

"It was Lord Phineus's doing! He *made* me do it!"

It didn't take very long for the three men to hear from Mr. Ratikan what Lord Phineus had planned to do with the bag of orange dust. As they walked back to the house to tell the others, Mr. Ratikan couldn't help thinking to himself, *Lord Phineus will be furious. What will he do to me?*

The men in the Highlands grew weary of a curious boy lingering about, and soon they forgot about Samuel, for they had the business of a potential war to handle. Samuel felt a small thrill as he escaped from view, hidden in the tall trees before the edge of the Highlands. He stayed in the trees all day and wished more than once that he had brought a book to pass the time.

When night came, Samuel was out of water, and he decided to search for the channel. He fought his way through the tall yellow grass until he grew tired of the effort and veered toward the edge of the Highlands once more. When at last he reached the end of the golden field, he parted the grass and found he was close to the top of the waterfall. There he saw a figure standing in the water.

It was a man, and though the light was faint, Samuel could see that it was Lord Phineus. He was standing in the middle of the channel close to the drop, the water slowly rippling past his knees, pouring the powdery contents of an open bag into the water before him. When the bag was almost half empty he stopped, tied it shut, and stepped out of the water on the other side of the channel.

As if just an apparition, Lord Phineus slipped quietly through the tall grass and disappeared, leaving Samuel to wonder where he'd gone and what he could have possibly been up to.

The three men walked toward the house, ducking under limbs as they made their way through the grove. Charles and Briney were talkative as they went, but Wallace remained quiet, and the two men began to wonder about their new friend. They didn't realize he had spent countless days in a field of sheep without speaking a word, and this made him thoughtful in nature.

"Are you alright, Wallace?" asked Briney. Wallace motioned to his companions to stop.

"You know, Charles, your trick with the dust in that bag has given me an idea," said Wallace. He scratched his wild red beard with the back of his hairy hand and continued.

"I've been stewing on it all night. How can we use what's in the bag without spreading it among ourselves? We can't grab handfuls to throw in the faces of any attackers. It's not a very practical weapon."

"I agree," answered Briney. "It seems as dangerous to us as it is to them. At least Lord Phineus can't use it against us as he had planned."

"But the way you dipped that stick in the water and then in

the bag," said Wallace. "That's given me an idea. Couldn't we do the same thing with a black fig?"

Briney was beginning to understand. "Why, that's brilliant!" he said. "The dust would dry on the fig, and we could use the slings to throw them wherever we want!"

Charles interjected with a dose of truth. "None of us knows how to use a sling. We're as likely to throw a poison fig at one another as we are apt to hit the approaching enemy."

This took a little of the wind out of Briney's excitement, but Wallace was undeterred. "Then we best be getting back quickly," said Wallace. "That daughter of yours has some teaching to do, and we've got precious little time to learn."

The three men hurried through the grove to find Isabel and put Wallace's inspiration to the test. As they were nearing the village, Briney inquired whether or not Charles knew a remarkable boy named Edgar.

"Yes! He's an orphan of the grove, a very hard worker. Come to think of it, I haven't seen him about of late."

"He's gone in search of something," said Briney.

"What do you mean? You've talked to the boy?" asked Charles.

"I have. You'll never believe where he's gone off to. You'll think I've made it up."

The three men didn't know it, but everything they discussed was heard by someone hiding in the grove nearby. Isabel had put the children to work and wondered where her father had gone. She knew the grove as well as Edgar knew the cliffs and could slip between trees as quiet as a whisper. She listened as

Briney told of Edgar's encounter with the man from the High-lands, how Edgar had torched the man's hair off, and how her friend had gone over the edge to the Flatlands below.

Isabel crept away unheard and unseen before they could discover her missing. Her friend had gone too far this time, she knew. She wondered if she would ever see Edgar again.

CHAPTER

20

CLEANERS

It may be difficult to see at first glance, but Edgar had actually gotten an equal measure of bad and good luck all at once. It was a stroke of screaming misfortune that he'd come upon a place to where a group of unsavory creatures with enormous mouths and rows of crooked teeth had escaped. It was also true he'd fallen twice — being hurt both times — and that the creatures lurking nearby wanted to eat him.

But it must be said that Edgar's good luck greatly out-weighed his bad, for there was a hunter who had been tracking these dangerous and unpredictable beasts from a distance for many hours. He was a grave-looking man whose hair was thin-ning on top, though what hair he did have grew long and tan-gled over his ears. He was dressed in dark clothing that made him hard to see, save for his very wide, hooklike nose that curved toward his face. The man's name was Vincent.

In the waning light of day, Vincent saw Edgar scaling down the side of the cliff and wondered with utter astonishment how anyone could have made it so far — and why they might have come to begin with. He had no way of knowing how old the figure was, but he wrongly assumed it to be a man who was either bringing trouble with him or who was in some trouble of his own. He proceeded with great caution, unsure of whether or not the greater threat were the creatures he was stalking or this unknown person making his way down to the Flatlands.

After Edgar's spectacular fall, it crossed Vincent's mind to let the creatures do away with the intruder, but it was not in Vincent's nature to permit such a cruel act. And then there was the matter of the creatures themselves, who were prone to losing all sense of direction in the dark — there was no telling whether or not their gruesome mouths would stumble onto Edgar. It would be best to keep with the plan. He would kill the four beasts first — and then he would deal with the fallen body.

The four beasts were what Vincent called Cleaners. There will be plenty of time to talk more of them later, for they are terribly important dwellers of Atherton. For now we must remain uneasy in the presence of these beasts, each about the length of two grown men, with a great many legs and teeth that rattle like broken bones.

Vincent had killed Cleaners many times before, but he had to be careful not to make a mistake, or there could be quite a lot of trouble. He used a long spear with a very sharp point, but even so, he always waited until it was almost dark to do his ghastly work.

What made it possible to attack a Cleaner without daylight was the fact that these creatures, while dreadful to look at and vicious in the extreme, were rather stupid in just about every way imaginable. They may have been very fast on their many legs, but they weren't smart enough to change course when a spear was pointed right at their throats, and on they'd charge, crooked teeth flying toward him at ferocious speed, until they were skewered clean through.

There are three things a hunter must remember when encountering Cleaners:

1: WITHOUT A SPEAR, THERE'S ALMOST NO CHANCE OF SURVIVING AN ENCOUNTER WITH A PACK OF CLEANERS. NEVER LEAVE HOME WITHOUT AT LEAST ONE SPEAR TIED TO YOUR BACK, TWO IF YOU CAN MANAGE IT.

2: NEVER ATTACK MORE THAN ONE CLEANER AT THE SAME TIME. IF THERE ARE THREE OR FOUR, THEY WILL ALL COME AT ONCE FROM DIFFERENT DIRECTIONS. WHILE YOU MIGHT KILL ONE OR TWO, THE OTHER ONES MAY EAT SOME PART OF YOUR BODY THAT YOU'D ALMOST CERTAINLY PREFER TO KEEP. IT'S BEST TO LURE THEM APART, AND THEN ATTACK THEM ONE BY ONE.

3: IF YOU DETECT THEM FROM FAR OFF — AND THIS IS COMMON, FOR THEY ARE VERY LOUD ABOUT THEIR

The cyclic movement of a walking leg consists of two parts — the power stroke and the return stroke. Internal neural circuits are responsible for the creature's motion.

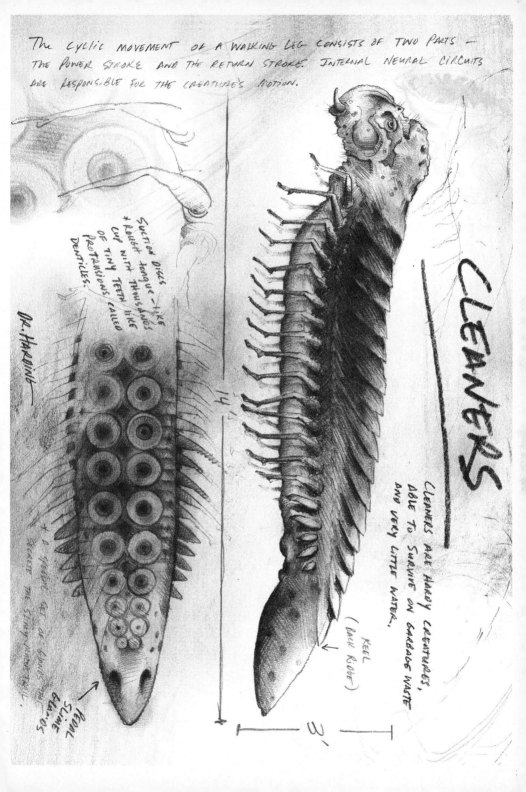

CLEANERS

Suction discs — like a rabbit tongue + Thousands cup with Thousands of tiny teeth, like protrusions, called denticles.

Dr. Harding

Cleaners are hardy creatures, able to survive on garbage waste and very little water.

Keel (back ridge)

14"

3'

BUSINESS — STALK THEM QUIETLY UNTIL NIGHT, FOR
THEY HAVE TERRIBLE SIGHT WHEN THE WORLD GOES
DARK. CLEANERS ALSO HAVE TROUBLE HEARING, FEEL-
ING, AND SMELLING AFTER DARK, FURTHER INCREASING
THE ODDS OF SUCCESS.

Vincent had followed each of the rules, and so he had no trouble at all slaying the first two Cleaners. He simply walked up to them and put the spear through their open mouths. Unfortunately for Vincent, by the time he got to the third one it had gotten darker, and as a result his margin of error had grown. When he thrust his spear, it glanced off to the right and only injured the Cleaner, causing it to thrash about with an earsplitting shriek.

This startled both the remaining Cleaner *and* Edgar, the latter of whom woke up and began making a lot of noise of his own. First there was a shout and then cries of pain, which Vincent assumed were the result of the fourth Cleaner eating one of the climber's legs or arms. Vincent became alarmed when he heard Edgar's voice, aware for the first time that it was a boy and not a man who had fallen into the Flatlands. If the boy were in serious trouble with a Cleaner, which it appeared that he was, Vincent would never forgive himself. A meddling man from above was one thing, but an innocent boy was something entirely different and unexpected.

Vincent flew into action. It was dangerous work because the injured Cleaner flopped on the ground violently in every direction, the teeth searching for something to latch onto, but he quickly finished off the third Cleaner with a series of brutal blows to the head.

The last of the Cleaners had moved off a little and had become still in the darkness. Vincent listened carefully for the sound of teeth grinding and chattering. The beast was looking at him, though it could not see. It was instinctively chomping its teeth in the air to protect itself.

"What is that thing?" It was Edgar, who had jumped up and moved behind Vincent in the dark. The sound of Edgar's voice sent the Cleaner charging toward them, and Vincent had to act quickly to stop it.

"Hold onto that question for a moment, if you would," said Vincent, pushing Edgar away. "I can't let this one escape."

The Cleaner charged past and turned, wasting no time in a second attack. This time Vincent was ready, and when the sound of breaking bones came directly at him, loud and fast, he aimed, thrust, and finished the last of the Cleaners.

At last Vincent could turn to face Edgar. In the darkness he could barely make out the boy's features, though he could see his eye was swollen as though he'd been hit.

"How did you get down here?" asked Vincent. He looked up toward Tabletop in wonder. "It's impossible. No one's ever done that before."

Edgar sat down with exhaustion. The stump where his pinky used to be was pulsing with pain, but his shoulder bothered him even more.

"You didn't make it here in one piece," said Vincent. "When did you lose the finger?"

At first, when Edgar had seen Vincent fighting the Cleaners, the man had seemed wild and violent. But now Edgar saw that Vincent had a kind face. Beneath the hooked nose, in the darkness, Edgar could make out a thin but earnest smile.

Edgar told Vincent how he had fallen in the night, how his little finger had been torn free, and of his crippling shoulder injury. Vincent nodded knowingly.

"I can tell that the bone has been pulled from its socket. Will you let me have a look at it? I have certain skills that may be of some use."

With Edgar's approval, Vincent took the damaged arm in his hand and moved it slowly from side to side. Edgar cried out, but Vincent managed to get the arm up over Edgar's head.

"Lie down, won't you?" asked Vincent. Edgar was delirious with pain and fatigue, and he simply fell over onto his side. Vincent stood over Edgar and held the arm out straight, shifting it until he was satisfied it was in the right place and then, with sudden force and speed, he pushed down the arm. There was a loud *pop,* and Edgar screamed.

The shoulder was back in place, and Edgar had gone limp, which were the two things that Vincent had hoped for. The boy was feverish, he'd lost blood, and his body was seriously weakened from lack of food or water. He picked up Edgar, and it shocked him to realize how little the boy weighed.

"What are you doing down here?" Vincent wondered aloud, though he knew Edgar wouldn't hear him. His eyes ran up the monstrous wall of rock leading to Tabletop, and then lowered to marvel at the boy in his arms. Vincent shook his head. *Could he really have come all this way?*

What followed was a long night journey in which Edgar remained asleep but alive in the arms of a man of the Flatlands, taking him to a place he could not have imagined.

CHAPTER
21

SIR EMERIK'S SURPRISE

Upon their return to the village, Briney, Charles, and Wallace were pleased to find a dozen children sitting on the ground in a circle around Isabel, each of them hard at work making slings. While they watched, two young boys approached from behind with bags full of black figs.

"We've made another nineteen slings in the past hour and we're getting faster," said Isabel. "They'll work all night if they have to, won't you?" She gazed at the group around her and they all nodded. A tiny boy who couldn't have been more than five walked into the circle carrying a handful of leathery squares.

"Twenty more rabbit skins for you," said the boy, pleased with his progress. He handed them around the circle, and the children began tying them to the braided ropes as Isabel had taught them to do.

"Can they work without you?" asked Isabel's father, aware that hundreds of slings would be made in the night, perhaps more than they could find use for. He had picked up a sling to examine it. "It's time we began training some of the adults how to use one of these."

Isabel was pleased to comply and she left with the men, leaving the others of her age to gawk at the way she moved among adults in a time of danger.

All through the night, hundreds of people streamed into the grove from the Village of Rabbits and the Village of Sheep. Some spent hours dipping figs into water and dust with sheep-skin sheaths over their hands, filling bag after bag with encrusted black stones. About a hundred learned to use a sling with reasonable skill under Isabel's direction, while others took to wrapping a hand in rabbit skin for protection and practiced throwing the black figs.

When morning came, the villagers returned to their broken houses, everyone carrying a bag of crusted black figs and a sling or a rabbit skin. In the light of a new day, everyone could see how close the Highlands had come, so close that the majestic trees near the edge seemed like a wall of intimidating guardsmen just a fig's throw away. The villagers had agreed to take shelter under the rubble of their homes. If they needed to go outside, they were instructed to act as though they were feeling ill. But it was hard not to look up with awe at the ruling land they'd never known.

In the Village of Sheep, Wallace worried over his animals, as shepherds often do. It was a green place at the foot of the cliffs, sleepy and peaceful. The trembling had become so constant that his animals didn't seem to notice it any longer. It was the only place outside the grove where grass was allowed to grow. But still he paced back and forth, scratching his hairy red belly, calming the animals with his gentle voice.

"Don't you worry now," he said. "I won't let anything bad happen. I've learned to use a sling. I can protect you." He drifted into a silent meditation, waiting for the Highlands to arrive.

Lord Phineus felt a certain unease as the morning broke, and he looked down over the edge of the Highlands. Since last evening, the fall had progressed even faster than he'd imagined, and so he was glad to have gone about his business at the three waterfalls in the night. Everyone would get their cup of water as the sun rose and he would command them in their illness to stay back. It would give him time to impose his will on a changed world. These thoughts eased his mind as he moved away from the edge.

He, Sir Emerik, and Sir Philip were stationed somewhere between the Village at the Grove and the Village of Rabbits, and all three of them were sitting atop horses, something with which Sir Emerik was exceedingly uncomfortable. He had never liked horses very much and hadn't taken the time to learn how to ride in the same way that Sir Philip had. It annoyed Sir Emerik immensely to look over at Sir Philip and see him in command of his steed.

"We are fully prepared, then?" asked Lord Phineus.

"Yes. Absolutely prepared, sir," replied Sir Philip. Sir Emerik reeled around on his horse in an effort to get closer to the two of them but quickly found that he was facing the wrong way, and the butt of his animal got the better position. The scabs and missing hair on his head made him look even more ridiculous.

"Get off the horse, Sir Emerik," said Lord Phineus. "If you can."

Lord Phineus was in an uncommonly jolly mood as he conferred with his men. He seemed content astride the animal, about to come face-to-face with a world that had previously been beneath him.

Sir Philip proceeded to give a last assessment of the strategy he would employ while Sir Emerik dismounted and held the reins on his horse, glad to be on two feet again.

"There are forty men on horses above each of the three villages," he began. "They are trained in the use of a spear and have been instructed to attack at the slightest provocation, Lord."

"That's all very well," said Lord Phineus. "But you may discover I've already subdued them for you."

Sir Philip appeared puzzled. "In the event they are not subdued upon our arrival, my men will handle them without difficulty."

Lord Phineus nodded his approval, though he was hopeful the precautions would not be necessary.

"They'll be begging for water soon," said Sir Emerik from the ground, observing the low water levels above the falls.

But Lord Phineus was not listening to Sir Emerik. "At times

like this I almost wish we had shown them how to read. This would have been so much easier if we could have sent a note, don't you think?"

The dark humor troubled Sir Philip but seemed not to bother Sir Emerik.

"To your posts, then," said Lord Phineus. "When we're close enough for them to hear, we must tell them that their lives will not change. They are still our subjects and they will remain in their villages, or else pay a heavy price."

Lord Phineus would give the instruction to those in the Village at the Grove, Sir Philip to those in the Village of Sheep, and Sir Emerik would do the same in the Village of Rabbits. Sir Emerik was glad to be already halfway to his post without much more riding ahead of him.

"Sir Philip," said Sir Emerik. "Might I get a bit more instruction on the keeping of this beast before you go off?"

"Give the man some help, Sir Philip," Lord Phineus told him. "Stop and see me as you pass to the other side. I may have more for you to do."

Lord Phineus kicked his horse and galloped away. Seeing him majestically astride the charging animal gave him the aura of an even greater power that sent a shiver down Sir Emerik's spine.

When Lord Phineus was gone, Sir Philip turned to Sir Emerik. "How you could have waited until now to master the simple skill of riding a horse is beyond me." Sir Philip shook his head in disgust. "Quickly now! You'll have to get on first if you want me to help you."

"I have a better idea," said Sir Emerik. "Why don't you come down here. I have something I want to discuss with you. Something private."

Sir Philip came down from his horse, at once exasperated and intrigued by Sir Emerik's invitation.

"You've done a fine job putting this all together, Sir Philip," complimented Sir Emerik. "Very impressive, I must say."

The feeling was not mutual. Sir Philip wanted nothing more than to be rid of Sir Emerik. Seeing him sitting on a horse with his hair burned off only confirmed his suspicion that the man was a fool and didn't belong in the inner circle at all. Sir Emerik was quickly losing respectability, and soon he would be on the outside looking in.

"What is it you have to say, Sir Emerik? We have important business to attend to and I must be getting on."

"I have some information that I think you might find interesting," Sir Emerik offered.

They were still a hundred feet above the ground of Tabletop, and Sir Emerik beckoned Sir Philip to walk with him nearer to the edge. Sir Philip followed, not entirely willingly, but his interest had been piqued. The two men stood very close to the edge of the Highlands, only a few feet away.

"What kind of information do you have?" asked Sir Philip.

"When I was in the village just yesterday, I found the boy Edgar *and* the missing page."

"You *what*?"

Sir Emerik carefully followed the script he'd made in his mind. "Sir Philip, you and I both know that Lord Phineus is simply too powerful. You will never be able to surpass him, nor will I. But together we could bring him under our control. Or better still, we could move him aside."

Sir Philip was unmoved. He realized then that the poor man had become desperate for power he could never have. Unseat Lord Phineus? It was unthinkable, and it was outright madness coming from someone as inept as Sir Emerik. But Sir Philip was a clever man, and he sought to use the situation to his advantage.

"What have you learned that Lord Phineus couldn't already know?"

This is perfect, thought Sir Emerik. *He is even more a fool than I imagined.*

"First, you must swear that it is you and I, then, against the one man. Am I right?"

Sir Philip nodded, but he gripped the spear in his hand tightly, prepared to take Sir Emerik prisoner the moment the treachery was complete.

"I read the missing page, and I know where the boy went."

Sir Emerik held back from telling more, for suddenly he felt sure that Sir Philip would betray him. There was something in the man's eyes and the way he held his hand on his spear. For his part, Sir Philip's cleverness was no match for Sir Emerik's powers of perception — and he had underestimated his opponent in the matter of ambition.

Sir Emerik leaned his shoulder out over the edge.

"Did you hear that?"

"Hear what?" asked Sir Philip.

"That noise from down below. They are right beneath us!"

Sir Philip made the catastrophic error of turning to look below, and for a split second his watchful eyes were not on Sir Emerik. It was then that Sir Emerik moved swiftly behind him and pushed Sir Philip with a sudden, vengeful force of strength. Sir Philip's eyes grew wide with shock. He managed to swing his spear towards Sir Emerik as he tried to catch his balance, teetering on the very edge of the Highlands. But it was too late. Sir Emerik lunged once more, and Sir Philip fell backward into the open air.

Sir Emerik watched as the body careened off the cliff, Sir Philip's limbs thrashing ghostlike in the wind until he slammed into the ground at the bottom.

Now there is only one to contend with, and I shall reach the very top.

Sir Emerik gathered himself, went about the tricky business of getting on his horse, and rode away toward his post, where he would find forty men waiting for him.

CHAPTER

22

AN OLD MAN WITH DROOPY EARS

The sensation of being chilled to the bone woke Edgar up. A blanket had been placed over him, but he was still shivering quietly. The cold air in the Flatlands radiated from the ground and held firm until mid-morning, when the rocky land finally warmed up, and one could walk barefoot and almost enjoy the coolness.

The ache in Edgar's shoulder had passed from sharp pain into a dull soreness. But his finger — or the place where his finger used to be — was another matter. It radiated a striking hot pain. Edgar felt the place where the finger had been. Someone had put a bit of worn cloth around the stump.

Edgar let his eyes dart back and forth across the rock ceiling above, certain that he was underground. He felt a panic rising in his throat. He'd slept in the open of the grove under a canopy of

trees his entire life, but this new place was like being in a black
coffin that he could not escape. He would gladly listen to Mr.
Ratikan yell at him if only he could go home. For the first time
in his life, he regretted that he'd learned to climb.

Edgar knew that lying on his back was the worst place to be
when he was about to start crying. Even the tiniest tear that escaped his eye would run straight and fast down the side of his
face right into his ear. Edgar remembered this from the days
when, as a young boy, he would sometimes feel lonely after the
others had gone home. He had made a rhyme for himself that
he would say, looking up at the night sky with thousands of
leaves dangling overhead.

There's nobody here, only me and the trees.
I can swing if I want, as much as I please.
There's no one to see me, no one is near.
No need to cry, no reason to fear.

He would grab hold of a limb over his head, swinging back and
forth and saying the words until the wind dried his eyes and he
grew tired once more. By the time he lay back down, he'd usually forgotten what was bothering him.

And so as he lay there with his hand throbbing and his head
full of dark thoughts, he began to whisper the old rhyme as he
turned his head slowly in the gathering light of the room.

Edgar was not underground, as he had supposed. He was in
a large cave, and the light he saw streaming ever-brighter into
the space was morning coming on in the Flatlands. The cave

was a place of natural earth and stone with a high ceiling, sloping down to a long tunnel at one end, and it was shaped, Edgar thought, much like a ripe fig cut lengthwise and laid flat. Edgar was lying in the wide end. He was looking toward a round circle of light at the narrow end of the room, wondering how he might escape, when there came a black figure into the distant entryway. It moved slowly closer to him.

Edgar stared at the ceiling once more, his heart racing, and felt the odd tickle of water inside his ears. By that time, the figure had found his way to the foot of Edgar's bed.

"You're not used to the cold," the voice said, unrolling another blanket over Edgar.

Edgar risked opening his eyes, the way children do when they want others to think they're asleep. It was just enough to see through the forest of his eyelashes and the watery blur of his tears.

The man was standing just above Edgar. Edgar couldn't make out the features of the face before him, but he was oddly comforted by the man's presence. Edgar had long been able to sense danger when it was close, and though he still trembled, he felt reassured.

Edgar blinked two or three times and then looked directly into the face of the man hovering over him.

"So you've decided to wake, then, have you?" said the man. "I was beginning to wonder if that fall had put an end to you after all."

"Who are you?" whispered Edgar.

"I'm Vincent. We met last night, though I can see how you might not remember. You were, shall we say, in a bit of a predicament."

Edgar had a vision of himself plummeting to the ground, and now recognized the man who had been there when he awoke.

"What is this place you've taken me to?"

Vincent craned his neck about the stone room and looked back at Edgar apologetically.

"I'm afraid this is where I live. It's the only place I'm aware of where the Cleaners can't get in. *Nasty* creatures."

Cleaners. Edgar recalled the awful monsters he'd seen in the darkness. He'd thought they were only in his nightmares.

"What are those things?"

"You have a lot of questions! But I have one for you, and I believe it's well past my turn." He had his concerns about *anyone* visiting the Flatlands.

"Why have you come here?" Vincent's brows slanted downward. "And *how* have you come here?"

Edgar was about to answer when both he and Vincent were distracted by the sound of someone — or something — moving outside the cave. Shadows snaked on the wall near the light at the opening of the cave, and Edgar instantly became alarmed.

"I thought you said those creatures couldn't get in here!" Edgar tried to sit up, wincing in pain as he pushed down on the injured hand. But to his relief, it turned out to be a human figure that was approaching.

"Ah, Vincent! Where have you been all night?" the figure

called out. "I was worried about you. I do hope you managed to bring us something to eat. I've been out walking since before dawn and I'm feeling sure of it now, I just —"

The man broke off suddenly when he came close enough to notice Edgar lying on the bed. There was a deep and long silence as the man stared at the boy in wonder. He was old, older than anyone Edgar had ever known, and as he stood there gazing into Edgar's eyes Vincent broke the silence.

"I found him on the hunt, coming down the side of the cliff."

The old man had a big round nose and prominent ears that hung low from a head covered in gray hair. When Vincent spoke, the old man looked at him, quickly and incredulously, and his ears flopped back and forth. He looked back at Edgar with sparkling hazel eyes too young for the face that contained them.

"What is your name?" asked the man. He was keenly interested in both the person before him and the way in which he'd arrived in the Flatlands.

"My name is Edgar."

Only a deeply drawn breath penetrated the silence. The old man reached his hand out and placed it on Vincent's arm.

"Leave us," he said. Vincent went without protest, and when he reached the entrance to the cave the old man called to him. "And bring two plates of Black and Green."

When Vincent was gone, the old man crossed the room and returned to the side of the bed with a stool to sit upon. He was visibly moved as he beheld the fragile boy before him: the swollen eye, the missing finger, a body so thin it made him embarrassed of his own comparatively normal weight.

"I simply cannot imagine how you've come to find your way here," he said, his voice full of compassion. He was a fidgety man full of energy that he liked to expend most of all by talking. And so he blurted out his next surprising words in his usual manner — quickly and clumsily, bursting with emotion.

"It's me, Edgar. Don't you remember? I brought you here all those years ago. It's me, Luther — Dr. Luther Kincaid."

The two looked at one another, both of them feeling conflicted for entirely different reasons. Edgar could not bring himself to believe it was possible. Could this really be the man Edgar had lodged in his memory for so long? What was he doing in the Flatlands? Why did seeing him stir such a strange mix of emotions? Anger: *How could he be so close and leave me alone for so long? How could he lead me down such a treacherous path?* Uncertainty: *Not only does he not love me, but it seems he wants to kill me!* Joy: *I've found him at last. He cares for me; he* must *care for me.*

And as for our complicated and brilliant Dr. Kincaid, a whole different set of feelings and questions pressed upon him: Wonder: *How could this boy have come here? It's absolutely impossible and yet here he is.* Happiness: *He is alive (injured for certain and far too skinny, but alive).* Guilt: *He will hate me for what I've done. He should hate me. How can I possibly explain?*

"Come with me, Edgar," said Dr. Kincaid. "Let's go outside where it's warm and you can get something to eat. We can talk all day if we want to."

Edgar sat up with some help from Dr. Kincaid. He wobbled back and forth as he tried to escape his blankets.

"Put this on, won't you?" Luther had quickly fashioned a sling for Edgar's arm, and the two of them had an awkward time getting it on, for the shoulder still ached. It felt better in the sling, though the relief only served to remind him that his hand hurt even worse. Dr. Kincaid tried to refocus Edgar's attention on more positive changes.

"You've grown!" he said, seeing that Edgar was now nearly as tall as he was, and realizing for the millionth time that he himself was a very short old man.

"Is it really you?" asked Edgar, tears welling up again as he tried to comprehend the man who had reentered his life.

Dr. Kincaid put his arm around Edgar to steady him and was at once overcome with emotion. He really was a blubbering old fool, the truth be told, and so he hugged Edgar as a grandfather might a grandson he hasn't seen in a year or two or three.

It was a strange and confusing reunion of two souls, and it would take the better part of the morning for them to understand what had happened and why.

CHAPTER
23

A PLATE OF BLACK AND GREEN

"Come on now, Edgar — you can't imagine how good the food is down here. And there's water — as much as you like! There's only me and Vincent to use it, so we have more than we could ever drink. How does that sound?"

Needless to say, it all sounded *very* good to Edgar. When they arrived outside, Dr. Kincaid wasted no time in getting them settled at a table. Edgar had never seen dark wood like what had been used to make the table and chairs, and Dr. Kincaid picked up on his curiosity.

"It's not like what you're used to," he offered, not sure how or when to explain all of the newness and strangeness of the lowest world of Atherton. "You will find there are a few other oddities in the Flatlands that I can clarify for you, but it's perhaps not the best place to start our conversation."

Dr. Kincaid followed Edgar's gaze to the cliffs beyond, which rose high into the air.

"I always take my breakfast outside, where I can look and wonder about all that's happening up there."

The table and chairs stood on a flat surface surrounded by huge rocks — each at least the size of Mr. Ratikan's house — which towered around Edgar like misshapen eggs tipping into the sky this way and that. He could see through the gaps between these boulders, as if a lopsided stone fence had been put there by giants without much care. A pathway led around the mass of rocks and over the edge, for Dr. Kincaid's home was high off the ground. Behind them the entrance to his cave looked dark now, as if it were sleeping and wanted to be left alone.

A bowl filled with water sat in the middle of the table, and two big wooden cups were placed in front of Edgar and Dr. Kincaid. Edgar began by sipping the water. It was wonderful — so cold and clean and plentiful. It instantly awakened all of his senses. He gulped, slurped, and even put his finger inside the cup, swishing it around luxuriously. He entertained himself this way for a while — Edgar lost in a dream of water — until he was surprised to find the cup empty, and he returned his attention to Dr. Kincaid.

There was a tangled mess of questions brewing uncontrolled inside Edgar's head, and it was difficult to know where to begin. Dr. Kincaid seemed to be having the same problem as he reached across the table and dipped Edgar's cup in the bowl, setting it back down in front of the boy.

"I suppose I should tell you how I got here and why I came," said Edgar hesitantly. "It started with a memory I had of something hidden in the cliffs, something I had tried to find for a long time."

"The notebook I left for you!" said Dr. Kincaid. "You remembered our little conversation and retrieved it when it came to you, just as I'd hoped."

Dr. Kincaid was feeling rather proud of himself at that moment, and then realized the implications. "So then it's true, the Highlands have moved down?"

Edgar nodded. "They have, but I found the book before that. I climbed up the cliffs every day, searching for it."

This information was like a blow to the head for Dr. Luther Kincaid. He had never imagined the boy would risk his life to find the book he'd hidden.

"So you climbed up and got the book, then you climbed down here?"

"First I had to climb into the Highlands to find someone who could read it to me. Then I came down here to find the second book of secret things."

Dr. Kincaid was devastated. He had sent a mere child down a treacherous path. "I expected you to wait for Atherton to come to you, not for you to go to Atherton! When the Highlands came down — it was *then* that you were to find the notebook hidden where the symbol was, not before. Hiding that book was a foolish whim to begin with. I see now it was a terrible mistake to have left it for you. . . ."

Dr. Kincaid's voice trailed off and he rubbed his big earlobe between his thumb and finger.

"I brought you to Atherton because I care about you, Edgar, and because it was the safest place for you. I've never stopped thinking about you while we've been apart, and I've always known that someday we would reunite. I just never thought it would be so soon."

"What about the second book of secrets? Do you have it?" asked Edgar.

"I'm afraid I have no idea what you're talking about. I made no mention of such a thing."

Edgar pulled the last page of the book out of his front pocket. It was crumpled and torn but legible.

"But it says right there!" Edgar insisted. "That's why I came — there's another secret book down here. You must have forgotten. . . ."

Dr. Kincaid took the page from Edgar and flattened it against his knee. He examined it carefully and then handed it back to Edgar.

"You see there!" said Edgar. "It's why I came — to get the book."

Dr. Kincaid knew that what he was about to say might harm the boy, and he hesitated to tell him.

"Edgar, who read that page to you?"

"Why do you ask?" It had never occurred to Edgar that the man at the inn might have lied to him.

"I'm sorry," said Dr. Kincaid. "I never would have brought

you down here in search of a book. It's far too dangerous. I can scarcely believe you made a go of it. But you should be very proud of yourself! You did something I didn't think anyone could ever do — nor did Dr. Harding! You climbed down. You found me!"

Dr. Kincaid smiled at the boy and waved his hand through the air. "Anyway, I'm full of secrets. I'll tell them all to you. We have all the time in the world now that we're together."

Edgar was stunned. He'd banished himself to the Flatlands forever and had lost a finger in the process. He would never see the grove again, nor Isabel or Samuel, Briney or Maude. Tears welled up again in his eyes.

"What *does* the page say?"

Dr. Kincaid had been thinking all the while about a good answer, and he'd come up with the best response he felt he could offer.

"I promise you, Edgar, you shall know what the page says. But please trust me — it will be better if we wait a little longer. I believe it will be better if I *show* you what the page said, and I can't do that just yet."

Edgar wiped the tears from his eyes. Letting himself cry had actually made him feel better, and it crossed his mind that things could have been a lot worse. He might have lost his entire arm in the fall or ended up in the mouth of one of those nasty creatures. And he was talking to the man who'd written the book for him. In many ways the journey he'd begun so long ago had come to a good end.

He sniffed and rubbed his nose with the sling, then asked

the question he'd been afraid to ask until this moment. "Dr. Kincaid, are you my father?"

Dr. Kincaid knew the question was bound to arise, but hearing it now didn't make it any easier to answer.

"I'm afraid not, Edgar," he said. "But I have tried to act as a father would. I know it seems as though I've put you in enormous danger, but you have to believe me when I tell you it was not my intention. I only wanted to protect you. You were safer in the care of Mr. Ratikan in the grove than you would have been here in the Flatlands with Cleaners at every turn. I had hoped to solve the Cleaner problem by now, but my efforts to control them have failed. I'm sorry, Edgar."

Edgar saw how regretful the old man was. It was true that the hidden book had unintentionally sent Edgar on a perilous journey, but to his great surprise, Edgar was beginning to feel a growing comfort with Dr. Kincaid and a certain contentment with these twists of fate.

"No one else can climb like I do," boasted Edgar. "I'm the only one."

This seemed to revive Dr. Kincaid, and he prodded Edgar to go on.

"If you hadn't left the book, I would have spent all my life in the grove, tormented by Mr. Ratikan. I *love* to climb. I would go straight to the wall and do it right now if not for those creatures and *this*," said Edgar, giving his own hand a wistful glance. "It was an odd gift you gave me, and it didn't get used the way you might have thought it would, but it has given me an adventure others could only dream of."

A smile of relief spread across Dr. Kincaid's face, as if a great weight had been lifted from him. Edgar told him what had happened in the world above, and the old man listened with enormous interest. He told of Lord Phineus, the bag of poison, the grove, the Village of Rabbits, and on and on until his memory met with the second book of secrets — at which point Vincent came up the path carrying a tray.

"Ahhh — here's our breakfast, then," remarked Dr. Kincaid. "I think you're going to enjoy this very much."

"Getting acquainted, are we?" asked Vincent as he set on the table two plates covered with pieces of cloth. Vincent turned to Dr. Kincaid.

"I see you haven't told him yet," he said.

"Told me what?" asked Edgar.

Dr. Kincaid glared at Vincent but spoke to him in the way old friends do when they share a secret.

"Don't you have some hunting to do? It's getting awfully late."

Vincent smiled knowingly at Dr. Kincaid and went into the cave. When he emerged there were two spears on his back.

"I'll be back before nightfall, as I'm not killing anything today. There was plenty of that last night."

When Vincent was gone, Dr. Kincaid rubbed his hands together with anticipation and theatrically unveiled both plates.

There were two items on the plate in front of Edgar. One was something black and meaty, but he knew it wasn't rabbit or mutton. The other was a chunky green pudding that looked a lot like something Edgar had seen blown out of noses when people had gotten sick after the third-year trees hadn't been cut down in time.

Dr. Kincaid picked up the meat on his own plate with his bare hand and dipped it into the green pudding. He raised it toward Edgar as one might ready to toast with a cup, and then he took a bite so big that Edgar was certain the old man would choke on it. By the time Dr. Kincaid had swallowed most of the food, Edgar still hadn't moved.

"Eat up, Edgar. I'm quite sure you'll enjoy it," he said through a mouthful of gooey food, which only served to increase Edgar's distaste for the meal before him.

But Edgar couldn't remember when he'd been so hungry, which was no small thing, since he'd been hungry almost every day of his life. Hesitantly he picked up the meat and started to put it in his mouth.

Dr. Kincaid made a disapproving sound and scowled, showing Edgar that he should first dip it in the green pudding.

"I call it Black and Green for a reason," he said. "The two go perfectly together and it would be a shame to eat them separately."

Edgar was about to ask what Black and Green was made of, but something told him that he might be better off not knowing. He followed Dr. Kincaid's lead, dipping the meat into the pudding, and found that Black and Green was indeed very tasty. It was salty and sweet at the same time, and it filled him up unlike anything he'd ever eaten.

Now that the boy was enjoying a plate of Black and Green,

Dr. Kincaid knew there was nothing else to do but begin telling Edgar about the world he lived in. It was difficult at first, because Dr. Kincaid could only use words and concepts that simply made no sense to Edgar at all: microscience, biomechanics, DNA, metal and machines. It was as though Dr. Kincaid spoke a different language, and Edgar leaned back in his chair, exasperated.

"This meat is very good," commented Edgar as he swallowed the last bite, not having understood a word Dr. Kincaid had said. "Where does it come from?"

"It comes from the Cleaners, those beasts that almost ate you last night."

Edgar laughed nervously, which so delighted Dr. Kincaid that he continued on the topic.

"The Cleaners are remarkable creatures, really. They are but one invention of the mind that created Atherton."

"Did you create Atherton?" asked Edgar. Luther smiled wryly.

"I'm afraid not. This world is far too complicated even for me to wholly understand." Dr. Kincaid was about to start explaining the origin of Atherton in scientific terms, but he was able to stop himself.

Must keep this simple so that he will understand. Must not scare the boy.

"Let me say it this way, Edgar. You weren't born on Atherton. You were born someplace else. Where that place is doesn't really matter because you can't ever go back there — and I can assure you, you wouldn't want to. While I may not be your father, I *am* your guardian, and I wouldn't agree to come to Atherton unless you were allowed to live here with me."

"I don't understand," said Edgar, which was something he felt he would be saying quite a bit when listening to Dr. Kincaid.

"Where you come from, there are almost no trees. Can you even imagine a place so unlike the grove? The air is filthy, nearly impossible to breathe. A person can live where you come from — lots of people do — but it's not the beautiful world it used to be. If you must know, it's called the Dark Planet, and it's closer than you think."

"But how did I get here? How did anyone get here? And why don't I remember my life before Atherton?"

Again Dr. Kincaid slipped into speaking in terms Edgar couldn't understand. He lectured about computers and machines and something called the third wave, until Edgar shook his head. Science, skyscrapers, televisions, cars, pollution — all of it was lost on the boy. It made the divide seem impassable to poor Dr. Kincaid.

"Try again," suggested Edgar. "And pretend you're a boy like me. Maybe that will help."

Dr. Kincaid pondered this approach a moment before he continued.

"There came a time on the Dark Planet when I and a group of other scientists — those are people who try to solve problems — had the idea of building a new place where people could live. We worked on it for a long time and found ourselves going in circles, not getting anywhere. But then we found someone who could help us."

He took a drink from his cup and dipped it back into the bowl.

"There was a boy, Edgar, a very smart little boy who was an orphan just like you. His name was Max." Edgar recognized that this was probably part of the story that Samuel had begun to read to him in the book of secret things.

Dr. Kincaid seemed to light up at the thought of this other boy, but Edgar felt a little sting of remorse. He realized then that he was an orphan of not just one, but two worlds.

"We all called him Max at first," continued Dr. Kincaid. "But very soon we were in the habit of calling him Dr. Harding."

"You mean as a joke? To make him feel a part of things?"

"No, I mean he was a lot better at fixing and making things than the rest of us were."

Dr. Kincaid was getting better at speaking in terms Edgar could understand.

"What did Max do that was so special?" asked Edgar.

"To be fair, by the time he was twenty none of us really understood all of what he was working on."

Dr. Kincaid wanted the boy to know how that could be possible, and he struck upon an idea that might make it clearer.

"There is a thing on the Dark Planet called an airplane. Do you know what that is, Edgar?"

Edgar thought for a moment that he might know, but then he drew a blank. He shook his head.

"An airplane is a man-made thing that can carry you around

in the air. But it's a complicated machine, very complicated, and many are far bigger than these rocks towering around us. It takes hundreds of people to put one together. Everyone works on a small part but nobody makes the whole thing. They each learn about the one part they are building, but they can't know how to build the entire airplane. It would be too much information for a single person to understand all at once."

Dr. Kincaid wasn't sure if he'd lost the boy, but he thought he was doing all right, and so he continued.

"Now, Edgar, imagine something a lot more complicated than an airplane, so complicated in fact that it would involve thousands of different kinds of smart people doing extraordinary things all at the same time. And now try to imagine one person who designed it all, who created it completely in his mind by the age of thirty. If you can imagine such a person, then you have come closer to knowing why we took to calling Max by the name of Dr. Harding."

"So Dr. Harding created Atherton, is that it?"

"In the simplest terms, yes. But there were . . . complications."

"What sort of complications?"

Dr. Kincaid thought for a moment before responding.

"Let's just say that Dr. Harding wasn't altogether normal. He was . . . troubled."

"What do you mean, 'troubled'?"

There was no sense hiding it now. The boy would have to know sooner or later.

"Dr. Harding was what we might call a 'mad scientist,' Edgar. He kept a great many things from us. Some we now know about, some we do not. I'm afraid the story gets a little darker from here. Do you want me to go on?"

Edgar could think of nothing he wanted more (there being no more Black and Green to be had), and so Dr. Kincaid began to unravel the mystery of Dr. Maximus Harding.

CHAPTER
24

TWO WORLDS COLLIDE

"Isabel."

"Yes."

"Are you ready?"

"Yes, Father, I'm ready."

Light streamed under the door of her small room as she touched the bag of figs at her side.

"As we said, remember?"

Isabel nodded. "Just one shot, then I run and climb into the tree."

Charles pulled her near, having second thoughts about allowing her out of the house at all.

The two stepped outside and found that no one else could be seen in the village. There was an eerie quiet that took Isabel's breath away. The children had all been sent to climb trees in the grove, and the familiar sound of their little voices could not be heard. Was that the sound she missed, she wondered? It was not. It was a silence more maddening than peaceful — the sound of a world gone dry.

There had never been a time when Isabel could not hear the waterfall, but today the sound had gone. Lord Phineus had stopped the water flow entirely. The exhilarating sound of water crashing across rock would very soon be a thing of the past in Tabletop. They would speak of it as if it were a dream and try to remember, but the sound would soon be forgotten.

Isabel raised her eyes to the Highlands and saw a wall of men astride horses along the edge. They were close enough that Isabel could see the expressions on the men's faces and hear strange sounds emanating from the creatures.

"Those aren't men," she croaked, terrified. "They're giant beasts with four legs and two arms!"

Charles hadn't thought to warn Isabel of the strange creatures he had seen for the first time earlier that day. He was in something of a state of shock himself.

"We've been watching them as they grow near," he said. "They're not attached. The men are riding those beasts. Like when you were little and we put you on a sheep and rode you around. Do you remember that?"

Isabel did not, but the idea that these men were in command of such huge animals made her wonder if trying to fight them were a good idea after all.

"Are we making a mistake, father?" asked Isabel. "Maybe we should listen to them first and do as they say. If we do, then

Tabletop might not change too much. . . . We could rebuild the houses, and you could run the grove."

Charles knelt down next to Isabel. "I'm afraid it's too late for that." There was sadness in his voice as he gazed back into the grove behind them. "I'll miss the simple life of the grove, the days of trimming and pruning." He looked back at Isabel and she saw fire in his eyes. "But I won't miss watching you go hungry and without water whenever the mood strikes them."

As if to make his point clearer, Isabel's stomach rumbled. She wasn't certain if it was from hunger or from nervousness.

"You're too young to have your innocence taken from you," he said. "That they would poison us, *all* of us — the children included — is unjust. The truth is the Highlands are filled with cruel people, and they have come to rule over us with force."

With that thought echoing eerily in her mind, Isabel stared at the men on horses expecting to see evil looks on their faces. She did not see any evidence of it. For a fleeting moment she wondered if maybe they were just as stunned by the fall of the Highlands as everyone in Tabletop had been. But trusting her father's words, she cast her own look of fire and anger across the line of men — and just as she did so, the ground began to shake.

There was a horrifying sound, like a vast row of grinding teeth, and the Highlands crashed toward Tabletop as though whatever had been holding it in place had been kicked out from beneath it.

The line of horses scattered in every direction. One of them, unaware of the peril at the edge, came so near as it turned that its back legs careened over the edge. Moments later the High-lands lurched to a stop ten feet from the bottom, and the horse and man were thrown off the edge with a dramatic crash into Tabletop. The two of them were injured but not dead. The horse remained on its side, whining pitifully as the man tried to free his leg from beneath the animal.

The horses that lined the Highlands returned to their positions. Isabel heard the men in the Highlands yelling, "Stay back! Stay back!" When she looked behind her, she saw the men and women of the grove rushing into position. It would take them a minute to arrive — and in that minute, a great many things were about to take place.

"Isabel! You must do it right now!" her father shouted.

Isabel's eyes darted back and forth among the men, and she now noticed a man in the middle of the line who was not like the others. He wore a dark robe that draped over the sides of his horse, dangling against black boots. The widow's peak of his hair pointed down at her, and he had a bold look of triumph on his face as if daring her to turn against him. It was Lord Phineus — the target she was seeking.

A fig caked with dust was already poised in her sling, and she began swinging it over her head with a fierce whirling sound that seemed to set the rest of the world to silence. The people from the grove — fanning out behind her — stopped and waited. As the men on horses in the Highlands became aware of this bold girl from the grove, a mixture of amazement, indignation, and curiosity hushed their shouting. It was a frozen moment that buzzed with anticipation.

I'm going to miss him. I know I'm going to miss him, thought Isabel as the sling spun faster and faster over her head.

Lord Phineus sat high on his horse, almost amused by the child's play. Shifting his gaze to the land beyond, he wished the Highlands would finish its descent so that he could ride through the villages, aiming his spear where he chose. He could almost imagine spurring his horse into a grand leap over the edge of the Highlands. She just might make it without breaking a leg, and then he could lead his forty men as a general should.

He chose to speak instead.

"If you can hear me, I order you to turn back! Do not dare to think that you can enter the Highlands. There will be bloodshed if you try!" He felt the power of his voice rippling over the village and into the grove.

It struck him then that the people weren't sick as he thought they ought to have been. He had thought only of victory as the Highlands crashed downward, but now he understood that his plan had somehow gone horribly wrong.

Then: *Snap!* Isabel had grown accustomed to the long sling, and she watched as the black fig shot through the air toward her target.

Lord Phineus had been unwise to dismiss the threat of a small girl. He saw the approaching object too late, a mere second before it was about to hit him. He ducked to the side and the black fig, which Isabel had aimed at his chest, hit him square in the meat of his shoulder.

The pain was sharp and instantaneous. Lord Phineus pitched forward on his horse and found that he was in a haze of orange dust. He waved his hands and felt his throat constricting, and then he began to cough as he had never coughed before.

Isabel had agreed to throw only one fig, to show those from the Highlands what she and the others were capable of, to show them they should not come into the grove. But in the tension of the confrontation, she couldn't help herself. She thought that if she could hit him just once more, their leader would be down and the will to fight would leave the rest of them. When Lord Phineus looked up, Isabel was already swinging the sling over her head again.

He heard the *snap!* once more.

In that instant, he pulled the reins of his horse, and the animal reared onto its hind legs. The fig slammed into the horse's neck, and a plume of dust shot into the air. Lord Phineus got his wish to fly off the cliff on his horse, for the startled animal bolted the moment its legs hit the ground, and over the edge the two of them went.

The horse landed surprisingly well but seemed in a mad rage when it hit the ground, charging at full speed toward the grove with Lord Phineus coughing and wheezing on its back. None of the other men followed suit. They seemed more inclined to wait a little longer until the fall wasn't quite so steep. Some were already contemplating a retreat at the sight of a hundred men and women from Tabletop in a line of their own, readying their slings.

The Highlands came alive again, and this time the grinding of the last ten feet was so deafening that everyone in Tabletop covered their ears and looked on in wonder. The horses bucked and ran in every direction until the Highlands were but a few inches from the bottom. It lurched to a violent stop, then seemed to crawl the last few inches with a soft, gurgling noise.

The Highlands were no more.

When Lord Phineus reached the first trees of the grove, he found that he could not sit up on the horse without smashing into a tree limb. He hung around the animal's neck as the animal darted between trees, racing in mad terror until its lungs were so infected with the orange dust it could run no more. The horse began to act as though it might topple over, and Lord Phineus briskly dismounted, buckling over and coughing so hard it dropped him to his knees. When he stood up again the horse was on its side, wheezing painfully.

Lord Phineus now realized he was approaching the clearing where Mr. Ratikan's house had been. He had drawn his sword and wanted to use it on someone, anyone on whom he could unleash his rage. He couldn't possibly run with his lungs so tight, and it would be a long walk back to find his men. He was badly in need of water, and for a moment wished he'd not restricted the supply to Tabletop.

"Mr. Ratikan?" It hurt his throat to say the man's name. "Where are you?"

There was no reply, but soon he thought he heard a man coughing. Turning to his left, he saw Mr. Ratikan tied to a tree.

"You didn't hear me when I called?" said Lord Phineus, his voice raspy and labored. He approached Mr. Ratikan with a fury.

"I had been sleeping . . . ," Mr. Ratikan said, and immediately wished he hadn't, but it was too late.

"You have failed me," said Lord Phineus. "*They* have the dust you gathered from the trees." He coughed ferociously, and a great orange ball of something very nasty flew out of his mouth and dripped from his chin to the ground. He wiped his face with his sleeve.

Lord Phineus listened to Mr. Ratikan berate the people who worked for him, promising he would soon bring things under control if only he were freed from the tree. But Lord Phineus responded by pointing his sword at Mr. Ratikan. The man begged for mercy, which only served to enflame Lord Phineus's cruelty.

I'm afraid we shall not be hearing anything more in this story from mean Mr. Ratikan.

Sir Emerik's skill at climbing the ranks of power did not carry over to the battlefield, and he found an instant distaste for the management of men at war. The people in the Village of Rabbits wasted no time in hurling hundreds of poisoned black figs at Sir Emerik and his men. By the time the Highlands crashed into Tabletop, Sir Emerik had grave doubts as to whether he could subdue the people of the village.

Half of his forty men were already coughing so hard they could barely stay atop their steeds, while the other half seemed completely unsure of what they should do. When Sir Emerik called the charge, he himself turned his horse and bolted for the safety of the House of Power. The rest of his men endured a violent shower of black figs until they felt no choice remained but to retreat.

There were two, however, who truly were men of violence, and these two rushed into the village between the flying figs with their swords drawn. But two men with swords and horses are no match for a hundred angry villagers. Briney and Maude had instructed everyone not to throw poisoned figs in the village, to protect it from the poison's effects. Instead, they were to use clubs fashioned from trees in the grove.

It was a second line of defense, and the moment the two riders met with it, they wished they'd never come so close. They were both overcome by the mob, struck over and over again until they were knocked free from their horses. Once the two men were down, the horses galloped away, leaving them on foot to face a throng of club-wielding men.

"That's enough!" said Briney as the men prepared to beat the two until they dropped their swords. He looked at the Highland men. "Leave your weapons and go."

The two stood back to back and seemed unwilling to comply.

"We won't harm you," said Briney. "But you must leave those to us." He pointed to the swords.

One of the men seemed ready to agree, but the other had always held that those in Tabletop were there to serve. Enraged, he lunged at Briney with his sword. The moment he did was his last, for clubs rained down on his head more quickly than he could have imagined. The second of the two men dropped his weapon and backed away, then ran all the way back to the House of Power.

Owing to a complete lack of guidance in the absence of Sir Philip, the forty men of the Highlands who presided over the Village of Sheep met with similar results. Having no true experience with warfare only added to their confusion when hundreds of hard black objects laced with poison were thrown in their direction. Still, they did not enjoy the luxury of a man such as Sir Emerik, whose cowardice would have pointed them home sooner than they went. All but three of them were hit at least once, and some as many as three times, by flying figs and orange dust. A tremendous roar of coughing and wheezing increased the clamor of battle as they rode on through a storm of figs, and a heavy engagement ensued.

It was this battle, along with the one in the grove that we shall speak of next, that set Atherton's course to violence. Men on both sides fell in the Village of Sheep that day, and when it was over, most of those from the House of Power had sustained injuries of one sort or another. It was the only battle of the three in which the Highland horses were captured and kept, for shepherds are very good with animals and see the beauty and gentleness of them no matter the size.

When Lord Phineus finally found his way back to his troops, it was quickly apparent the battle hadn't gone as he'd hoped. Many from his small army had already fallen by the club. He spotted ten men who remained on horses. All the rest had, it seemed, turned back or lay lifeless on the ground.

One horse and rider had wandered close to the grove, searching for their leader. Both the animal and the man on it seemed uninjured. Lord Phineus broke into a run, which was terribly painful on his heaving chest, and met the man halfway.

"There you are, Lord!" shouted the man. "I've been looking everywhere for you!"

"Get off that horse!" commanded Lord Phineus. The man hesitated to dismount the steed. If he were left on this side of the opposing forces, how would he make it back alive? He reached his hand down toward his master.

"We can both ride to safety. Take my hand," said the man.

Lord Phineus drew his sword and commanded the man on the horse once more, and then he heard a sound from the grove — *snap!* A split second later a black fig hit the man on the horse square in the forehead with a loud *pop!* The man's head jerked backward and then his whole body flopped forward onto the neck of the horse and he slid off the side to the ground.

Lord Phineus mounted the horse and kicked it brutally, listening for another *snap!* from the grove. He heard the sound as he rode off, but the black fig missed its target and whizzed high past his head. Lord Phineus looked over his shoulder and spotted Isabel running toward him.

That girl! She has been the cause of all my trouble today!

He turned his horse sharply, but the moment he did Lord Phineus saw that Isabel had loaded her sling once again and was swinging it over her head.

Lord Phineus knew that he'd been beaten, and the thought of it enraged him. And yet, there was still one way known just to him that would allow him to maintain his power. He needed only to get back to the House of Power.

With a renewed vigor he sped past his own men without a word, and those who were able fell in behind him amidst a triumphant roar from the people of the grove.

CHAPTER

25

THE DARK PLANET

Dr. Kincaid pushed his chair back from the table and stood up. He was old, but he was in surprisingly good condition. It was true his face was aged, but the rest of him seemed slow to catch up.

"Let's go inside out of the sun for a while, shall we?" He helped Edgar out of his chair, though Edgar was feeling a new strength. He had rested a full night, drank like he never had before, and had a belly full of nourishing food. For a boy of Edgar's background, this was more good fortune all at once than he had ever received.

When they entered the cave, it was difficult to see. Dr. Kincaid hurried into the darkness as someone who knew his way. There was a single wick lit in the corner, and Dr. Kincaid took it around and lit other wicks. When he was finished, he returned to each one and covered them with a tube of glass — a substance not known to Atherton, or at least not to Edgar. Light flooded the room with a brightness Edgar hadn't seen before.

"What are those things?"

Dr. Kincaid said something about the reflective properties of glass, and Edgar realized asking questions about strange objects in the room would send his companion on long explanations that were beyond Edgar's understanding. Like the waterfall near the grove, Dr. Kincaid's voice was a distant, oddly comforting rumble in the background as Edgar looked at the tables in front of him that were covered with all sorts of objects he'd never seen. Edgar couldn't guess what a single one of them did. He also observed with some unease that there were a great many books and journals lying everywhere.

". . . You were asking about the Cleaners earlier, weren't you?" asked Dr. Kincaid. The word *Cleaners* got Edgar's attention. "The trouble is there are too many things to explain. We must focus on the important items, and Cleaners are *very* important."

Dr. Kincaid motioned Edgar farther into the cave and asked him to sit down on the bed to rest.

"Cleaners do seem awful, don't they?" asked Dr. Kincaid.

"They do," answered Edgar, surprised that anyone could think differently.

"I agree we could have prettied them up a bit and made them less dangerous, but they do such a marvelous job of cleaning everything up. That was why we made them — to keep Atherton clean. Everything runs down, Edgar, and when it does, it ends up in the Flatlands. Those creatures will eat just about anything they find in their path. And they leave almost nothing behind, only an odorless trail of bright green excrement wherever they go. Perfectly harmless. Without Cleaners, I'm afraid Atherton wouldn't be much better than the Dark Planet."

"Then why not let them loose there, instead of making this place? Why not let them clean the Dark Planet?"

"Excellent question! Excellent! Unfortunately, as I've already said, they eat everything. On Atherton this is a tolerable situation, so long as they remain contained in the Flatlands. But on the Dark Planet I'm afraid a lot of important things would get eaten, like children."

Edgar made a sour face. "Then why haven't you and Vincent been eaten?"

"Because the Cleaners stay near the cliffs, where most of the food comes down, and this cave is well away from there. Our home is high off the ground, which protects it. They don't climb very well with all those bony legs."

"And it's only you and Vincent down here, no one else?"

"That's right, just the two of us. Vincent was sent here to protect me; I was sent here for other reasons."

Edgar was glad to be leaving the topic of Cleaners for the moment.

"I know this is all very hard for you to understand," said Dr. Kincaid. "So I'm going to make it as simple as I can for you. Just listen carefully, all right?"

Edgar nodded, wanting to know as much as he could but realizing there would probably be much that he couldn't fully grasp.

"When Atherton was in its early stage of development — when it had grown to about the size of a house — we could begin to see that levels were forming, and we asked Dr. Harding about this strange occurrence. He said the center would hold water and that the levels would grow apart from one another. The bottom had to be very heavy to get it away from the Dark Planet, in order for it to sit in space the way it would need to once it was launched. It grew its own air supply and began orbiting around the Dark Planet. I have a drawing here that will help you understand," said Dr. Kincaid. He crossed the room, and he returned with a notebook. Fanning through it, he came to a page and turned it toward Edgar.

"But if it's so close, why have I never seen the Dark Planet?" asked Edgar, seeing how big it was in the drawing and wondering how it would be possible for it to hide from view.

"Because you are always facing away from it, of course. Gravity from the Dark Planet stops Atherton from flying out into space, but it also holds Atherton in one *position*. In other words, the bottom of Atherton is always facing the Dark Planet. If you leaned over the edge of Atherton here in the Flatlands, you would see the Dark Planet for yourself."

Edgar wanted to go there right away. "Will you take me? So I can see the place that I've come from?"

Dr. Kincaid hesitated, thinking now that he'd revealed too much too fast and the boy might wander off on his own and fall off the edge of the world.

"Let's wait until Vincent returns and ask if he'll accompany us. It would be safer."

THE ORBIT OF ATHERTON

ENLARGED VIEW

* ATHERTON ALWAYS FACES AWAY FROM DARK PLANET.

ATHERTON

23,000 Miles

ATHERTON

29,000 Miles

(DP)

(DARK PLANET)

* ATHERTON ROTATES AT SAME RATE AS (DP)

O. HARDING
2.5.20

This satisfied Edgar for the moment, and he asked something else that had been on his mind.

"Dr. Kincaid, where did all the people come from? Why don't they ever talk about the Dark Planet?"

"Another excellent question!" said Dr. Kincaid. "You can't imagine the clamor of people who wanted to go to Atherton. *Everyone* wanted to go. It was new, light, and clean. There would be trees and grass. You have to remember, the Dark Planet is just that. *Dark.* It's dirty. It's hard to breathe if you're not inside, where the machines make the air clean.

"But there was one thing that made it a little undesirable to come to Atherton. To be perfectly honest, it was actually a rather *big* problem for a lot of people."

"What was it?"

"Well, the thing of it was, if you wanted to come here, you had to go through a period of . . . shall we say, *readiness* training."

"What's readiness training? What does it do?"

"It makes you someone who's from Atherton, not from the Dark Planet. You remember certain things — some new, some old — but you feel as though Atherton were the only place you've ever known. You're still *you,* mostly. It's just that a lot of people felt that if you couldn't remember experiences and people from your previous life — such as your loved ones, your happiest days or your most painful learning experiences — you wouldn't *really* be you anymore. It was for this reason that we chose mostly people who had something of a loose connection with the Dark Planet to begin with. People with no children, very little ties to the community, people who *wanted* to forget their past, that sort of thing — and so it's very possible we may have let a few individuals with some character defects slip through our screening. After all, Dr. Harding developed and demanded readiness training, and it was he who decided who would inhabit Atherton. Who can say what a madman's motives are from one day to the next?"

Dr. Kincaid added that he himself had not been through readiness training and hoped he never would. He was on Atherton because he helped create it and had been sent to watch over it.

"While Dr. Harding shared much of what he was doing with everyone — all of the good things — he did not share the wrong things that he was also doing."

"What sorts of 'wrong things' do you mean?" Edgar asked, though he didn't know for sure if he wanted to know the whole truth.

"Atherton is moving, Edgar, because it's not finished yet. Dr. Harding made us believe it was ready, but it was not. He used us as an experiment. On the Dark Planet we might have said he used us as 'guinea pigs.' This is a dangerous place, Edgar, not suitable for people. At least not yet."

Dr. Kincaid sat down on the stool in front of the bed, wondering again if he were telling the boy too much.

"Dr. Kincaid, how old is Atherton?"

"Thirty-two years last month, but there have only been people here for about twelve of those. It wasn't inhabitable for the first twenty years, and then there were other complications. I visited here many times — there was a way you could get here that, trust me, you wouldn't understand — and then I came here with you seven years ago, and I have never gone back."

It was impossible to believe. The world that Edgar had assumed was ancient — the only world that existed anywhere — was not much older than he was. By now the questions were multiplying faster than Edgar could keep track of.

"Why have you never gone back, like you'd done before?"

For once, Dr. Harding seemed not to know how to answer. There was so much the boy couldn't comprehend, and he'd only scratched the surface of all that was involved. He chose to answer the question honestly, though he knew it would only bring more questions he wasn't sure he could answer.

"I can't go back," said Dr. Kincaid, his voice full with a sense of loss only he could understand. "The connection between Atherton and the Dark Planet has been broken, and to my knowledge there is no way to bring the two back together again."

Without warning there came a thunderous sound like a great wave on an ocean, a sound Dr. Kincaid knew and could remember from his days on the Dark Planet. Edgar, of course, could not place it in his memory of an oceanless Atherton. It grew in volume, and the glass covers on the lights began to shake until one of them toppled to the floor and shattered.

"Come! The Highlands must have finished their descent into Tabletop. Now you shall see what the last page of the book I left for you said!"

The two of them ran for the entrance to the cave, and the light of day burned Edgar's eyes. It took him a moment to see clearly.

"You see there! The last page of the book that I left for you foretold of this!" screamed Dr. Kincaid, falling to his knees, for the roar of grinding stone was much louder outside the cave than it had been inside. Edgar fixed his eyes to where Dr. Kincaid was pointing.

Tabletop was crashing down into the Flatlands.

They watched and listened as the fall continued for half a minute. Then the sound vanished in the air and everything was still again.

But the quiet could not calm Edgar, who was overcome with a surge of worry for Isabel and Samuel. He could not have imagined the battles that had broken out far above, the role Isabel had played, or the unexpected victory for those in the villages. The only thing Edgar knew for sure was that the world had changed.

And it was changing again.

Two Cleaners were clicking their legs quietly at the base of the cliffs. They had managed to avoid Vincent as they moved all the way across the Flatlands, at last arriving at the cliff leading up to Tabletop. The creatures grated their teeth against the rock, looking for something to eat, when they suddenly reared back on their legs in confusion. They approached the cliff once more and sniffed at the dirt with hideous, wet noses. Then they watched as the rock began to move slowly.

The movement had startled the beasts at first, but now the Cleaners were curious and clapped their teeth together with a powerful clanging noise. The Cleaners were amused. They seemed to understand the cliffs were descending, and the creatures were excited to think that fresh food might be on its way down.

I see by your eagerness, and the wonder and hope which your eyes express, my friend, that you expect to be informed of the secret with which I am acquainted. That cannot be.

Dr. Frankenstein
Frankenstein, 1818
Mary Shelley

PART
THREE

"You do realize we'll never get it back."

A maddening silence fell over the room in which only breathing was heard.

"Dr. Kincaid is a good man," came a new voice. *"But he's not a magician. He can't wave his wand and make it come back."*

"And what of Dr. Harding?"

There was a sterile clang of a glass being set on a metal table.

"He's gone, and with him all our hopes of a new world."

The sound of a man coughing filled the room, followed by a pause in which the two men looked at one another for long moment. It was the older of the two who broke the silence between them.

"Do you think God has forgotten us?"

It was a dreadful thought filled with hopelessness.

"Is there nothing else we could try? The fate of the Dark Planet hangs in the balance. One would think we could do better."

The two men were startled by the distant sound of breaking bones. They turned to a wall of thick glass facing the bleakness of their home on the Dark Planet. On the other side of the glass were a dozen Cleaners, trying with all their might to break into the room.

CHAPTER

26

A STRANGER IN THE GROVE

While Isabel watched Lord Phineus and his men race back into the Highlands, her eye caught a tiny movement away from the village. Someone was heading for the grove, fast and low to the ground. Isabel stayed along the line of trees and made her way toward the moving person until he was within striking distance. She loaded her sling and waited, wondering if it were a spy or the beginning of a second assault.

And then she realized it wasn't a man but a boy, dashing through the open space, trying to reach the grove without anyone seeing him. When he came near enough, Isabel called out a warning.

"Go back where you came from! We don't want you here!"

It was Samuel she had spotted. Startled by the voice, he tripped and fell forward in the dirt, a plume of dust rising around him. He struggled up onto his elbows and peered into the grove but saw no one. Whoever it was who'd detected him, he knew from the voice that it was not an adult — and it was a girl.

"I'm not going to hurt you!" yelled Samuel, assuming his appearance might have scared a small child younger than he. "Just let me into the grove, please!"

Isabel didn't know what to make of this boy trying to escape the Highlands. He could be an intruder sent to let loose more poison that she and Edgar may not have found. Maybe adults in the Highlands had sent this boy on a wicked errand. Isabel's own people had been willing to use her in their efforts to thwart an oncoming enemy. Why wouldn't grown-ups from the High-lands do the same?

"Don't come any closer or I'll have your head!" said Isabel, coming into the open area and swinging the sling over her head. Samuel saw that it was indeed a small child with dark black brows set coldly against him as he slowly rose to his feet. The moment he did, Isabel released a flying black fig, and it struck Samuel in the shin. A stabbing pain shot all the way down to his foot, and Samuel collapsed to the ground again. When he looked up, Isabel had reloaded her sling and was swinging it above her once more.

"That was a warning," she said. "Get up again and I'll aim a poisoned one for your head."

This was not the timid little girl he'd expected, but Samuel felt he'd be more likely get help from her than any adult he might encounter. He began pleading with her to help him.

"Do you know a boy named Edgar?" yelled Samuel. He saw

a glimmer of acknowledgment on Isabel's face. "I know him! He came to see me in the Highlands. I'm only trying to find him!"

"What do you mean you *know* him? How could you possibly know Edgar?"

"I tell you, he came to see me — twice, actually — and I only want to talk to him."

Isabel slowed the sling and let it come to a stop at her side. Could this be the boy Edgar had told her about, the one who read the book to him? She couldn't believe he would make the dangerous journey to the grove in search of Edgar, and she still felt unsure about Samuel as she stared him down.

"Tell me what he looks like," demanded Isabel. "If you get it wrong I'll put this black fig through your eye."

Samuel stammered a moment, trying to collect his thoughts.

"Quickly!" yelled Isabel. In the distance she had seen people coming toward her.

"He's got black hair, like yours. Small nose, big hazel-colored eyes. He had on a shirt with a big pocket on the front and old pants. He was sort of dirty, sort of like you, like he hadn't been cleaned up in a while. And —"

"All right, all right," said Isabel. "That's enough." She was insulted by the boy's calling her dirty, but she had to concede that he did know what Edgar looked like and must be the one he had chosen to trust. She motioned for Samuel to come into the grove.

The adults approaching her hadn't come close enough yet to see Samuel's belt, white shirt, and grey pants, which labeled him as a child of the Highlands. Isabel managed to help him climb up a tree for hiding as quickly as she could.

"You must be very quiet," she said. "Don't move until I tell you to, understand?" Samuel's nod was barely visible through the thick screen of green leaves. Isabel darted down the row of trees and then into the open, where her parents and some others from the village greeted her.

"Isabel! We've done it!" her father said. "We've pushed them back!"

There was a quick reunion and some celebrating, though brief, before Charles asked her to whom she had been speaking.

"It was no one — just a boy from the grove. He's gone to find his parents."

This seemed to satisfy her father's curiosity, and the group of them moved toward the village.

"I must go to the other villages and see how they fared," said her father. He gazed into the center of Atherton, fascinated by the first quiet glimpse of its otherworldly beauty. "Though it is very tempting to venture into the Highlands."

"That can wait," said Isabel's mother. She was a practical woman and didn't see any reason to get closer to the enemy just yet. As far as she was concerned, they needed to prepare for the evening. It was possible that Lord Phineus would make a night ambush with his men, his horses, and his swords.

"You should send some men into the grove," said Isabel. "Mr. Ratikan is still tied to the tree, but I'm afraid Lord Phineus was not pleased with him."

"Do you mean —" started her mother, but she didn't need to finish. Isabel nodded with an expression that told her Mr. Ratikan would not be alive when they found him.

"We best get things taken care of before more of the children see," said her father. "I'll get some men to handle it. Then I'm heading off to the Village of Rabbits to meet with Briney and Maude."

Isabel had never seen her father so animated. He had come alive in a way she'd never known before. It sounded to her as though he were leaving on a grand adventure.

When her father had gone, Isabel's mother draped her arm around Isabel as they walked, not wanting her to wander even a few steps away. When they arrived in the village, Isabel was surprised to find that there were people from the grove who had paid with their lives in the fight. She hadn't gotten that impression from her father. By the time she got back to her broken-down house, she was shocked to see many Highlanders and people of the grove who had been lost in the day's fighting.

"Where will they go?" asked Isabel. The question came from an empty space somewhere deep inside.

"What do you mean?" asked her mother.

"I mean, now that there's no life in them. Where will they go?"

Her mother thought she had an answer and started to say something, but it was like a faded whisper in her memory, and she had no reply. She shrugged as if to say she didn't know, and the two sat on a wooden bench made of limbs in front of their little house with their arms around one another.

While they were seated on the bench, they began to feel a trembling that quickly turned to something more. The feeling took their breath away, as if the ground were being pulled out from under them. A bottomless yawning noise came from somewhere far, far away, and they clung to each other even tighter.

Now that the Highlands had fallen, Isabel had thought the quakes would have come to an end. She looked at her mother inquisitively for an explanation, but again, her mother had none. The two tried to put the feeling out of their minds and focus on the work at hand.

"Mother," said Isabel. "I want to be of some use. Let me go and help with the children and collect more black figs. We might need them come night."

Her mother looked toward the Highlands and saw the tall trees and the golden grass. She was reflective as she held her daughter.

"It would be nice to go inside there, don't you think?" she asked.

"I don't know," answered Isabel. "Maybe. But I would never want to leave the grove. This is our home."

Isabel's mother looked at her and knew her daughter had grown older than her years in the past few days. She would have to let her go, her little queen of the grove.

"It's a shame things had to go this way," said Isabel's mother. "We say we want only to be treated with fairness, but to look at the Highlands brings some new feelings, don't you think?"

Isabel thought she knew what her mother meant, but she wasn't sure.

"We want it for ourselves. Before it came so near we never thought of such things. But now we must have it. I can see it in your father's eyes," said Isabel's mother.

Isabel was confused and didn't know how to respond. She knew that beyond the trees and the golden grass there were awful men with horses and swords. But there must also be plentiful water, shelter, and comforts she'd never dreamed of — and who knew what kinds of adventures.

Isabel's mother let go of her daughter's arm and put her hands in her lap, looking pensively out at the trees.

"Be careful, Isabel. Stay near the village and the grove. And come see me in an hour so I know you're safe."

Isabel didn't want her mother to change her mind and she was up in a flash, sneaking back to where she had left Samuel in the tree.

A distant sound had echoed through the grove, and Samuel became aware that the tree in which he was hidden had begun to feel as though it were sinking into the ground. When it stopped, he wished that the girl would return quickly to keep him company, but after a time he couldn't stand it any longer. He made up his mind to leave the safety of his perch and go in search of Edgar. When Samuel dropped down out of the tree, he found that Isabel was standing right in front of him.

"I told you to stay in the tree until I returned," she said. Isabel felt sure that if she called them, the children of the grove would stream out of the trees like little fairies and do her bidding.

"You were gone a long time," said Samuel defensively, but

Isabel had a disabling effect on Samuel. His mouth became dry, and when he tried to continue, his voice was shaky. "I was only going to look around and then come right back."

Isabel was beginning to warm up to Samuel, and she didn't see the point in scolding him further. Samuel cleared his throat, thinking of how he might change the subject.

"Did you feel that — when the ground went out from underneath us — did you feel it?" he asked.

Isabel nodded, and Samuel could see that she was beginning to trust him, if only a little.

"What do you think it was?" he asked, wondering if she knew as much as he did.

"I don't know."

Samuel realized the two of them didn't even know each other's names. "Do you have a name? Mine is Samuel."

"Isabel," answered Isabel.

"Do you know where I can find Edgar? It's important that I see him."

"He left the grove and hasn't returned." Isabel wasn't ready to tell Samuel what she'd overheard Briney say.

"Where has he gone to?" said Samuel, concern rising in his voice.

"I don't know for sure," said Isabel, still uncertain about Samuel's intent.

"Are you sure you don't know where he went? I really must find him."

Isabel couldn't hold Samuel's gaze, and he could tell that she was hiding something.

"He could be in real danger," said Samuel. "It would be best if I could speak to him."

"I don't think you'll find him in Tabletop." Isabel's resolve was beginning to crumble.

"What do you mean? He hasn't gone back into the Highlands looking for me, has he? That would be terrible news."

Isabel shook her head, which further confused Samuel.

"Where, then? Where did Edgar go?"

Isabel pointed to the ground. "Down there."

Samuel was mystified by her answer at first, looking at the ground and scratching his head. Then he caught on.

"You can't mean . . ."

"He's climbed down to the Flatlands," said Isabel. "Or at least he's tried to."

"It's unbelievable! Why would he do such a thing?"

The two of them thought about it, and both smiled hesitantly at the grandeur of what their friend Edgar had attempted to do.

"I wish I could have gone with him," said Samuel.

"Only Edgar could have climbed down there. How did you suppose you would go with him? Did you think he might carry you down?" said Isabel, unexpectedly feeling some competition for Edgar's affections. Samuel only smiled.

"I don't know why he did it, but I'd give anything to have found him before he left. I wonder if he knows what the last page of the book of secret things said."

Now Samuel had let slip his own secret, and Isabel was quick to demand an explanation. "What last page are you talking about?"

He looked at Isabel and thought he'd better tell her what he knew. The information was too important to keep to himself any longer.

"The page had some information that I think only very few people are aware of," said Samuel. "Maybe Edgar went below searching for someone who could read it to him. I hope not."

"What did the page you gave to Edgar say?"

The time had come for Samuel to share what he'd read. He had a hard time getting started. All along he'd imagined this would be a conversation he would have with Edgar, not a girl from the grove he hardly knew.

"Tabletop is sinking into the Flatlands," said Samuel. "That feeling of falling, that must have been the beginning. The page revealed that the descent of Atherton would continue even after the Highlands and Tabletop came even."

Isabel was dumbstruck, and for a long moment she could not respond. She reflected on the moment she'd sat with her mother and felt suddenly light as a feather. Then she thought of something else that scared her.

"What — what's down there? I mean, besides Edgar."

Samuel had come to something he had to share but didn't want to.

"I don't know for sure," he said. "But even if Edgar made it all the way down, he's still in a lot of danger."

Isabel asked the question again, with more force this time.

"What's *down* there?"

Samuel knew they had to let the others in Tabletop know what was to come.

"Some sort of . . . animals," said Samuel. ". . . Or beasts. They will want to do us harm."

Isabel took choppy breaths and imagined Edgar all alone in such a dangerous place. On the very heels of that thought was the realization that Tabletop would likely one day fall even with the Flatlands. Would the creatures find their way into the grove?

"I wish he hadn't gone down by himself," said Isabel.

Isabel and Samuel looked at one another as though they'd both lost their best friend.

"I must tell the others what you've told me," said Isabel. No sooner had she said the words then she was off to find her father in the village, leaving Samuel alone to contemplate the peril into which Edgar had descended.

CHAPTER
27
THE HOUSE OF POWER

When Sir Emerik returned to the House of Power, he was feeling some concern that he would be seen as a coward. Lord Phineus was nowhere to be found, and the gate was guarded by just two men. Sir Emerik awkwardly dismounted from his horse as he watched the rest of the men in his party ride their own horses past the House of Power to a stable. There was no one to take the reins from him, and he wasn't sure what to do with the beast, so he let it go and watched as it trotted away toward the other horses.

"Sir Emerik!" came a shout from behind him as he walked through the gate and into the House of Power. "Lord Phineus approaches!"

It was the guardsman, and he was pointing past the main

entry to the green fields in the distance. A rider clothed in black raced toward them, and Sir Emerik felt the cold stare bearing down on him from far away. He had a fleeting thought of closing the gate and leaving his master outside.

Instead, Sir Emerik took no action. He waited, standing at the gate, and in due time Lord Phineus arrived.

"Have you any word from Sir Philip?" asked Lord Phineus. He wasn't as sick as he had been. Riding through the fresh air had begun to clear his lungs.

"There is no word, Lord," answered Sir Emerik. "We are the first to arrive."

Lord Phineus dismounted his steed and towered over the shorter man before him. His gaze grew cold as he examined the scabbed head of Sir Emerik.

"And did you succeed in your efforts at the village?"

Sir Emerik chose his words carefully, for he knew the look on the face before him was that of a man about to turn violent.

"We did not, I'm sorry to say. They were armed with a method of defense we knew nothing of. It would seem they are not only willing but also *able* to rise up with force against us. We fought hard, but were turned back — although not before I discovered the thing we've been looking for."

This explanation seemed to pacify Lord Phineus, and his interest was piqued. But first, he turned to berate all of the men before him who didn't look as though they'd put up much of a fight.

"You have all failed me!" screamed Lord Phineus. He coughed

again and tried to clear his aching throat, craving the bucket of water in his room that awaited him. "But you shall not fail me again! All of my men — inside the gate!"

All fifty of the remaining men started for the gate, and Lord Phineus waved them off. "If you are part of Sir Emerik's party you will stay outside and keep watch. I shall not have a band of cowards eating my food and drinking my water!"

The men who had ridden with Sir Emerik backed off and glanced uneasily at one another. They were thirsty and tired and Lord Phineus had shut off the water to the Highlands. When would he let them in?

Lord Phineus cleared his throat and spat on the ground, then turned away from the rest of the men and motioned Sir Emerik to come closer.

"You found the page, then," whispered Lord Phineus.

"I did! There was a man from the inn — I recognized him from my visit before. I pinned him to the ground in the middle of a heated exchange of flying figs and slashing swords. He offered it in exchange of his life, and I felt it was a good trade."

"And the boy? What of him?"

"The man at the inn didn't know for sure. He only offered that the boy had probably gone back to the grove. But it doesn't matter now — I *have* everything we need!"

"Give it to me," said Lord Phineus. He held out his hand and waited for Sir Emerik to hand him the page from the book. Sir Emerik hadn't thought of this dilemma and had to come up with a very fast lie in order to cover the lies he'd already been telling.

"Well, sir, it's not — not quite that simple," stammered Sir Emerik. "You see I *read* the page, but I did not keep it. Trust me, Lord; it was far too sensitive to carry around. What if I'd been killed on the field and someone had taken it?"

Lord Phineus decided to let the story pass until they could find more private quarters to discuss the matter. All of his men had gone through the gate and awaited instruction on the other side. Lord Phineus first addressed Sir Emerik's men.

"Remember that those people in the grove tried to poison us!" He was quite sure only Mr. Ratikan was aware of his plan to poison *them* and wanted to keep it that way. "Next time you will show them no mercy."

He strode past Sir Emerik with the black robe dragging behind him. Four men pushed against the enormous wooden doors, which began to close with a groaning sluggishness. Lord Phineus yelled a parting word of instruction to Sir Emerik. "Stay with your men until Sir Philip arrives, then the both of you come see me. We have important matters to discuss."

Lord Phineus felt the full weight of his situation when he heard the gates close behind him. He had hoped for better news from Sir Emerik, and could only assume things had gone the same for Sir Philip.

As for Sir Emerik, he was busy with thoughts of his own as his men spread out in front of the gate and talked among themselves. He wondered how long he should keep secret what he had read on the last page of the book. It was a juicy bit of information and he relished the fact that only he was aware of it. *The boy Edgar certainly perished trying to fulfill a fool's errand — Ha!*

He dabbed his fingers on his scabbed head gingerly, and another thought crossed his mind. Samuel had said he'd never read the book, but Sir Emerik wasn't so sure. Samuel might know the same information Sir Emerik did. *He must be done away with before Lord Phineus questions him once more.*

The field of green parted in the distance, and the bouncing heads of riders came closer. What few remained of Sir Philip's men approached.

"Ah, it's Sir Philip!" cried one of the men guarding the gate. "It will be good to have him back."

"Indeed," said Sir Emerik, his eyes narrowing as he peered out over the Highlands. "I do hope no harm has come to him."

Lord Phineus sat alone in the main chamber, looking out the window toward the gate. He was disturbed not to find his snaggle-toothed general among the few returning men. Frowning, Lord Phineus took a long sip of water, then he crossed the room to Mead's head. He put his hand on the stone hair and talked to the statue as if it were alive.

"Where did you come from, Mr. Mead?" he said, the tenor of a madman entering his voice. "Here you sit, day after day, keeping watch over nothing at all. What will become of you?"

Mead's head had been in the House of Power for as long as Lord Phineus could remember. He knew its name only because it was carved into the side of the stone neck.

While Lord Phineus was having his conversation with Mead's

head, Sir Emerik raced through the courtyard and up the stairs
past Horace without a word, casting a pale shadow on the wall.
He wasted no time charging up the narrow steps to the room
where he expected to find Samuel. Before entering, he drew a
sharp wooden stake from his boot, intent on killing the boy and
putting the blame on Sir Philip.

He opened the door ever so slowly, catching the scent of
dusty air. Looking around the room, he was aghast to find the
boy had gone missing.

Wherever Samuel had gone, his mother was sure to know,
and it was she whom Sir Emerik decided to visit next. He made
his way down the narrow stairs and found Lord Phineus standing at the bottom.

"Horace tells me Samuel tricked him and has escaped," said
Lord Phineus. "Apparently the boy made a lot of noise, and
when Horace came to investigate, Samuel acted as if he'd been
locked inside by accident." Lord Phineus became reflective. "We
must be more forthcoming with our guards in the future. Horace had no idea we had use of the boy."

Sir Emerik agreed and made a move to continue on his way,
but Lord Phineus blocked the stairs so that Sir Emerik could
not pass. "Hoping to get some information from Samuel?" he
said abruptly, with an accusing look.

"Not at all," said Sir Emerik, unruffled by the allegation. "I
was only looking in on him."

Lord Phineus moved out of the stairwell and started for the

main chamber. "Even his mother has no idea where he's gone off to. There is talk from a few of the men that he may have slipped into Tabletop."

This pleased Sir Emerik immensely, and his worry over what Samuel might know subsided as he changed the subject to more pressing matters.

"My men still guard the gate for you, sir," said Sir Emerik. "But I'm afraid Sir Philip never even appeared at the Village of Sheep to lead his men. It would seem that he has deserted us, Lord."

What a delight it was for Sir Emerik to see the look of disbelief on his master's face. He saw his chance to redeem himself and used it well.

"I did not want to mention it before, in front of all the men," began Sir Emerik, "but Sir Philip seemed unsure of himself when I saw him last, before he left for his post. I wonder if he might have lost courage in the end."

They arrived at the main chamber, and Lord Phineus crossed the room and sat at the table. It had not been a good day for him, and the loss of Sir Philip, a trusted ally, seemed to drive him into an even darker mood. Even Sir Emerik became concerned when his master did not express aloud his wrath at the news of Sir Philip's alleged desertion.

"You must tell me now, Sir Emerik," Lord Phineus said. "Tell me everything you read on the last page of the book."

Sir Emerik felt a peculiar sensation rise in his chest. The tangled green web of vines on the ivy-covered wall behind his master seemed to envelop the black figure before him, and never before had Lord Phineus seemed so evil in his intent. It was as though the very vines in the room had wrapped themselves around Sir Emerik's beating heart and turned it so cold it would never again find warmth in the world.

He looked his master in the eye. "Atherton is not through changing. The Highlands have fallen, as the book said it would. But there is more change to come."

Sir Emerik let the words hang in the room.

"What changes?" said Lord Phineus, losing his patience. "Tell me!"

"Tabletop will collapse into the Flatlands. It's only a matter of time."

Lord Phineus was still for a moment, thinking it through. "Did it indicate when this would happen?"

"I believe it's already begun, but I can't be certain. Did you get a strange feeling earlier in the day, as though the ground had come out from under your feet?"

Lord Phineus had sensed it, too. It was as though he were floating on air and his stomach had caught in his throat. But he had thought that the poison from the orange dust had dizzied him.

"There's more," said Sir Emerik, a dark cloud of malice growing in his heart. "There are creatures of a sort in the Flatlands — dangerous creatures, and many of them. And they eat — everything."

"*Everything*?" repeated Lord Phineus, astounded.

Sir Emerik nodded.

"But they have one flaw, which plays to our advantage."

"What is this flaw?" asked Lord Phineus.

"They cannot climb cliffs," said Emerik. *"Nor walls."*

Lord Phineus pondered this ghastly new revelation. It was chilling to think of beasts invading the Highlands and devouring everything in their path. There was a part of him that felt a sudden desire to save all of Atherton from an unknown enemy. But there was a greater treachery in his heart that saw the benefit of the world being cleansed of his enemies. In the House of Power, he had water and gardens, and a great deal of food hoarded away. He could make the creatures die of thirst. *There's no reason why everyone should perish — at least, certainly not me.*

"If you have made up this story, it will be the end of you," said Lord Phineus. His eyes, rimmed in red, searched Sir Emerik's face for the truth. "Of that you can be sure."

"I swear it, Lord," said Sir Emerik. "And it will be quick this time, according to what I read."

"What do you mean?"

"Tabletop crashing into the Flatlands. It will be quick. The page said it would be faster than when the Highlands descended."

The two men regarded one another in the silence of the gloomy room. This was a catastrophic piece of information Lord Phineus was desperate to keep to himself as long as he could. It crossed his mind to put a sword through Sir Emerik then and there, to contain the secret so that it could not escape. But in the end he calmed his mind and realized the importance of a man such as Sir Emerik. He was deceitful to the core, but

Lord Phineus had few remaining allies, and he needed Sir Emerik to do his bidding for a while longer.

"How many of the men in the House of Power have wives and children in the Highlands?" asked Lord Phineus.

Sir Emerik hadn't the slightest idea. It wasn't the sort of information that interested him.

"I couldn't be sure," he said. "Why do you want to know?"

"Find out the answer as quickly as you can. Those who are here in the House of Power who have families should be sent home. Tell them I offer leave for a day and then get rid of them. If they have wives and children, their loyalties are compromised, and I must take only the men with complete allegiance to me."

"I don't understand," said Sir Emerik. "What do you mean to do?"

"It is time we made our stand alone, inside these walls," continued Lord Phineus. "The Highlands and Tabletop are one, and they shall all bow to me in the end. Or they shall have no water to speak of."

Sir Emerik let an ugly smile come over his face as he understood his master's intent. The source of water was *inside* the House of Power, hidden where only Lord Phineus knew. When the gate was closed, they could have all the water they wanted. It would give them power to ask for anything they wanted and needed. No longer would they be friends with the world outside. There was only Tabletop now — the Highlands were no more — and those in Tabletop did as the House of Power commanded.

There was one other essential detail that pleased Sir Emerik the most. He had his sights set on ruling Atherton alone, and he began to plot in his mind how he might discover the source of water and do away with Lord Phineus when the time was right.

28

THE FORCE OF GRAVITY

Edgar was already hoping to put his skills to the test, to see if he could climb with a sore shoulder and missing finger, but getting down from the cave perch was not a great challenge. Instead he found a disappointing path at a gentle grade that wound through the towering oval rocks. Along the way, Edgar was pleased to come across a thick pile of stones blocking the pathway. There was no way around them, only over them, and the wall was at least three times taller than Edgar.

"It keeps the Cleaners out," said Dr. Kincaid. "I've done this many times, and there is an easy way if you know it. I must find Vincent!"

"Can I come with you?"

"I'm sorry, Edgar. But with that shoulder and missing finger, you can't make it over, and I can't carry you as Vincent can. He's much stronger than the two of us."

Edgar scowled. There was a wall before him — a small one, but a wall nonetheless — and being told not to climb it was unbearable.

"Wait here and I'll find our companion," said Dr. Kincaid. "I don't think he'll be far away."

The old man took hold of the wall of rocks and began climbing up the side. It was slow going, and Edgar could see that he was taking the safe path, though not the fastest. When Dr. Kincaid reached the top, he grunted and kicked his way over the edge, then stood and looked down at Edgar.

"That's not the fastest way," said Edgar.

"What do you mean it's not the fastest way? Of course it is."

"No, it's not," said Edgar.

"I've done it a thousand times and I tell you it *is* the fastest way."

Edgar removed the sling from his arm, took hold of the stone wall before him, and climbed to the top in just a few seconds, using a different path. Dr. Kincaid was speechless. The boy had not only done it faster, he'd also done it beautifully, with only nine fingers and a swollen shoulder.

"One day I'll teach you to climb properly," said Edgar, completely unfazed by the effort. The sleep, the plate of Black and Green, and all the water he'd enjoyed had given him energy he'd only dreamed of in the past.

"You are the most amazing boy I've ever laid eyes on," Dr. Kincaid said at last, and Edgar beamed.

Dr. Kincaid had quite a lot of trouble getting down the other side. It took him twice as long to get down as it had taken him to get up. "Be careful," he called up to Edgar. "You'll find it's a bit more treacherous on this side."

Edgar descended so fast it was almost as if he were free-falling to the ground.

"Now you're just showing off," said Dr. Kincaid, chuckling, and the two of them trampled down the pathway.

At the bottom of the path the immense boulders that had surrounded him dispersed. The feeling reminded Edgar of leaving the shelter of the trees in the grove for the open land beyond. He made the final turn, and the last of the rocks fell away from his sight.

Edgar stood speechless before a view no child of Atherton had ever seen before, and it was not what Edgar had expected.

Dr. Kincaid continued calling for Vincent until he noticed the look of awe on Edgar's face. He remembered the first time he'd seen what the boy was seeing, and so he let Edgar enjoy the view a minute longer before breaking the magic of the moment.

"Stay here," he said. "There are no Cleaners about the place right now, but if they do come, run to the stone ladder and cross back over. I'm quite sure you can manage it."

Edgar nodded slowly, without really hearing what Dr. Kincaid had said, and the man hurried out of sight in search of Vincent.

There were two things that stunned Edgar into silence at the bottom of the path, each in a different direction. The first of these things was his initial broad view of the Flatlands

itself — vast and open, scattered with towering groups of gigantic stones. Running between clusters of smooth, grey boulders —
like the ones surrounding Dr. Kincaid's home — were jagged,
dangerous-looking rocks of red and orange. Wild, curving lines
of green fuzz darted this way and that between the sharp stones.
And it was all decorating a desert ground of deep brown and
black. It seemed as though the Flatlands were at once entirely
dead and threatening to explode with life.

The second thing within Edgar's sight was even more
breathtaking. He faced the very edge of Atherton, which was
closer than he'd imagined it would be. It would seem that Vincent had carried Edgar all the way across the Flatlands in the
night and that Dr. Kincaid's home sat very close to the edge of
the world. He could hardly believe that this really was the end
of everything. He began to walk toward the edge and felt his feet
carrying him almost without effort.

"Stay back," said Dr. Kincaid. He had returned without
Vincent and was watching Edgar carefully. "You won't want to
be near the edge if a Cleaner comes near."

Edgar listened carefully for the sound of bones clanging together and heard nothing. He felt so drawn to the very edge it
was hard to stop. "I won't get that close, really I won't."

The boy had come this far, and he needed to see the rest.

"All right, Edgar." Dr. Kincaid came and took Edgar's hand
in his, and the two of them began walking. "We must go quickly
and be done with it. Be careful — it has an unbelievable pull
when you get nearer to it."

When they came within twenty feet, Edgar began to feel as

though the edge were pulling him closer, like there were strings tied to his toes and they were drawing him forward.

"This feels very strange," Edgar commented. "Why does it feel this way?"

"The bottom of Atherton is shaped like a half circle, and it's extraordinarily heavy. As you get closer to the edge of the Flat-lands, you are actually closer to the bottom of Atherton. It pulls you toward it. That's what keeps you on the ground instead of floating in the air. It's a thing we call gravity, Edgar."

As they walked a little farther, when Edgar lifted his feet he noticed how they were dragged forward in the air. He made a game of watching his feet move of their own accord.

When they came within a few feet of the edge, Dr. Kincaid sat down in the dirt and told Edgar to do the same. They nudged forward until they reached the very edge, and Dr. Kincaid swung his legs over, holding them out in the open air. Edgar faltered a moment, unsure if he could go through with it, then he, too, lowered his legs over the edge.

If you could have observed Edgar and Dr. Kincaid from the space beyond the edge, it would have been quite a sight: the cliffs of Atherton towering above two small people with their legs curling over the edge of the world. Dr. Kincaid leaned out and Edgar followed hesitantly.

The Dark Planet came into view for the first time. It was monstrous in size and stunningly close. It was dark, as Dr. Kincaid had said it would be — a huge, round world in varied shades of grey and brown. There was a sadness about it, as though it were coming to the end of a long life of pain and suffering. The sight stirred mixed emotions in Edgar: Even as it made him almost want to cry, he felt a strange longing to go there, to see the world where he had been born.

"If you were to fall off, you wouldn't fall straight down into nothingness," said Dr. Kincaid. "Gravity would draw you back in toward the round bottom until you crashed into it. The impact could certainly kill you."

Edgar wanted more than anything to turn over, slide down, and climb around on the bottom of Atherton. If what Dr. Kincaid said was true, wouldn't gravity hold him? He looked at his hand with the missing finger and felt a phantom pain where the pinky had been. This was not the day to climb around on the underbelly of the world.

Edgar thought he heard a faint clicking sound, though he might have imagined it. The idea of a Cleaner taking hold of him with those monstrous teeth and ripping him from the edge proved too much, and Edgar pulled his legs back into the Flatlands.

"It's good you got that out of your system," said Dr. Kincaid. "It was something you needed to see, and I'm very glad we could come here together, but there are other pressing matters at hand."

The two of them crawled away from the edge until they felt comfortable enough to stand and begin walking back to the pathway.

Vincent was waiting for them at the foot of the path with a rope slung over his shoulder, carrying something under one arm. "What do you think of the Dark Planet, Edgar?"

Edgar said the first words that came to his mind. "It looks sad. And dirty."

"You have captured it better than most in a mere five words," remarked Vincent. "Well done."

As they approached, Edgar realized that Vincent was hauling a large chunk of a Cleaner. It was a slice about the width of Edgar's foot. Six bony legs with sharp claws at the ends hung from the bottom and thick, green liquid that looked like pudding was dripping from it.

"Excellent!" cried Dr. Kincaid. "It looks as though Vincent has done some hunting today after all. Have you any water?"

Vincent leaned over, and the rope rolled down in front of him. It was attached to a jug and it was glistening with water, as though it had recently been dipped in a pool and hadn't dried off yet.

"Perfect!" said Dr. Kincaid. "Now, come with us, Vincent. You simply must see this boy climb. You've never seen anything like it!"

CHAPTER
29

UNLOCKING DR. HARDING'S BRAIN

By the time Edgar and his new companions had returned safely to the flat, it was clear that Dr. Kincaid and Vincent were planning a journey. The two of them had talked endlessly of what to pack and what routes would be the safest, and Edgar had carefully listened to everything they'd said. Still, he was confused about where they were going and why — until the three of them sat down for another plate of Black and Green. It was then that Edgar was able to sneak in a question while the two men were chewing their food.

"Why must you travel so far?" asked Edgar.

Dr. Kincaid and Vincent looked at one another between bites and seemed unsure of what to say.

"Look closely at your old home," said Vincent. Dr. Kincaid

nodded and seemed to comply with where Vincent was going. "Do you see it moving?"

Edgar stared hard at the top of the cliffs, but he could see nothing.

"It's not moving very fast, but it is steady," said Dr. Kincaid. "It will keep coming, and it will not stop moving until . . ."

"Until what?" pressed Edgar.

"Until it reaches the very bottom," said Dr. Kincaid. "And our world is flat. Then it will stop."

Edgar was surprised, but not as much as he would have been had he not seen the same thing happening to the Highlands only a few days before.

"How long will it take?" asked Edgar, who hadn't yet eaten a bite. He finally took the meat from his plate and dipped it into the slippery pudding.

"We're not entirely sure," said Vincent. His long brown hair was dangling close to the green pudding as he leaned over his plate. "It could be all the way down by tomorrow, or it might take a few days. We're not completely sure."

Edgar hadn't realized the change would occur so fast, and he suddenly had a vision of Cleaners running free in the grove, devouring trees, sheep, rabbits, and people.

"How about a change of subject?" said Dr. Kincaid. He could see the fear in Edgar's expression. The boy hadn't yet had his question answered about how far they were traveling, and Edgar began to sense that they didn't want him to know where they were going and why.

"Why not tell Edgar more of our Dr. Harding," said Vincent. "I can't help enjoying tales of the strange scientist myself."

Dr. Kincaid nodded and stood up. He'd always been a better thinker on his feet. "The man had many eccentricities. He hated birds, bugs, most of the various large animals. Unlike most modern scientists, he thought there were far too many species on the Dark Planet, which he felt complicated the natural world and caused untold illness. In designing Atherton, he settled on rabbits, sheep, and horses and not much else. Those, he said, would do just fine. He was very proud of the hybrid fig tree he'd designed and saw it as the perfect source of food and other resources. It was troubling to him when he discovered they were poisonous after the third year. He'd not worked out a solution to that before. . . ."

Vincent saw that Dr. Kincaid was veering into sensitive territory and redirected. "He also had strong opinions about books, didn't he, Luther?"

"Indeed." Dr. Kincaid cleared his throat, shifting his attention to Vincent's question. "He believed books only belonged in the hands of those who were worthy of them, those who could understand and put them to a good use. There were those who worked — in the grove and with the animals — and those who studied. Dr. Harding saw the two as mutually exclusive. One either worked with his hands or with his mind, and mixing the two created all sorts of problems. A laborer with a book had questions, curiosities, and in the end, demands. He believed that many of history's most violent uprisings were caused by the educating of those who ought to have been left to the fields.

And so the Highlands have books — albeit some pretty ancient ones — and Tabletop is without them."

"I wish I could read," remarked Edgar.

"Don't fret, Edgar — I have a great many books of my own, and one day I shall teach you to read. There are a lot of very old books up there in the Highlands, things that wouldn't spark a memory of life on the Dark Planet. My books are better, and you shall read them! In fact, I see no reason at all why everyone on Atherton shouldn't be shown how to read again. Readiness training may have hidden that talent from many, but it will make a quick return for those who have the will to learn."

Dr. Kincaid paced back and forth as he continued to tell about the man who had brought Atherton into existence.

"Dr. Harding kept a great many secrets from us. He even kept them from himself, if you can imagine such a thing. He would use a technique in which he could lock vast groups of complex information behind numbers in his mind so that he didn't have to remember them all at once. He assigned a number to each set of information, which worked like a key in his mind. Once the lock was undone, it would open the storehouse of information he had hidden there."

Dr. Kincaid darted off toward the cave without warning.

"He does that sometimes," Vincent said casually. "Gets an idea in his head and then dashes off to pursue it without telling me a thing. Give it a moment. He'll be back."

In no time Dr. Kincaid stood before Edgar and Vincent with a journal in his hand. It had a worn cover and faded yellow pages with torn and dirty edges not unlike the book of secret things.

"This happens to be one of Dr. Harding's journals."

Edgar noticed that as Dr. Kincaid flipped the pages, every one of them was filled with columns of five-digit numbers and keywords.

Inner workings	44857
Rock formations	22302
Secretion	32439
Memory glands	32441
Outer worlds?	13120

"Each of these numbers unlocks something he'd hidden away in his mind, or I should say it unlocks the first chamber, which sometimes leads to another, and another, and who knows how many beyond that. Dr. Harding made hundreds of these journals. Countless equations, ideas, and inventions were locked away in his mind — and he could find any one of them whenever he chose by following the path he'd set out for himself. But there came a problem that was the beginning of all the other problems."

"What sort of problem do you mean?" asked Edgar.

"This is the only journal that remains. All the others are gone."

"Gone? Did someone take them?"

"He burned them. All but this one, which was the very first. He made this when he was still a boy of twelve, and I don't think it has anything of great value in it."

"Why would he burn the numbers?"

Dr. Kincaid sat back down in his chair and closed the journal.

"It's another great mystery, Edgar. Perhaps Dr. Harding reached the end of what his mind would hold. Maybe he thought if he could destroy the existing numbers, his mind would be erased and he could fill it up again. I don't know. He was a very complicated person."

"Dr. Kincaid," said Edgar. "Why have you never returned to the Dark Planet as you used to?"

"When I left you on Tabletop, I didn't know. I couldn't have known."

"You didn't know what?"

"Oh, I *knew* there was trouble, big trouble ahead. I didn't know what it would be, but I knew it was coming."

"Don't torture yourself," said Vincent. "We've been over and over this, and it wasn't your fault. There was nothing you could have done."

"Dr. Kincaid, what are you talking about?" asked Edgar.

Dr. Kincaid pulled something out of his pocket that he'd brought from the cave with the journal. Edgar had never seen anything like it. It was as shiny and black as a fig, but it was oblong and made of a material unknown to him.

"There was a time when people on the Dark Planet, so far away, could hear my voice with another object like this. I could talk into it, and even if they were very far away, they could hear me."

This seemed like a fantasy to Edgar, and he couldn't bring himself to believe it.

"It doesn't work any longer," continued Vincent. "Dr. Harding wouldn't allow much of anything onto Atherton that might contaminate it . . . anything like machines and computers that might turn it into a place like the Dark Planet."

Dr. Kincaid jumped back in. "But this thing did work for a time. And it wasn't just people from the Dark Planet that contacted me on it. There was another. . . ."

"Dr. Harding?" asked Edgar.

"Yes, Dr. Harding," answered Dr. Kincaid, turning somber as he thought back. "It was Dr. Harding who disconnected. We didn't know it then, but he was able to cut all links between Atherton and the Dark Planet. He severed Atherton from its home forever. We're floating free around the Dark Planet. They can see us but they can't contact us."

"Where is Dr. Harding now? Is he dead?"

Dr. Kincaid set the device on the table and breathed a deep sigh of frustration. Vincent ate the very last bite of Black and Green from his plate and wiped his bare arm across his face.

"My boy," he said. "You have finally come to a question the good doctor cannot answer."

CHAPTER

30

SAMUEL MAKES HIS CASE

A small group of men crouched beneath the tall trees, waiting and wondering whether or not they should move. All but one were leaderless members of Sir Philip's brigade. They had endured a long morning of fighting and returned to a House of Power unwilling to take them in. Concern over whom they could trust had compelled them to approach the Village of Rabbits and see what allies they might find.

One member of the group in particular had grave doubts about Lord Phineus. He was the only one who had not been among Sir Philip's fighting men in the Village of Sheep. It was Horace — from the House of Power — who had been asked to leave his post a few hours before. When he'd returned, the gate was locked and Horace was refused reentry, so he went searching for others who had also been refused at the gate.

Some of the men had scattered, trying to find a way into the House of Power or simply going back home with no plan for getting water or food. But Horace had pulled aside five of Sir Philip's men, and they'd all agreed: Lord Phineus was a violent man, and his way of ruling Atherton had not worked. He had to be stopped.

In the absence of Sir Philip, Horace took the lead of the five men, for he had held an important post — very close to the seat of power — and the men were in search of a leader.

"We can't wait here all day," said Horace. "One of us will have to go to them."

He glanced at each of the men's faces and saw not a volunteer among them. This turned out not to be a problem for Horace, for when he gazed back at the Village of Rabbits, he saw a group of men with clubs heading toward him and his men.

"Leave your swords in the trees," said Horace, "and come with me." He felt certain there would be no hope of a peaceful encounter if both sides came with weapons of war. The men reluctantly followed the command as Horace stepped out from the protection of the trees and walked toward the oncoming mob, his men following hesitantly.

"Get back to your own land!" screamed someone from the Village of Rabbits. "We're prepared to protect ourselves if we must!"

Horace held his arms up and told the rest of the men to do the same. "We've brought no swords with us. We're unarmed and only want to talk. Have you a leader among you who would listen to us?"

There was some chatter in the group, and then one of them ran to the inn and disappeared. When the messenger reemerged, Briney and Maude were with him.

There was arguing Horace couldn't discern, though he was sure they were debating whether or not he and the others from the Highlands had come to trick them.

Eventually, Briney and Maude ventured closer to Horace without the rest of their group. "Are you here on errand from Lord Phineus?" asked Maude. She was the most matter-of-fact in the group and had no trouble getting to the point.

"We weren't sent by anyone," said Horace. "We just want to talk."

Maude and Briney whispered to one another.

"What's your name?" asked Maude. Horace told her.

"All right, Horace. You alone can come with us to the inn. Send your boys back to the trees."

A vision of Horace's little boy flashed before his eyes, sitting at their kitchen table with bowls and spoons, watching the stream flow by in front of their little house. And then he remembered how the water that had always run in front of his house had disappeared, how it had felt on his feet to walk the dry bottom of the stream bed.

"Go on," he said to the other men, motioning them back to the trees. They were not willing at first and wished they'd brought their spears, but Horace convinced them that it was the only way.

"If we find you've been sent by Lord Phineus, you'll never see those trees again. You might want to take a last look." Maude still didn't trust this man of the Highlands with droopy eyes and no hair on the top of his head.

When they entered the inn, it was dark but for a few wicks burning, and Horace was escorted to a table. Rabbits were being cooked on the fire as a group of men and women stood nearby.

"That table," said Briney, pointing to the same corner where Sir Emerik had been questioned by Edgar. Horace crossed the room and sat down while Maude told the rest to set the rabbits on the stick aside and wait outside. Soon the inn was empty but for the crackling fire and three people seated in a gloomy corner.

"Why have you come here?" asked Briney. He regarded the man before him thoughtfully, trying to read his expression.

"Because I think we misunderstand one another," said Horace.

"I understand Lord Phineus planned to poison us, and that you are one of his men," said Maude.

Horace tried to answer, but Maude wouldn't let him.

"I *understand* how you've taken every fig and rabbit and sheep you could force from us."

"Yes, but —"

Maude slapped her hand on the table, and the man was silenced. To Maude, Horace symbolized everyone and everything in the Highlands, and she would say her piece whether he liked it or not.

"You gathered the orange dust," she said. "Something that those in the grove have worked so hard to subdue in the face of your demands for more, more, more figs! How *dare* you try to harvest it to use against us!"

"*You* tried to poison *us*," said Horace, surprised by the accusation. This seemed to set Maude back on her heels, and he took advantage of the silent moment. "Do you deny it? Do you deny using poison against us? Men have died. There are others back in the Highlands who can barely breathe. How do you respond? They have sores on their hands and faces. What would you have us think? That you are a peaceful people?"

Briney could take no more of this man insulting Maude and pointed a finger in Horace's face.

"Your Lord Phineus asked Mr. Ratikan to harvest the orange dust and to test it on us in the water, which he did. We were lucky enough to find it before it could be used against us, but I have no doubt Lord Phineus planned to poison the whole lot of us. It is *you* who tried to poison *us*. We have only tried to protect ourselves all along."

Horace didn't exactly know how to respond. If what Briney said were true, everything was altered. He had never been told of such a plan. None of them had. Could Lord Phineus be so cruel?

Maude got her wind back. "Why have you always been so stingy with the water? From what I can see of the Highlands, you've had all you could use for far too long."

This was a point Horace had trouble disputing even in the quiet of his own mind. He'd known for a long time that the Highlands enjoyed more water. Seeing the dryness in Tabletop firsthand had made him realize how truly miserly Lord Phineus had been.

"The water is one of the reasons I've come," said Horace, feeling as though he might have arrived at a point on which they could agree. "Lord Phineus has shut himself in the House of Power with his closest allies. He has plenty of food, for much of it is stored there. And he controls the flow of water from a secret place known only to him."

Horace looked across the table and couldn't tell if Briney and Maude understood what he'd meant, so he repeated himself.

"He's locked the gate to the House of Power and he controls the only source of water from within," Horace said again. "It would seem that Lord Phineus has turned against not only Tabletop, but the Highlands as well."

"How can he shut himself away like that?" asked Briney. "It's not possible."

"You are wrong," answered Horace. "The wall around his fortress is very high and well protected by his most dedicated guards."

"Who knows of this place where the water comes from?" asked Maude.

"Only one — Lord Phineus. Once there were three, or so I've overheard from my post in the House of Power. Sir Philip — who passed in battle at the Village of Sheep today — and Sir William, who was lost a while back in an unfortunate accident. There is one other, Sir Emerik, who seems to have been left out of the loop, I imagine because he couldn't be trusted, though he wields considerable power."

"Then we must get to Lord Phineus!" yelled Maude. "We must go to the House of Power and force him to make the water begin flowing again. And then we must kill them both — him and this Sir Emerik."

"That, I'm afraid, will be more difficult than you imagine," said Horace. He rubbed his hands together, trying to decide how he should tell them.

"I and those five men I brought with me are the only fighting men I know of who will help us. We will meet with resistance not only from the House of Power, but from a great many more men who don't want anyone from Tabletop in the Highlands. Just because they can't get into the House of Power doesn't mean they will tolerate your entering into the Highlands."

"Can't you talk to them? Convince them we only want the same thing they do?" asked Briney.

"Do you want the same thing?" asked Horace. "Can you say you only want water? Can you say you do not also want to live in the Highlands as we do? And will you still give us food when you're no longer forced to do so?"

"He has a point," said Maude. "I see it in the faces of almost everyone in the village. They want to go in. They don't want to be ruled any longer."

The door to the inn flew open, and light poured into the room.

"Briney? Maude?" It was Charles and Wallace from the other villages. They were both breathing heavily, as though they'd tried to run the entire distance between villages.

"We're here, Charles," said Briney from the dark corner of the room. "What's happened?"

Charles had to catch his breath before he could speak. His voice was a thin, raspy whisper, and it was difficult to hear what he was trying to say. They pulled him and Wallace over to the table and set them down on a bench.

"What is it, Charles?" asked Briney. Horace looked on with a mixture of concern and bewilderment.

"Isabel," murmured Charles. "She talked to a boy from the Highlands, a boy who knew Edgar from the grove. She made him tell her something before he escaped to his home. It's happening again, only much worse this time!"

Charles swallowed, wishing for a cup of water, but there was none to be had in the inn.

"What's happening? What do you mean?" asked Maude.

Charles was so agitated by the news he hadn't thought to use some discretion. But Wallace had been looking at Horace, half hidden in the shadows, since the moment he entered the inn.

"Who is this man?" Wallace asked before Charles could go on.

They all looked at one another, unsure of how to proceed, and then the ground began to move beneath them.

Samuel and Isabel were hiding in the deepest part of the grove, sitting among the leaves and branches of a third-year tree.

"The grove's being neglected," she said. "And there's no water in the pool."

Samuel touched one of the wilting leaves.

"Lord Phineus has turned off the water," said Samuel.

"I didn't know he could do that." Isabel was beginning to think Lord Phineus held even more power than she'd been led to believe.

Samuel wasn't sure if he should tell Isabel all that he knew. Growing up in the House of Power with a father who was part of the ruling class had exposed him to much more information than anyone realized. He had always been a secretive boy, especially once he had only his mother to trust. The thought of her in the House of Power alone, and his selfish act of leaving her, made him hope he could trust Isabel with one of the most important secrets of Atherton.

"The way to control the water is hidden beneath the House of Power," said Samuel. "It is known by only two."

"Who are the two?"

Samuel kicked at the dirt, trying to form the words.

"There used to be three men who knew how to control the water: Lord Phineus, Sir Philip, and my father. My father would never show it to me, but it didn't matter."

"Why didn't it matter?" She felt as though she were slowly pulling the story out of Samuel's mouth on a string, bit by bit.

"I know every nook and cranny of the House of Power. Nobody ever watched me."

He looked at Isabel until she caught his eye.

"Besides Lord Phineus, I'm the only other person who knows where the source of water resides. It's not an easy place to find, and it's a scary place to go, but I know the way."

He paused and shook his head in frustration.

"What?" asked Isabel.

"To get to the water would require us to first get inside the House of Power."

"That shouldn't be hard," said Isabel. "We can tell my father and he'll go there with a lot of men. Lord Phineus will have to listen to him."

Samuel almost smiled wryly at Isabel's simple view of the challenge ahead. Of course, she had never encountered a fortress before, or any security more formidable than the guards who had strolled near Tabletop's waterfalls and streams.

"I don't think it will be that easy," said Samuel. "There is only one gate, and it's heavily guarded. It's surrounded by a wall that only Edgar could climb. It's flat and smooth as water. If Lord Phineus doesn't want people inside, he can easily keep them out. But there is one place we might get in. . . ."

Isabel waited, letting the words rest in the air, and then she pulled on the string once more.

"Where is the place?"

Samuel feared for his mother. The longer he sat in the tree the more he felt that he needed to return to her and make sure she was safe.

"Isabel, if we're to do this, we must go alone."

Isabel began to protest, though she was secretly excited about the idea of entering the Highlands with someone who knew the way, free of her mother's will. She imagined the adoration from the other children in the grove when the water would flow thick through the trees again and they would find out that it was Isabel who had made it happen.

"We're little, Isabel. We can hide more easily, especially once we're inside the House of Power. I know many places where we can remain concealed, but they are small places. And there is a more sensible reason we must go alone as well."

"Why?" asked Isabel, though she was already touching her bag of black figs, wondering if she had enough of them for a perilous journey.

"The hidden way into the House of Power is only big enough for us. An adult won't fit."

And so it was decided that the two of them would go alone when night fell on the grove. Isabel would spend the late afternoon gathering food, water if she could find it, and the very best black figs. She had an extra bag in her room filled with figs dipped in orange dust, which she would also bring.

As they plotted their journey, the feeling of the ground falling from under them came again, and the haunting groans from far away rippled through the air. It went on so long that finally Isabel rushed off to make her preparations with the tremors still afoot.

After she was gone Samuel reflected upon some of the details he'd left out of his story, and he felt badly for not telling Isabel everything. But if he had, she might not have agreed to come, and he needed her skills with a sling to make the journey and reunite with his mother.

There were two things he did not tell her in the tree. The first was how deep underground the source of water was and how perilous the way to it would be. But that wasn't the most troubling part. He also hadn't told her that even if they did find their way inside the House of Power and to the deep underground passage, it wouldn't matter. For at the end there was a door that required a key only Lord Phineus possessed.

CHAPTER
31

THE SPIRIT OF A BOY REMAINS

"What do you think, Wallace?" asked Charles. "Shall we trust him or not?"

Charles had finished telling Briney and Maude about the descent of Tabletop and the horrifying creatures they could expect to find in the Flatlands. The group of them had sent Horace outside to wait, and now they had to decide if he should be told.

"Threats mounting on all sides," Wallace muttered. "This changing world is a curse."

Wallace was a thinker and a waiter, less prone to action than the rest. And yet his quiet, philosophical way had a calming effect on people, as if they were his sheep and he were only trying to herd them in the right direction.

"We don't know what's coming," he continued. "The danger

from the Flatlands is a mystery, but it sounds to me as though it threatens everyone." He looked at the others and saw that they didn't understand what he was driving at.

"It would be unwise to wage war on two fronts if there is a chance we could wage one, together, against the greater foe."

There was a silence at the inn as each of them pondered the risks.

"Could this boy from the Highlands have lied to Isabel, to scare her? Could Lord Phineus have sent him?"

"She's not easily tricked," said Charles. "She came to me not with a rumor or a possible lie, but with the truth. She was convinced the boy came to warn us."

"And yet even the boy could be deceived, couldn't he?" asked Briney. "This page from the secret book — it might be filled with lies."

They all listened to the deep moan of Tabletop slowly moving down. Eyebrows raised and chins nodded around the table as they silently agreed that some predictions from the page were already coming to pass. It would be foolish to expect a peaceful meeting with the Flatlands.

"We trust this man at our own peril," said Maude. She remained unconvinced. Horace, the secret book, and the boy could easily be part of an intricate deception by Lord Phineus. And yet, she grasped the wisdom Wallace had shared. How could they fight two enemies at once when they'd only just begun to understand how to fight at all? They were doomed to fail in both endeavors.

"Who wants to bring Horace in and tell him what we know?" asked Charles. "Show of hands."

Wallace raised his hand almost before the words were said. Of them all, he was most certain they were on a precarious path. He had tasted battle and even victory, but in the hours that had passed after the fight, he had felt a terrible unease and a growing belief that in the end they would fail. Ongoing war was no place for a peaceful people, and it did not suit him.

Charles was next to vote in favor. Then Briney looked at Maude as if to say he would not raise his hand if she did not want him to. His heart was torn between his devotion to her and his hope to work with the Highlands instead of against them. He was very pleased when Maude sighed deeply and raised her hand.

"Wallace, you do the talking," said Maude. She was determined to force some part of her will on this table full of men. "The men he leads fought in your village and lost friends to its clubs, and the trust must come between the two of you if I am to be convinced."

Once Horace had settled back onto the bench where he had been seated before, he looked nervously at the faces before him, wondering why no one spoke. Wallace relished the silence in the room, but it clearly made Horace uncomfortable.

"Tabletop feels like it's moving," remarked Horace, as if to break the ice. "I wonder what it means."

Still not a word from the group at the table. Horace was not a rash person prone to babble in order to fill an empty space, and said no more. Charles nudged Wallace on the shoulder, thinking maybe the man had nodded off to sleep, but Wallace was not sleeping. He was waiting for the right words to come to him, something very few people are apt to do in times of tension.

Wallace looked intently at the man before him. The heavy jowls told him Horace had eaten too much for too long. In his eyes he felt the man's exhaustion and worry, the worry of a father.

"You have a wife and children," said Wallace, breaking the silence. "I have only my sheep, but they mean as much to me as anything I've ever known."

Another silence ensued in which Horace thought of the sheep his five men had probably trampled over with their horses. *My child is safe, for the moment, but some in this man's care have perished before their time.*

"Your men fought well," said Wallace, folding his hands on the table.

"From the looks of things, so did you," said Horace, thinking of the many fallen men from the Highlands.

"No, that's actually not true. I don't know how to fight well. *We* don't know how to fight well." Wallace glanced at his friends. "We were very lucky. Briney has told us you have your doubts about Lord Phineus. We haven't any doubts at all. History tells us he will use his power to control us, but we have some hope that your visit is a sign that not all in the Highlands feel as he does."

"Your hopes are well founded," said Horace. "I don't claim that everyone in the Highlands feels as I do, but there are some. How many, I can't say."

"We have a new enemy, one that might bring our two peoples together."

Horace was baffled by the comment. "You mean Lord Phineus?" he asked.

"I'm afraid he is only part of our problem, the rest of which I should like to ask Charles to explain to you."

Charles was about to begin when Wallace touched him on the arm, prompting him to wait a moment more.

"Horace, I'm sorry for the loss of your friends in my village. I would have wished for another outcome."

Horace felt the sincerity of the words. He wanted to tell Wallace he too was sorry for a great many things, but he seemed unable to get started. Wallace nodded, seeming to understand what the man felt without hearing the words.

It took only a few minutes for Charles to tell Horace everything he knew from Isabel and her mysterious visitor about the fearsome creatures in Tabletop. In the telling, Horace began to realize that it might be Samuel who'd come to the grove with the news. The thought of it was worrisome, for he had some paternal feelings toward the boy. But Horace was a man of action and wasted no time shifting his thoughts to the peril at hand, as if he were trained for just such an encounter.

"We should send someone to the edge as quickly as we can. We need to know how close we are to the bottom. Soon enough these creatures, whatever they are, will be close enough to see. We must know our enemy."

"I'll go," said Maude. "And I'll bring Morris and Amanda with me. The three of us can be back here before dark with news."

She didn't wait for an answer from the rest, and Briney knew his place was at the inn, overseeing the village. He was glad she'd thought of bringing someone with her. For the time being he wanted her as far away from the Highlands as possible, at least until Tabletop had descended closer to the Flatlands.

After Maude left the inn, Horace was the first to speak.

"She's a strong one," he commented.

"You have no idea," said Briney. The four men smiled and together began discussing how they would begin to prepare for a day when Atherton would be flat. It was a short conversation, for their mouths were growing parched and sticky, and they began to realize they would have to conserve their energy.

Horace rose to go, and the rest of the men followed him out. They stood at the front of the inn.

"I will leave a man in the woods, just there," said Horace, pointing to where his men were awaiting his return. "When Maude returns with news, you must go to him. He will find me. If we've come near the bottom and there is a threat as the boy said, I'll go directly to the House of Power and try to convince Lord Phineus we must fight them together."

"Take your men to the Highlands by a new way," said Wallace. "Follow the rim where the two lands had been separated. There is a man and a horse in that direction, if you keep walking, and I wonder if he might be someone you know."

Before long Horace would find Sir Philip where he'd fallen, away from all the villages in the middle of nowhere, and wonder how he had come to an end in such a desolate place.

It was one of those times when Isabel wished with all her heart that she could write and her parents could read. She wanted more than anything to leave a note for her mother and father telling them not to worry, for she would return soon. And yet she also knew that if she told them, they would surely come looking for her and meet with violence in the Highlands. No, she could not risk losing the chance of helping Samuel on this important mission.

She decided to tell her most devoted follower from the grove, a very affectionate, loyal girl of seven.

"Tell my mother something for me, will you?"

"I will," the little girl said.

"Wait an hour, then go to her and say that I've gone to do something that could not wait, but that I'll return tomorrow."

"Where are you going? She'll want to know." It was really the little girl who wanted to know.

"I can't tell you, and she can't know."

"Will you come back?" The little girl's voice trembled, and Isabel got down on one knee before her.

"I promise to come back. There's something I can do to help save the grove, but she cannot come after me. You just have to tell her that I *will* return."

"I can do it," said the girl. "I'll wait until an hour after dark and then I'll tell her."

The little girl ran off and Samuel jumped down out of a nearby tree. Early evening had come; and as the sky was turning grey, Isabel tore a leaf from one of the trees. There was a subtle change, something only someone who'd lived in the grove all her life would be aware of. The leaf was just a little dry, starting to turn a slightly different color. Isabel thought of the saplings across the grove and wondered how long the fragile young trees would last. They were delicate, requiring great care and lots of water. If they failed, the future of the grove was in question. The grove might be lost.

"We must go quickly," she said. "There's no time to lose."

And so Isabel and Samuel began a journey that would take them through lands dangerous and beautiful, on a quest to bring water to a barren land and a thirsty people. It would be more perilous than either of them suspected.

Isabel and Samuel crept across the hardening mud where the bottom of the waterfall used to be, and they both thought of the boy who had brought them together.

"What do you think Edgar is doing right now?" asked Samuel as they passed into the Highlands unseen.

"I wish I knew," answered Isabel.

"There's still a chance the three of us will return to the grove."

The two looked back at the trees as they slipped into the tall green grass. Even in the grey light Isabel had seen how lush the Highlands were, but all of the beauty of the Highlands paled at the sight of the precious fig trees she loved. The grove had taken her heart and would not let go. It was filled with the power of memory, and above all with the spirit of the boy Edgar.

By the time she'd return to the grove, it would not be as she remembered it.

CHAPTER

32

MEAD'S HOLLOW

Throughout the day Atherton released a dull roar as if it were taking a final, labored breath of air in its drive for the very bottom. The steady descent was easier to hear than feel, a lullaby of dark sounds that seemed to play forever and fade into the background as the clamor of the waterfall once had. Now and then it would rumble and howl, falling fast, then grinding slower, reawakening the senses of everyone on Atherton. But it never stopped completely as the Highlands had during the many days it took to crash into Tabletop.

The nearer Maude and her companions came to the edge of Tabletop, the more parched and bleak it became. Dusty rocks marred the ground, and the air became harder to breathe. Maude stopped well short of the edge and pointed to a faraway place. Already they could see the Flatlands in the distance. Tabletop had moved lower than they or anyone else would have believed. The three of them looked back at the center of Atherton, where the Highlands had once risen from the land.

"This isn't home anymore," she said. Her voice was dry and quiet. Morris wished he could pour a cup of water over the words, making them wet and fluid again. Maybe then they wouldn't sound so hopeless. But he had to agree the absence of the cliff made Tabletop feel wrong somehow. Atherton looked empty. The cliff had been something to huddle against and make them feel sheltered and safe, but it was gone now, replaced by a feeling of dread Morris couldn't shake.

"It's getting late," he said. They had spoken little on the way, and he was surprised to hear his own fractured voice.

The three of them continued toward the edge, slower now, but with purpose. When they came within ten steps, Amanda stopped.

"I can't go any farther," she said. She was not a fierce woman like Maude, and the closer they'd come to the end, the more she'd wanted to turn back. She let Maude and Morris go the rest of the way alone.

When they arrived at the very edge, they leaned out and looked down.

"This cannot be," said Maude, overcome. It was as if a vast monster had crept up behind her in a nightmare and now stood at her feet. It was not the same feeling she had felt when the Highlands had come within view for the first time. The Highlands were filled with *people*. What she saw before her now was a mystery that made a dark terror well up in her throat.

Maude and Morris could see the jagged stones on its surface and the odd tangled green lines everywhere. But they could also see the strange creatures that caused them.

They had arrived at the place where the waste from the village was dumped, including the bones and unwanted insides of the rabbits. Cleaners gathered here in great number before dark. Edgar had climbed down at night, when most of the Cleaners are wont to hide amidst the jagged rocks and only a few venture in search of a bone that might have been missed. But in the light they came by the hundreds to this place, searching for bones and blood, anything thrown over the edge that might feed their insatiable hunger.

Maude's and Morris's stomachs turned at the sight of the squirming shapes below and smelled the scent of death wafting up. Maude had to fight back the urge to be sick, and she stumbled back from the edge in a daze.

The sound of Tabletop working its way down drowned out the distant noise of Cleaners moving and snapping their teeth, but if it had been a quiet day, Morris and Maude would have heard the faint sound of bones breaking from below.

"We may not be alone come morning," she said.

Morris nodded and stepped away. There was a large rock twice the size of his head nearby, and he picked it up, struggling to carry it back to where he'd stood. When he hurled it off the edge, he nearly lost his balance and went over with it. Amanda screamed and told him to get back, but Morris stayed and watched.

The rock smashed directly into the head of a Cleaner. The injured animal jerked in every direction as if it were trying to take flight. Morris was appalled as he watched dozens of ravenous creatures attack the fallen beast.

"We must warn the others," said Morris. "If these creatures enter the villages, we'll have no place to hide."

Maude went to Amanda and put her arm around her shoulders. "You and Morris will go to the grove. When you get there, send someone to the Village of Sheep. I'll go back home and warn everyone."

Morris and Amanda hastened toward the grove, and Maude started off alone. She would go directly to Briney, then find a way to get word to Horace and his men. *Tabletop and the Highlands must unite against the one foe.* She repeated the sentiment Wallace had expressed earlier in the day. *It's our only hope.*

Maude was better at thinking alone, always had been. She preferred the solitude of pushing her broom at the inn and letting Briney talk to the villagers. She had often thought of moving to the Village of Sheep and becoming a shepherdess, where she could be alone and think. But Briney would never leave the inn. She thought on these things in an effort to forget about what she'd seen in the Flatlands, but the sight of the stone hitting the creature below and the others attacking it kept firing back in her mind. She became obsessed with one thought near the end of her journey as the Village of Rabbits came into view in the distance.

We must find a way to turn these monsters against one another.

Lord Phineus stood before Mead's head in the main chamber and studied it as he loved to do, running his fingers over the white nose, up to the forehead, and over the waves of hair carved into stone. He was thinking of Sir William, for some unknown reason, remembering what a challenge it had been to keep him in line.

When Lord Phineus reached the back of Mead's head, his mind cleared, and he put his other hand on the face, holding the entire piece firmly in his grip. He applied pressure one way, and Mead's head began to move to the right. He did the same to the left, and then back again. When he pushed left once more, a sharp *click!* came from the floor behind Mead's head. Something had been unlocked.

He repeated the turning of the head in reverse order, which produced a different sort of clicking sound. Lord Phineus then enfolded the head with his arms, lifting it from its pedestal. He put his arm deep inside a shaft where the head had been and pulled out a key.

Lord Phineus replaced the head and checked the locked door to the main chamber for any sound of someone outside.

Carefully pushing aside the ivy that ran down the wall to the floor behind Mead's head, he found a large stone slab below him with notches on each side that allowed him to lift the sheath of stone. Lord Phineus dragged it away with a loud grating noise, then looked down into the hole underneath. He drew a deep breath as he listened carefully for any unusual sounds.

Lord Phineus felt a heavy dread come over him as his lighted wick illuminated the stairs leading down into the black. On the first stair were carved the words he'd read many times before on each journey to the source of all water: MEAD'S HOLLOW. It was not a friendly passage, and the sight of it always made him shudder, but he had gone many times and knew the way well.

When he was far enough down the steep stairs to seal himself in, he set his small bowl of fuel and flaming wick on a step at his feet. He listened carefully once more, gazing down the narrow passageway. Lord Phineus pulled the stone over the opening and was enveloped in darkness and shadow, only a weak orange light dancing from the wick at his feet.

He carried with him two sharp wooden stakes to protect himself, and the key from Mead's head. He also had a bag hanging from his side, which he touched nervously. It was filled with clumps of dry bread, for there were dangerous creatures in Mead's Hollow. They would leave him to his errand as long as he gave them something to eat.

Lord Phineus held the small flame out into the darkness, searching for the first of the small torches that he would light to guide his way. The walls before him were utterly covered with dead vines of brown and black ivy. They looked like the dried bones of some wild beast that would not let him pass. He shivered once more and began his journey beneath the House of Power. After a few steps, he heard a familiar low growl and put his hand in the bag of bread.

Sir Emerik had indeed been standing at the door, quietly listening for the sounds he had heard before. He knew of the power of Mead's head and of the passage known as Mead's Hollow, but he had never known the pleasure of opening the passage. He wasn't even sure until that moment where the key lay hidden, but now he felt certain that it was within the head itself, for he had heard the sounds of moving stone. Sir Emerik smiled grimly, thinking only of how he could do away with Lord Phineus, take control of the water, and rule all of Atherton.

CHAPTER
33
INVERSION

The grey of early evening was gone and only a dull smolder of light remained. It was approaching deep night on Atherton, and three figures were making their way across the silent world. The sound of quaking ground and grinding earth had vanished. There were no waterfalls roaring in the distance. The Cleaners were hidden quietly away in the jagged rocks. All of Atherton was hushed as a whisper.

Edgar was used to making his way without much light, but the eerie silence made the world seem haunted in a way he'd never experienced at night before. It felt to Edgar like Atherton was dead.

"Will it always stay so quiet?" asked Edgar nervously. "I don't like it."

"It's very odd," said Vincent, who was walking in front of Edgar and Dr. Kincaid, leading the way.

"I don't mind the silence," said Dr. Kincaid. "It's far better than the sound of Cleaners filling the air."

It had been a long way across the Flatlands, but they were nearing the edge of Tabletop at last. They went on a little more without speaking a word.

"Dr. Kincaid?"

"Yes, Edgar."

"Thank you for bringing me with you."

There had been some arguing between Vincent and Dr. Kincaid about whether they should leave the boy behind in the safety of the flat. They wouldn't tell Edgar where they were going, only that they would keep him safe.

"You've been on your own for a long time," said Dr. Kincaid. "Best you make these decisions for yourself."

"Why won't you tell me where we're going?"

Dr. Kincaid didn't answer right away, but he had been wondering how much to tell the boy for a while and thought he could tell him a little more.

"There's not a lot of time, Edgar. A few days, maybe a week, and our chance will be lost."

"You mean the Cleaners?" Edgar imagined them overrunning the grove and the village.

"Not exactly," said Dr. Kincaid, trying to pacify the boy's imagination. "Our course is set, Edgar, but our destination must remain a mystery to you awhile longer. For now you must focus on the present."

Edgar had grown used to adventure, and the old man's words appeased him, though he remained concerned about the days ahead. Dr. Kincaid tried to change the subject.

"You should call me by a more friendly name, don't you think? 'Dr. Kincaid' is so formal."

"What shall I call you?"

Dr. Kincaid pondered the idea a moment, rubbing his big earlobe between his thumb and knuckle.

"My full name is Luther Mead Kincaid. 'Mead' is rather odd, don't you think? I don't know what my mother was thinking. Why don't you call me Luther?"

"I'll try," said Edgar, but he knew it would be difficult.

Vincent motioned for the two of them to stop talking and be still. Hardly breathing, they heard a soft clanging sound. Vincent waved them to one side and guided them slowly through the waning light. As they continued on, the sound went away, and Vincent turned to his companions.

"A den of Cleaners," he said. "Bedded down for the night. We are likely to find at least a few moving about in small groups, but most of them won't come out until they can see again."

"How many Cleaners are there?" asked Edgar, hoping for a small enough number that Vincent could kill them all.

"More than there are people on Atherton," said Vincent. "When light comes, they'll crowd the edge, if there is an edge."

The idea of thousands of Cleaners coming out in the morning light to find no edge to stop them from advancing was more than Edgar could dare to imagine.

"I must go straight to the grove," said Edgar. He'd been

concerned all along for Isabel and the others in the village, but being so near had reinvigorated his determination to find his friends.

"We will make a point of going through there," said Dr. Kincaid, feeling the gloom that surrounded the boy.

They walked on in silence for a long time, until the sound of the sleeping Cleaners was too far away to be heard, and the three of them were all alone in the Flatlands. The farther they went, the more he couldn't believe Vincent had carried him all that way on the night he'd fallen.

"Are we coming near the edge of Tabletop?" asked Dr. Kincaid, his feet beginning to hurt from the long walk. The words were just out of his mouth when the sound of breaking bones came from somewhere in front of them and very near.

"Get back!" cried Vincent. He'd been using the butt end of a spear as a walking stick, but now it was turned with the pointed end straight out to protect them.

"There are two! Stay back!" Vincent yelled again.

Without thinking, Edgar took his sling from his pocket and two black figs from his bag. He held one in his hand and put the other in the sling, stepped out of the way, and began swinging the sling over his head. Dr. Kincaid didn't know what Edgar was doing.

"Edgar! What is that you've got there?"

But Edgar was deep in concentration and didn't respond.

Vincent thrust his spear over and over at one of the two Cleaners as it charged and swung its head viciously. Its tail thrashed wildly, pulling a dozen of the Cleaner's back feet off the ground. Vincent finally found a good position and stabbed it through the open mouth, but when he did, the Cleaner clamped down on the spear with its jagged teeth and wouldn't let go. It lay dying on the ground, the spear stuck deep in its middle, but the spear had been lost.

The second Cleaner charged for Vincent as he tried to pull a second weapon from where it was stored on his back. It was then that Dr. Kincaid heard the *snap!* of the sling as Edgar hurled the black fig through the air.

The black fig slammed into the Cleaner's head, and the creature reeled back in pain and surprise. Edgar loaded the second black fig and began swinging it over his head.

"Wait until he comes for us," said Vincent. Whatever the boy was doing would not kill a Cleaner, but it did appear to inflict some damage.

Edgar waited until the Cleaner began to charge toward the sound of Vincent's voice. Then he released the fig with a *snap!* and the weapon flew through the air, crashing into the Cleaner's face and cracking off a jagged tooth.

The Cleaner stopped cold and snapped its teeth in shock. Vincent was able to move in close and thrust his spear into the mouth of the stunned beast. It was one of the easier kills he could remember accomplishing in his many years of hunting in the Flatlands.

Dr. Kincaid crept up and put an arm around each of his companions.

"Well done!"

Vincent grinned at Edgar, shaking his head. "It looks as though I may have found a hunting partner."

Dr. Kincaid was pleased. "We may make our destination yet!"

"Luther," said Edgar. The name felt strange, and he was quite sure it would be the last time he used it. "Where are we going?"

"On a miraculous journey," said Dr. Kincaid. "And I'm glad to have you and Vincent to protect me."

Vincent cut away a chunk of one of the Cleaners and handed it to Edgar. He did the same for Dr. Kincaid, then himself. The fresh Cleaner was sopping with slimy green goo that bubbled and squished around Edgar's teeth as he ate.

"Let me ask you again, Vincent," said Dr. Kincaid. "Are we nearing the cliff or are we not? You've traveled this way many times, but I can't quite get my bearing."

Vincent had a large bite of Cleaner in his mouth, and Edgar could see that he'd gotten a good deal of slime on his face. It glistened like black water in the fading light.

"I'm afraid we have already passed into Tabletop," said Vincent. He wiped one side of his face against his shoulder. "The cliffs are no more."

Edgar looked back into the Flatlands and realized the Cleaners he'd been fighting were lying dead *in* Tabletop. It was a stunning revelation. It had been one thing to *imagine* the Flatlands and Tabletop as one, but the reality felt like a blow to the head, leaving him dizzy with thoughts of the transforming world he lived in.

He looked toward the grove and couldn't see it, though he could imagine exactly where it would be somewhere off in the distance. A moment had come in Atherton when there were no more cliffs to be climbed, and Edgar said the only words that came to his mind.

"The world is flat."

Dr. Kincaid gazed off into the darkened horizon, astounded by the changes before him.

"Indeed it is."

Vincent seemed the least moved of the three, for he was completely unable to put anything in front of his obligation to protect Dr. Kincaid and Edgar on their journey. He had known the time would come when the cliffs would vanish and thought only of how complicated the work would be of shielding his two companions from harm.

"We're barely on the other side," said Dr. Kincaid. He had moved off a few steps and was kneeling down. "Here. This is where the cliff used to be. I can hardly believe it's gone."

His two companions knelt down with him and examined the place where a great wall of stone had once been.

"This one is not so perfect as the last," said Dr. Kincaid. "It is as I suspected."

"What do you mean?" asked Edgar.

"What I know of the Highlands' descent leads me to believe that it will have come down without leaving gaps of any significance. Look there." Dr. Kincaid walked along the vein of rubble, pointing as he went. Edgar followed the line of his finger out into the depths of night and thought he saw the ground turn darker still.

"That darkness you see is a crevice, a place where the two lands met without matching. There will be great chasms such as these all the way around the seam," said Dr. Kincaid. "Some will be the size of your foot, others big enough to fall into. A great many of them will be deep and inescapable."

"I wonder if we could dispose of the Cleaners in some of the large breaks," said Edgar. "Maybe we could find a way to push them in or herd them."

Vincent looked down the line, wondering how deep and wide some of the gaps might be.

"Time will tell," said Dr. Kincaid. He looked off toward the Highlands and grimaced as he thought of the long journey ahead, cursing his old feet for their unwillingness to go along without complaint.

"We will do well to keep moving," said Vincent. "The grove is still a good distance, and we must be clear of it by morning."

It came to the blackest part of night, and the three figures made their way across Tabletop. It was a peaceful trek of quiet thinking for the three of them, each alone in his own thoughts of what the morning would bring.

Vincent prepared his mind for a great many battles to come in which his skills would be desperately needed. Dr. Kincaid thought of the place they were going and the complicated challenges awaiting them there. Edgar wondered where Samuel and Isabel were and if he would ever find them. He wondered if he would ever climb again. He thought of the grove and the villages, the Highlands and Lord Phineus, the vast army of Cleaners that would invade his home and rip the trees from the ground.

And yet Edgar was not afraid of the morning and what it would bring. He was no longer a lonely orphan who slept under

trees in a fig grove. He had dared to visit every realm of Atherton, and what was more, he'd made friends wherever he'd gone.
The sun would rise on a world of grand and perilous adventures at every turn, companions by his side, fighting a good
fight to save things that mattered.

What more could a boy hope for?

While Edgar and his companions traveled across Tabletop,
something began to happen that no one had expected. Not even
Dr. Kincaid knew of its coming, for this was a secret known
only to Dr. Harding. The first two people to notice it were Samuel and Isabel, who were hidden in the tall grass of the former
Highlands, preparing to sneak into the House of Power.

"Did you feel that?" asked Isabel.

"What?"

Isabel put her hand flat on the ground, but there was nothing.

"I thought I felt something. It was different than before.
Closer."

"I didn't feel it," said Samuel. "We should go now. It's the
darkest hour."

But Isabel felt compelled to go somewhere else first.

"Come with me a moment, will you? There's something I
must be sure of."

She ran out of the tall grass, and Samuel followed until they
came to the place where the Highlands had merged with Tabletop. In the darkness, Isabel came upon something hard against

her knees and fell forward on her hands. She stood up, rubbing her shins and feeling confused.

"You're suddenly a lot taller than me," said Samuel, his voice shaking and unsteady.

There was a haunting noise in the air, barely discernible but constant. It was a familiar sound — too familiar.

The two stood facing one another — Samuel in the Highlands and Isabel in Tabletop — and they found that Isabel was ever so slowly growing taller.

The Highlands had begun to sink into the middle of Atherton.

END OF ONE
ATHERTON TWO REMAINS.

EXPLORE SUPPLEMENTAL DATA FLOW FOR MORE ON
DR. HARDING AND THE MAKING OF ATHERTON.

Supplemental Data Flow of
Dr. Harding's Brain

Readers may refer to *unlockdrhardingsbrain.com*
for drawings, audio files, video segments, and more
information about the following topics.

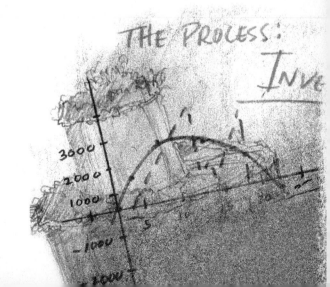

CLEANERS.

DR. HARDING'S JOURNAL 47,
LINE 6, NUMBER 22395

Cleaners were originally developed by Dr. Harding in a lab environment after a long string of failed efforts to assemble a creature whose singular purpose was to sanitize the underside of Atherton (unlock Dr. Harding's brain to better understand why this was important). Thousands of failed attempts at the cellular level were never fully developed. Early versions of the *Cleaner* concept included a mouth that was turned sideways, longer legs, and a much wider body. Early *Cleaner* prototypes and other material can be seen by unlocking number 22395.

THE DARK PLANET.

Dr. Harding's journal 16,
line 35, number 43682

The Dark Planet is Earth in the year 2105. Pollution has turned the Dark Planet into a place where people stay within containments most of the time. The air is thick with smog and unbreathable for more than a few minutes without the aid of Disposable Compact Filtering units (DCFs). A view of the Dark Planet from space lacks the blues and greens it once exhibited. The oceans are dim, the forests are mostly dead, and the Dark Planet is filled with the sharp coldness of metal.

In the history of the Dark Planet there were three waves of advancement. The first was agricultural, in which mankind settled into distinct places and managed to grow crops and create herds of animals for consumption and use. The second wave was the most dangerous, and set the Dark Planet on its eventual path to ruin. This was the wave of industrial machines, which made life easier for mankind. The third wave saw the rise of information technology and thinking machines, allowing mankind to create habitats and food sources in ways that hadn't been thought of before, ways that did untold harm to the Dark Planet. In time, the three waves of advancement overwhelmed the Dark Planet's natural resources, and it could not recover. By 2085 its former beauty was lost forever. For more information about the Dark Planet, unlock number 43682.

MAD SCIENTISTS.

DR. HARDING'S JOURNAL 154,
LINE 18, NUMBER 37782

Dr. Harding follows in the footsteps of another literary mad scientist, Dr. Frankenstein. The two have many things in common, and Dr. Harding carried around an old paperback copy of the famous Mary Shelley novel *Frankenstein* wherever he went. He was obsessed with its portrayal of a scientist gone mad with the idea of reanimation. Of particular interest to Dr. Harding was the struggle Dr. Frankenstein faced once he knew how to bring a dead person back to life. Did knowing how to do it mean he *should* do it? The consequences for carrying out his insane plan were devastating in the case of Dr. Frankenstein, and Dr. Harding wondered if the same would be true if he made Atherton. Unlock Dr. Harding's brain for more on the two scientists.

GRAVITY, ORBIT, AND DISCONNECT.
DR. HARDING'S JOURNAL 267,
PARTIAL DATA, FILE LOST

Gravity: It was necessary for the round bottom of Atherton to weigh an enormous amount. Without a heavy bottom, people would either float in the air or weigh almost nothing. Part of the bottom half of Atherton is filled with water, but some of the bottom is made of a living organic material with a mass similar to that of solid lead. If you were to visit Atherton and stand on any of the three levels, you would feel somewhat lighter than you do now. A 100-pound person from the Dark Planet weighs 81 pounds on Atherton.

Orbit: Atherton orbits the Dark Planet in such a way that a day and night on Atherton is generally the same length as a day and night on the Dark Planet. In addition, Atherton is always facing away from the Dark Planet so that those living on Atherton never see the place from which they originated. The closer an object's orbit to the Dark Planet, the less time it takes to make one trip around, and the faster it must go. Atherton orbits the Dark Planet exactly 22,300 miles away in the thermosphere. Unlock Dr. Harding's brain to see Atherton orbiting the Dark Planet.

Disconnect: There was a time when communication and boarding of Atherton from those on the Dark Planet was possible, but Dr. Harding severed contact, and there is currently no way to reestablish a connection. There are some on the Dark Planet who believe they will eventually find a way to make contact with Atherton again.

BIRDS, BUGS, AND ANIMALS.
DR. HARDING'S JOURNAL 82,
LINE 7, NUMBER 29430

Dr. Harding had a strong dislike for the enormous array of species on the Dark Planet. He blamed pollution, mass consumption, overpopulation, and a host of other problems on what he termed "mass variety," and while he was not in favor of destroying vast species of animals, he was determined not to have the same problem arise on Atherton. Birds and flying bugs of any kind were of particular concern, due in part to Dr. Harding's desire to maintain biological purity on all of Atherton's levels, but also because he had a terrible case of ornithophobia (the fear of birds) and simply could not bring himself to put flying creatures on Atherton. There are, however, bugs that do not fly on Atherton.

Dr. Harding was very fond of rabbits and sheep, and for a time he tried to create genetic versions of these animals with even greater usefulness. After a period of failed experimentation, he settled on the animals as they were. There is also the secret matter of the creatures that reside in Mead's Hollow.

Dr. Harding added horses primarily as beasts of burden. He did not intend them to be used as weapons of war, although war was a topic that upset him and was not discussed, so it could be that he gave some thought to the matter.

THE FIG TREE.
DR. HARDING'S JOURNAL 304,
LINE 92, NUMBER 15943

Agro science was a passion for Dr. Harding. He combined
countless varieties of trees and plants in an effort to create
something new and useful. The fig tree was at once his most
beloved invention and his greatest failure. He wanted desperately to create a food source that was easy to maintain, caused
minimal or no damage to the environment, and was almost
entirely edible or useful. He succeeded on all of these counts
but was later devastated to find that the tree he had created
was poisonous after the third year.

ACKNOWLEDGMENTS

First and foremost I need to thank my editor on this project, the incomparable Andrea Spooner. She had the skill and courage to give me a shovel and tell me where to dig, and knew when the time was right to take the spade from my hands and leave well enough alone. She got lost in Atherton as I did, and we came away together with a much better book than I could have written on my own.

My hat is off to David Ford. It was an honor to be chosen by him and his talented staff at Little, Brown and Company.

Thank you Sangeeta Mehta for patching me through, routing my stuff, and always sounding genuinely pleased to hear the distant voice of Eastern Washington.

Many thanks to my agent, Peter Rubie, for leading me across a tightrope with precision and grace and not letting me fall off. You knew our course and never wavered, even in the presence of my colossal indecision.

Thank you to the ever present (and never more appreciated) creative team in my hometown of Walla Walla, who helped make this project so much fun to work on (and gently reigned me in when I was good and lost somewhere deep in the woods): Squire Broel for inspired drawings and model building, Jeremy Gonzalez for film work, and Matt McKern for interactive content.

Thanks to Corey Smith, a loyal friend and mentor, for believing in me at his own peril and never giving up; Remy Wilcox for a character trait inspiration that shall go unmentioned here; and Marcus Wilcox for lively scientific discussions over sandwiches and Cokes.

Thank you, Skip Lee, for founding Agros, an organization that brings hope to thousands of people trapped in the cycle of poverty (and helps this one writer remain clear about what really matters). And three people I don't know, but acknowledge for their ability to change my mind, make me think, and challenge me to stop taking and start giving back: Al Gore, Bono, and David James Duncan.

In the end, there are no books without Karen. She makes everything possible.

—P.C.